JIDDY VARDY
High Tide

Praise for *Jiddy Vardy – High Tide*

"What an absolute page-turner! I couldn't put this down. A thrilling triumph of an adventure and such evocative descriptions of Robin Hood's Bay. I loved *Jiddy Vardy – High Tide*. Amazing!"

– Louisa Reid (*Gloves Off* and *Wrecked*)

"Ruth Estevez's Jiddy Vardy books are not just thrilling, tightly plotted adventures, but also beautifully written love-letters to the North Yorkshire coast. At their heart is a complex, memorable and very real central character and it is impossible to read these books without falling in love with Jiddy and her world."

– Bob Stone (The Beat Trilogy and owner of Write Blend Bookshop)

"Jiddy Vardy is a passionate and strong-willed young woman who you'll be routing for as she fights to find her place in her community of eighteenth-century Yorkshire. You'll soon lose yourself in Estevez's rich writing and discover a world of passion, smuggling and romance. Perfect for fans of Poldark."

– Anna Mainwaring (*Tulip Taylor* and *Rebel with a Cupcake*)

"Jiddy Vardy was good; this second instalment was brilliant. From the dark, impactful beginning through to the hopeful end, I was hooked.

Estevez' writing is wonderful here. The Yorkshire coastline and countryside is described in all its strong and stunning glory; rugged yet beautiful, calming yet fierce, with the opening scene being particularly powerful and atmospheric – I had chills. Estevez also managed to make the sea itself as much a character in this story as any other. It is both enchanting and unforgiving and plays such a pinnacle role in the tale.

Plot-wise, I was just as impressed. *High Tide* is fast-paced and pretty action packed. I found it completely gripping and chock-full of drama that kept me reading! It had plenty of substance too, though, exploring themes such as gender, class, politics and the North-South divide against a late 18th Century Yorkshire backdrop.

…I would…recommend to fans of historical fiction with strong female leads. Jiddy is certainly a girl you can root for! As a Yorkshire girl myself, it was great to see our beautiful county and its people, particularly its women (of all classes and situations), given a voice."

– The Pages of Mrs D (Eryn Davies)

JIDDY VARDY

High Tide

Ruth Estevez

Beaten Track
www.beatentrackpublishing.com

Jiddy Vardy – High Tide

Published 2021 by Beaten Track Publishing
Copyright © 2021 Ruth Estevez

Paperback ISBN: 978 1 78645 492 8
eBook ISBN: 978 1 78645 493 5

Cover Design: Debbie McGowan

Beaten Track Publishing,
Burscough, Lancashire.
www.beatentrackpublishing.com

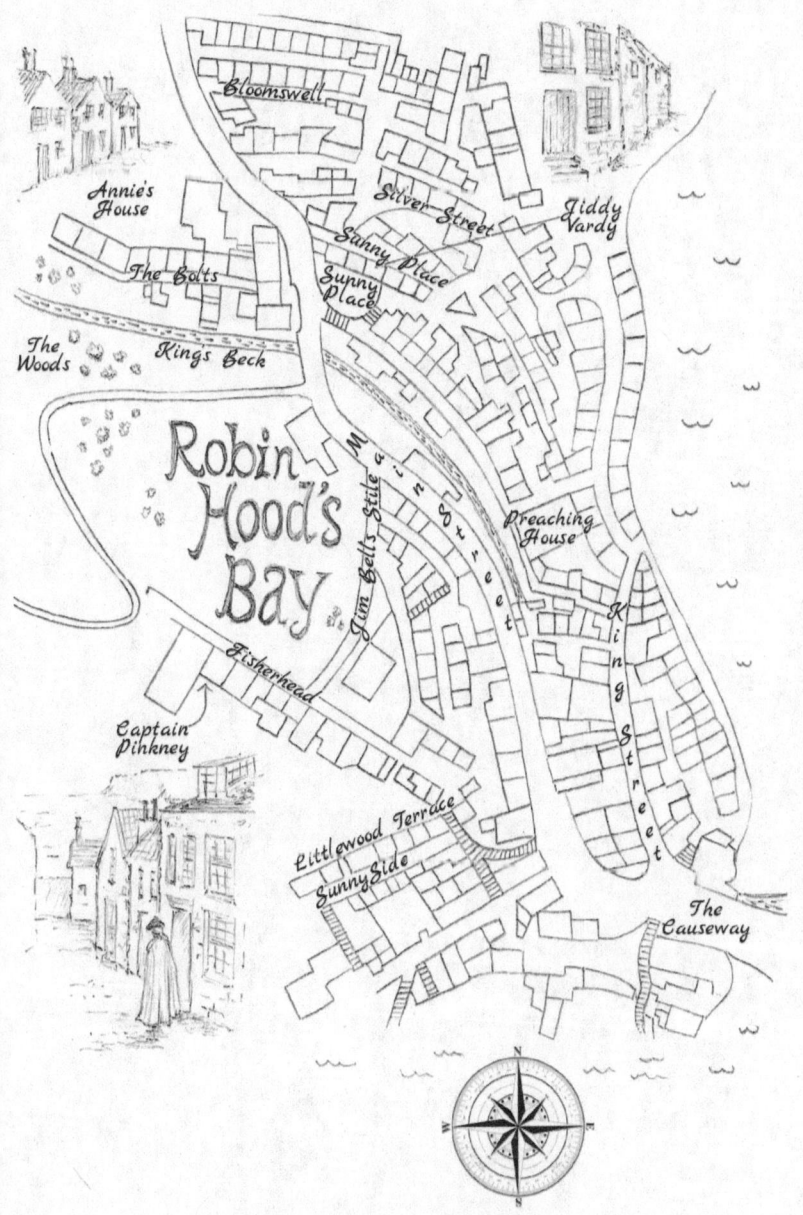

Bloomswell

Annie's House

The Bolts

The Woods

King's Beck

Silver Street

Sunny Place

Sunny Place

Jiddy Vardy

Robin Hood's Bay

Jim Bell's Stile

Main Street

Preaching House

King Street

Fisherhead

Captain Pinkney

Littlewood Terrace

Sunnyside

The Causeway

N
W E
S

ACKNOWLEDGEMENTS

With thanks to all readers who have loved Jiddy Vardy and who want to know what happens next.

Thanks also to Debbie McGowan, editor and MD of Beaten Track Publishing, for her support and reassurance as well as her superior editing and cover design prowess. To beta-readers, Bob Stone, Genevieve and Miranda Estevez-Baker and the Society of Children's Book Writers and Illustrators (SCBWI) North West YA group for their generous and expert suggestions, advice and enthusiasm. Anna Mainwaring and Louisa Reid, as always, thanks for your wonderful support. Plus, early readers, Deborah Grace, Jennifer Page and Jane Thorpe – thank you.

With respect and thanks to all the independent bookshops who have supported me too, specifically Book Corner, Saltburn, Chorlton Bookshop, the Grove Bookshop, Ilkley, Whitby Bookshop, and Write Blend, Liverpool.

And finally to Robin Hood's Bay, and Yorkshire.

This work of fiction is inspired by real-life female smuggler Jiddy Vardy and historical figures from the area. The map on the previous page is to provide a guide to the Bay rather than accurately depicting the area in 1797.

CHAPTER ONE

Robin Hood's Bay, England
Spring 1796

Three figures stared up at the rigid corpse hanging from the gibbet. A gust of wind made the wooden structure creak, and the girls, rounded by thick shawls, stood still. Beyond, moorland disappeared into darkness. A lone cloud released a bright cusp of new moon, and the structure revealed itself at the sandy crossroads.

Jiddy handed her lantern to Betsie. "Hold it up."

Betsie raised it with both hands.

"Higher."

"What if someone comes?"

Jiddy looked over her shoulder, then in every direction. Face shrouded in wool and shoulders hunched, Annie whimpered.

"No-one's coming," Jiddy said. She pushed down her shawl and, hoisting her skirt, clambered onto the platform.

Annie gasped. Betsie stepped closer and the light fell on shrivelled black feet. Betsie promptly retreated, and the dangling limbs disappeared as the light dropped to the ground, leaving Jiddy lit like a ghost.

"I can't do this," Betsie said.

"We agreed."

"I've changed my mind. Here." The light swung into Jiddy's face, glowing in her dark eyes.

"Annie, you hold it," Jiddy said, swivelling to reveal Annie, who shook her head. For a second time, the wind rippled their skirts.

"You should have got Jonas to help," said Betsie.

"We're Nellie's friends," said Jiddy. "This isn't for lads to do. It's our job to set her free."

"We can't reach. This is stupid! We need someone tall."

"I can reach." Jiddy drew a knife from under her skirt. It gleamed in the moonlight. "One of you hold the lantern so I can see the rope, other get ready to catch her."

Betsie raised the lantern higher. "You heard her, Annie. I'm holding the light. You get ready to catch."

Hugging the post with one arm, Jiddy straddled the supporting blocks and reached up, her other arm at full stretch to saw through the rope. The figure twisted, and straggling hair brushed Jiddy's face. She stared into two rotting holes, greened by sea frets, a gristle of nose and a lopsided leer of a mouth.

Retching, she dropped the knife with a clatter and released her grip. Her foot slipped. Annie screamed. The light bobbed, revealing tattered clothes and the shiver of part flesh, part skeleton. Jiddy reached for a hold again, grabbing the slime of rope, and pressed inadvertently close to the corpse. Screwing up her eyes and turning her head, she held her breath against the damp odour of mould and rot. The gallows groaned.

"Help!"

The others scurried, light bouncing, hands outstretched, as Jiddy grappled to reach the wooden beam.

Wind gusted, and she and Nellie shifted. She pushed the body away with her feet and the wood splintered with a loud crack. Still holding the rope, she fell.

"Jiddy!"

She landed on the block with Nellie's remains in her arms. The broken beam hit her back, and she half scrambled, half fell onto the ground, shoving away the decaying body. Annie squealed.

"Look what you've done!" said Betsie, skipping further away.

Jiddy pushed against the wooden block to stand and, grabbing the lantern from Betsie, she held it up to look at the jumble of tatters and shapes that remained of Nellie.

"It's disgusting." Betsie gagged.

"I want to go home," sniffled Annie.

Jiddy swung the lantern into their faces. Annie squinted in the glare and Betsie covered her eyes.

"We'll be arrested," Betsie said. "Wait 'til preventives see this. Wait till my mam and da hear about it. They'll kill us."

"They'll think we're traitors, they'll think—"

"They'll think we're good friends," said Jiddy, "and we take care of friends."

"Didn't think you were Nellie's friend." Betsie scowled.

"We grew up together, didn't we?"

"I'm scared," said Annie.

3

"Preventives'll want to know who took her down."

"That's why we'll leave scraps of her skirt," said Jiddy. "Wolves took down Bob Slater. They'll think same has happened to Nellie."

"He were fresh."

"Nobody asked questions. They'll not now."

They studied the skeleton folded over on itself and the curve of skull under a whimper of hair.

"I'm not touching it," said Betsie.

Jiddy crouched to look closer. "She won't be heavy. Annie, have you got the sacking?"

Jiddy and Annie lay the withered corpse on the blanket and looked down again at the more recognisable shape of a young woman.

"She's shrunk," said Betsie.

Jiddy swept up the knife and looked around. Satisfied they had left nothing, she took the lantern from Betsie and blew out the flame.

"Hey! We can't see."

"We can see enough, but we must keep quiet."

Their figures shifted in the high moonlight. Without the lantern, the crossroads snaked quickly into darkness.

"We'll soon hear the sea," Jiddy said.

"There's four corners," said Betsie. "Told you we should have brought Jonas."

"We should wrap blanket around her," suggested Annie.

Jiddy crouched by the figure on the ground. "Nellie should have an open coffin for one last catch of Bay. I'll take the front two. You grab a corner each at the back."

They shambled slowly, their silence crackling the air as they approached Main Street. Rooftops tumbled all the way down to the sea and the sharp spring moon illuminated the shoreline.

"We'll never get down without someone seeing," said Betsie. "Let's bury her in woods."

"D'you want dogs digging her up? And we're struggling even now, we'll never make it all way back there." Silence. "Well then, just keep quiet, and we'll be fine."

Betsie and Annie exchanged glances, but Jiddy set off, pulling them to follow. The hill dropped steeply, and Nellie's feet pressed against Jiddy's buttocks. She held her corners tight against her hips, anxious all the way down the slope of the Bay that Nellie's corpse would topple and the shriek of her bones, hitting the ground, would awaken the entire neighbourhood.

"Lift her a bit," she whispered when she feared the corpse would be so vertical it would walk over her head.

The stretcher wobbled and Jiddy halted. In the dark, with the wind drawing up the hill and the waves crinkling over shingle, it would be easy to believe that Nellie would rise. Halfway down, they crept around the bend of road and listened. A rat shot across their path and scampered into the Bolts, making Jiddy jump and the stretcher tipple. Annie didn't utter a word, but Betsie swore as they righted themselves and waited until Jiddy tugged the blanket so that they shuffled forward again.

Jiddy's heart pounded but she couldn't let on how jittery she felt. She could only imagine how close Annie was to letting out a scream and she'd never known Betsie so quiet, but they were almost at the slipway, and the flat beach would be a relief. Finally, they reached the dock and, exposed in the open space, Jiddy sped up, tottering with the effort. The clatter of Betsie's clogs ricocheted around the buildings. Glancing over her shoulder, she saw their white faces bobbing behind. They couldn't stop now, and they half jumped, half fell onto the beach. where they almost tipped the body.

"Let's wrap her up," Annie suggested.

"Should have done this straight away," said Betsie.

Jiddy pulled a knot tighter and didn't answer. Soon, they were carrying Nellie between them, slipping and sliding and popping bladderwrack under their boots. Jiddy kept her eyes on the goal ahead and let the crash of waves be her guide.

***

When they rested near the promontory of Boggle Hole, catching their breath, Jiddy walked towards the water.

"How are we going to get her out there?" said Annie.

"Why, more like," said Betsie. "We should have buried her in the woods like I said."

"Nellie didn't like the woods," said Jiddy.

"She didn't like the sea, neither."

"She didn't like Robin Hood's Bay!"

"Nellie didn't like anything!"

They exploded with laughter, bending and giggling with the relief of it.

"Nellie should be laughing with us," said Betsie. "She liked to laugh."

If Nellie had been standing on the beach, Jiddy would not have been with them. She knew that. Betsie was right: she and Nellie weren't friends, but they had understood each other, and the memory of Nellie's desperation haunted her.

"We should say some words," she said.

"Annie reached for Jiddy's hand. "Yes, say something."

"I'll say something," said Betsie. "I were closest to Nellie."

"Go on, then," said Jiddy, putting her arms around Annie's shoulders.

Betsie cleared her throat and clasped her hands together. She nodded to them. "Do same."

They stood, Betsie on one side and Jiddy and Annie on the other, hands gripped tight, eyes closed.

Jiddy would have been happy if no-one spoke. The crumble of foam on the pebbles and the deeper sense of waves lifting and the wind catching their skirts seemed all that was needed. A sea burial. A warrior's grave. That's what she'd want for herself.

Betsie's feet shifted. The cold night air chilled their faces and Jiddy's hair fluttered free. She hoped Betsie would realise that there were no words to say and they could instead listen to the ebbing tide.

Betsie cleared her throat again.

"I wish Nellie were here," she said.

7

They waited. Jiddy opened her eyes. Betsie had turned her back to them. Taking Annie's hand, Jiddy led her to stand by Betsie.

"Shall we all hold hands?"

They stood in a circle, looking at each other, then away, then over each other's shoulders, unable to maintain eye contact.

"I love Robin Hood's Bay," said Jiddy. "I love the sea and the woods."

Annie glanced sideways. "I'm scared of them all, but I don't know owt else. Except Whitby, and I didn't like Whitby."

Jiddy smiled. "What about you, Betsie?"

"I dunno."

"Do you want to leave Robin Hood's Bay like Nellie did?"

"If Nellie can't leave, no-one can."

"Jiddy tugged Annie's hand. "Is that what you think?"

Annie stared at Betsie.

"I think we should have left Nellie on gibbet," she said.

"Nellie's spirit has already left Bay," said Jiddy, "but we can make sure her body goes as well." She looked from one to the other. "If Nellie could be, she'd be as far from here as she could. That's what she wanted. We understand that, don't we?"

Annie and Betsie nodded.

"So, we do this for her? We set her free?"

"It's not fair," said Betsie. "You can try and go off with a soldier when he leaves Bay or find some fisherman or whaler if you're lucky, but it's not fair you're killed for it."

Jiddy held her tongue. She couldn't say Nellie was a traitor and that she'd tried to push the blame on others. Now wasn't the time. Nellie had left herself no more choices, and that was the tragedy of it.

"Nellie could have walked away on her own two feet," she said instead. "We can all do that."

"With nothing in her hands or belly and all alone? What choice do lasses like us have?"

They fell silent again, listening to the tide. Jiddy had chosen smuggling, but that could also have you swinging from the gibbet.

"You two go," she said. "I'll take Nellie out."

"No, we'll stay," said Annie. "We'll wait for you."

"Won't Nellie come back when sea turns?" asked Betsie.

"I'll get her into slipstream," Jiddy said. "Current'll carry her down coast, and she'll not be recognisable if anybody does find her, will she?"

"Don't say that."

"We only know who she is because we took body down."

"Stop it."

"What I want is for tide to take her out. That's what I'm counting on. Don't worry, I'll make sure I get her out far enough."

Jiddy pulled off her boots and handed Annie her shawl. Together, they dragged the body into the shallows until Jiddy waded out alone, pulling Nellie with her. As the water deepened, the waves lifted so that Jiddy had merely to guide the body while the other two watched from the shore. With water lapping at her thighs, she pushed the shrouded body in front, so she could swim and then, with a final goodbye, Nellie drifted out to sea.

CHAPTER TWO

Spring 1797

The sea rasped with the shadow of a schooner. White foam roared against the headland, and spray fizzed in the night air. Jiddy tucked stray curls back under her shawl, watching the water. The wind had picked up, and a spring tide swept into the Bay. They'd not seen Nellie's body since they'd taken her out, but this was a rough sea, and they all knew corpses could wash up months after being lost. She tried not to think about it but rather about the task in hand and trusting Nellie would stay away.

Shrouded figures stood knee-high in the bitter water, tense and waiting. Jiddy stumbled as the shingle dragged under her boots.

Movement. Andrew splashed towards her, holding an oilcloth parcel. No-one spoke. It took all their effort not to drop the precious packages into the foam.

"Tek it," Andrew spat through his teeth, face a pale, dripping scowl. "And stand closer to me. You're wasting us time."

Jiddy grabbed at the parcel, but he let go before she had a proper grip. He turned his back, striding a few paces into the dragging backwash. Knees bent to hold the weight, she adjusted her grasp, wet fingers slipping.

She'd be damned if she dropped it. She was the only lass trusted on being tough enough for this lark, and she'd not let any of lads think they were better than she.

Passing the waxy package, she made sure the lad behind her had a good hold before turning back to the sea and whatever Andrew presented next. Wiping a hand over her eyes, she blinked away the fine mist whipped by wind off the water.

A package jabbed her side, and she startled. Andrew again. She grabbed the parcel.

"Don't do that, you frig pig."

He shoved the package into her arms. "Then be ready."

The lad behind was ready, standing so close she bashed into him and they swapped an anxious look. She'd have to buck up. They couldn't afford mistakes. This time, she was prepared and took the next parcel and passed it on even though her arms and back were aching and she shivered, damp under her clothes.

Glancing past Andrew, she checked to see if the schooner had started to pull away, but its shape still loomed near and its groaning tilt snuck through the dark.

It has to be finished soon. Please let it be soon. With three lines of folk passing goods, they'd surely be reaching the end of the cargo and be done and gone before preventives got word of the run.

Big Isaac was right. The howl of the wind and crashing of sea against the promontory round at Boggle Hole and along at the causeway meant no-one could reach them from either end. Soldiers could come over the tops, of course, and down to Stoupe Beck, but who'd risk that with a sky threatening a torrential downpour? They'd never think villagers would be out on a night like this or that a ship would risk a battering on Yorkshire rocks. But Baytown folk had to be out helping whether they wanted or not. Goods would have to be stacked at the back of the cave here at Stoupe Beck, and next day, those snug in their beds right now would retrieve the Valenciennes lace, rum and salt packages and take them up the tunnels, out over the moors and into rich folks' homes.

Carrying an oilskin parcel, she shook her head to clear her face of spray. This was madness, even for them. It was too hard in this weather, wind squalling and knocking them all sideways. In truth, if she wore breeches like men, she'd not be gusted like a ship at full sail. She'd like to see Andrew trussed up in mounds of material. Maybe she should borrow a pair of breeches; that was worth thinking about. She'd not dropped anything she'd been passed, though, even with skirts to battle, while others had dropped boxes and barrels, a couple even in the sea, splashing up water and curses from lads already numb-fingered.

"Let it be done," she wished. "Let it be done and we can be off up tunnels and home to our beds."

And then, in a flurry of activity, they were done. Big Isaac, Andrew and others emerged from the water and strode past her and up the beach. Still more followed. On the cusp of waves, the Dutch schooner turned, taking its rasping wood and snapping sails into the gloom. She'd not be a sailor tonight, not for all the silk and lace she could cram under her bed.

She envied Jonas, who'd be tucked up warm at the farm. Rightly, he should be out, waiting on the clifftop with his horse and cart to load and disperse goods inland, but it was too wild a night for carriers to be out, getting wheels stuck in mud and sodden ruts on the moor. Never mind; she'd soon be snug in her bed too, and tomorrow, when they met on the sand to check on each other, they'd kiss and cuddle and hopefully more besides, and she'd tease him for being a soft nicky-ninny.

Catching her skirt, she hurried up the beach, jostling with others as they neared the cave entrance. They were all eager to be out of the biting wind.

Once inside, people's anxieties and complaints of the night's conditions spilled into the dim space, lit by lanterns that hung on the back wall. Already folk had disappeared in the crack that hid a winding tunnel up to the cottages. Big Isaac organised the stacking and hiding of the night's contraband, and Jiddy, relieved to be done, slipped into the tunnel. It led narrow and steep through the rock, almost suffocating with someone close in front and another following right behind. Soon, she'd be sweating, not shivering.

A lantern glowed at the first junction, and several of those in front peeled away. She touched the damp, cold stone to steady herself. She was tired, but the night wasn't over yet. Rough breaths behind told her others were shattered too. Stealth was sometimes more draining than fighting because you had to hold your nerve and stick close to the plan. Not that they brawled with the enemy if

14

they could help it. They'd learnt that long ago. The leader of their smuggling ring constantly reminded them.

"The most successful smuggler isn't violent, but smart."

Jiddy was known for being smart. She held on to that because that was why folk called on her so often, even on miserable, stormy nights when her skirt did its best to trip her up.

She reached the next junction. Andrew was right behind. She turned. Nodded. They veered off leaving others to head straight up. Helen Drake had promised they could cut through her cottage, but she'd be furious if they woke her as they trod through her living room and out the front.

They came to another lantern, and Jiddy slipped into an alcove to find a door. It opened with a tug, and ducking low, she crept under a wooden shelf. Inside a cramped space, she reached with one hand and caught hold of a handle. A panel swung outwards. Shuffling through the opening, she stood in a kitchen, holding the door for Andrew so that a freak gust didn't make it slam. Helen had left embers in the fire stacked so they could see their way. That was thoughtful; last thing they wanted was to be crashing around, bashing into tables and chairs. Reaching the front door safely, Jiddy listened.

"What you waiting for?" Andrew said, jolting her aside and swinging open the door. A bitter draught burst in, dimming the burning peat on the fire and wafting the curtains. Andrew gained the front step and bounded down the ginnel before Jiddy could stop him. He might be her best friend's brother, but he was a right pillock.

15

She closed the door behind her. Dawn seeped grey tendrils across the cobbles. Wind lifted her skirt and the corners of her shawl, and she held them down with both hands. There wasn't a soul in sight. It was times like this when the thrill of being a smuggler rippled through her. She listened for sounds. The sea crashing up the causeway and smacking the end cottages reached her ears. Even here, she heard it battering. It sounded a vicious wind, tugging her black hair out from under the shawl. It drew her breath too, slipping icy fingers down her throat and paining her chest. No-one should be out tonight. Jonas was lucky to be good and dry in his bed. She held on to the fact that soon she would be.

She'd not far to go. She could follow Andrew down Main Street and cut up into Sunny Place while he hurried along The Bolts. It was then that she heard a scuffle of boots coming in her direction along Bloomswell. A Baytowner wouldn't be coming this way. It could only mean one thing.

Keeping close to the wall, she crept in the other direction towards Main Street. Readying to duck behind a peat store or shoot across to the woods, she snuck down the hill. It seemed clear. She couldn't believe it. If it had been Andrew's rough opening of Helen's door that had alerted preventives, she'd kill him.

She was almost past the Laurel Inn and then she'd be up the steps and in through her front door in moments. Reaching the slope up to Sunny Place, she stopped. Barring her way stood two preventives: Jimmy Dowd and Kenny McLean. They looked as shocked as she felt.

A second later, she was running, telling herself to stop, to say she'd been visiting a neighbour who was sick, visiting anyone, but she'd chosen to run, and now it was too late to talk and explain. Or was it? She knew them well enough. She'd charmed them many a time; she could do it easy. But she was in the momentum of the hill, her boots carrying her downwards, and they were after her, their footfalls making a hell of a racket, even with the wind and her harsh breaths in competition. Her boots weren't so quiet either. She was running the wrong way too. She should have headed uphill not down. There'd be no cover in the dock. She'd have to pick up speed and head up the steep steps to Covet Hill. She could lose them round the backs amongst the maze of cottages, but they were gaining, and she was tiring.

The street opened out. Ahead, the full tide foamed over the causeway that usually stretched like a road out to sea. She watched it seethe for a moment before bounding for the steps on the right.

"We're armed." Jimmy Dowd's voice followed her. "We'll shoot you."

She stopped on the first step. They'd get her in the back if she carried on running. Turning, she realised that in the dim light, they hadn't recognised her.

"Lads…" she began, pulling at her shawl to reveal her face. She'd tell them they'd scared her, but now that she knew who they were, she felt safe. She'd tell them she'd taken them for smugglers, and she was terrified of the wicked dogs.

17

The pair walked towards her, and she realised this wasn't the moment to explain. They hadn't noticed the sea raging wild, frothing its grasping fingers towards them. Since she was a bairn, she'd been warned of the high tide flooding up Main Street. Strict instructions to keep clear, and here they were, standing on the edge of a thick North Sea at its height.

"Jimmy, Kenny, shift yourselves..."

As they stood there, the whole dock oozed with dark water, massing around Jimmy's and Kenny's legs, swirling black whirlpools of treacherous sea. Jiddy backed up the steps.

"Get up here!" she shouted. "Now!"

A second wave swelled the water higher. The force knocked Kenny off his feet. He yelled out, and Jimmy splashed to help him. The tide sucked back.

"No!" Jiddy shouted. "You can't help!"

Jimmy stumbled, and the ebb dragged Kenny with it into the dark. Her head told her that no-one could be saved once the tide had them, but it was impossible not to help. She jumped down into swirls of water and the cold made her gasp. She braced herself. Even the shallow tongue of the sea dragged her ankles. Spreading her arms for balance, she waded towards Jimmy. If he could move quickly, he could be all right.

"Stand up," she shouted. "Take my hand."

She waded nearer, but the weight of her wet skirt made progress slow. He rolled in the water, too dazed to make haste. Water groaned further out, readying to surge. She took another unsteady step. The rise of sea approached the dock. It swelled, thundering a churning furrow over the stone, and she bent to withstand the blast.

The noise filled her ears. This was more frightening than anything she'd encountered. She reached out, and her hand scraped his leg. The water growled. The landing wave spewed foam. Waves surged into the dock, and he rolled with the force. Instinct told her to retreat, and clutching her saturated skirt, she hauled herself up several steps. The waves uncurled, sweeping Jimmy with them. She scrambled up a few more steps, turning to watch. The tide held its breath, Jimmy balanced on its lips. She took a step down, watching for the water's turn, but she was too far away and Jimmy too deep. She'd never reach him. He gurgled. Retched. His head disappeared under again.

Heart thumping, she studied the water. Even here, it could knock her off her feet. She inched up the steps, hating herself. His face appeared out of the foam, shimmering white and opened-mouthed in a howl for help. What could she do? Her soaked skirt was heavy. Even though she could swim, this sea was wild. He shouted, flailing, arms, legs, too far away. Balancing, half on one step, half on the one below, she clasped her hands to her chest as in prayer. Jimmy's face sparkled for a moment before his expression dissolved from hope to terror.

"Swim!" she shouted. "Swim!"

The sea pulled back; nothing would stop it. A leg reappeared, then a hand, then the empty smudge of wet dock. Waves smashed into themselves and clapped in retreat before the water flattened into a jet-black lake. She looked at the now shallow water. It was as if the soldiers had never been there. Sickened, she waited for the wave to return, hoping it would bring Jimmy, if not Kenny, with it. She couldn't move. Cold clung to her limbs, but she couldn't leave. When it did come back in, roaring further up Main Street than it had before, Jiddy scrambled to the top of the steps. She couldn't see either of them. It really was as if they'd never existed, but she knew they'd be out there in the blackness, unable to swim or tread water or stay afloat.

Hands shaking, Jiddy lifted her scarf back over her head. Only she and the sea knew what had happened. No-one could survive when it was in this mood. She hoped it would be fast. All she could pray for now was that they'd drown before being beaten and battered by waves pounding them against the rocks. The sea didn't care. It would take anyone who stood too close. If only they'd taken it seriously like folk who lived in the Bay did. If only they'd been properly warned by them that knew. If only she could have saved them.

She stood until the cold and wet numbed her skin and a chill seeped into her bones. She didn't want to leave them to die so far from home with no-one to know where they'd gone.

CHAPTER THREE

The next morning, Jiddy dragged herself out of bed and made her way downstairs. The clatter of pots met her, mixed with the familiar piercing voice of Helen Drake. The woman seemed a constant visitor at Sunny Place. If her dear Mary wasn't so ill, Jiddy would tell the woman, politely of course, that she would be better off in her own home on Bloomswell. Trouble was, Helen had let Jiddy sneak through her living room the previous night, and Jiddy might need to do that again.

"There'll be someone to pay," Helen Drake said.

Typical. Know-it-all Helen must have heard what had happened to the two preventives last night and couldn't wait to share her opinions.

Thankfully, their favourite neighbour, Gracie, had come in to help. Mary sat by the well-built fire, almost concealed in an armoury of shawls and blankets. At least they'd taken care of her while Jiddy had been out. Silver-haired Gracie stood by the table, pouring tea into cups. She was the first to notice Jiddy.

"Afternoon," she said, her voice warm as baked apples.

Jiddy looked at the dull light slumping through the window. She'd been playing these games with Gracie ever since she could talk.

"It's still morning for me," she said.

"Cockerel gave up trying to wake you hours ago."

Jiddy shambled over in her stocking feet and snuggled into Gracie's soft bosom. She looked sideways at Mary, who sat dappled in firelight and waiting patiently.

"Morning, Mary," she said, shuffling over the flags.

Thin and brittle as a gnarled stick, Helen Drake didn't wait for Jiddy to give Mary a similar embrace.

"I said there'll be a price to pay with them two preventives being swept out to sea." Helen Drake could drag a noon-day sun to the bottom of the ocean. "Did they see your face?" she asked.

"Wouldn't matter," said Gracie before Jiddy could answer. "They can't see 'owt from seabed. Come and have some hot tea, Jiddy love."

"Hell, lass. What were you doing down by dock?" Helen said, undeterred. "When I heard you come stomping through my house last night, I thought you'd at least have sense enough to head straight on home."

Jiddy kissed the shawl covering Mary's head. "I'm sorry if I worried you. How are you feeling today? Any better?"

Mary cradled a cup in her thin hands and, looking up at Jiddy, nodded. Jiddy glanced at Gracie.

"Hot tea is what we all need," Gracie said. "And I'm glad you're safe too, Jiddy. It were a devil of a night, and I can't think what them two beggars were playing at."

She held out a cup, and Jiddy pattered over to take it.

"Is it all right if you stop with Mary for another hour or so? Is that all right, Mary?"

"Where've you got to go, now?" asked Helen.

"Just an errand. And I did try to warn them about high tide, but they weren't quick enough."

"Seems peculiar to me. Those two would take a bribe any day rather than bother with an arrest and all that palaver."

Gracie shuffled in her clogs and plonked herself down opposite Mary. "I agree. This is a to-do," she said. "They'll be after us hotter than potato cakes, but we're not going to let that get to us, now, are we?"

Jiddy sipped the scalding tea. "It happened so fast," she said. "One minute, dock were dry. Next, massive wave swept up and dragged them away. Whatever folks say, I've no control over sea."

"So how come you're standing here, safe and sound, if tide were that forceful?" said Helen.

"Give it a rest," Gracie chided. "Can't be helped that they had more faith in their pistols than eyes in their heads."

"But we'll have to pay."

"Gracie told you to leave it be, Helen," said Mary, raising her head. "Jiddy knows danger of high tide on causeway. Those two preventives have been here long enough too. They should have known you don't turn your back on sea."

Helen ground her teeth and Jiddy winced. Everything that woman did got on her nerves.

"I still think it odd they've not got to bottom of Nellie Ashner's corpse," Helen muttered.

"At least storm's subsided," Gracie said.

"Storm is just beginning, if you ask me."

Jiddy strode to the window and peered out. "Seeing as you've got visitors, Mary, you won't mind if I make that errand, will you?"

It seemed wrong to be out, leaving the warm fire and Mary with neighbours again, no matter how happy they were to stay, but she couldn't bear to be questioned by Helen Drake about the sea and Kenny McLean and Jimmy Dowd and that she'd got away with merely a wet skirt and salt stains on her hem.

"I've come away with more than that!" she wanted to shout, but what was the point in railing against Helen Drake? Besides, Jonas would be waiting.

The early afternoon air made her shiver, and she hoped she hadn't caught a chill. She pulled her shawl tighter around her shoulders. There was nobody about; everyone was either sleeping off the night or lying low. Nobody would want to be questioned by soldiers about the whereabouts of two of their own. She walked quickly, hoping Jonas was back from delivering contraband to all the well-frequented houses over the moors and would be waiting in their usual spot. They always checked on each other after a run. It were first thing they did, and the relief of seeing each other never diminished.

She slowed as she reached the dock. All that remained of the thirsty sea was a slick of brine. The causeway rose out of the rocks and sand as if the sea couldn't possibly cover it as it had last night. Waves lapped far out, having left behind bladderwrack and empty shells. Gulls called out of low barriers of cloud. She didn't know if she'd expected to see the two preventives sprawled on the rocks, eyes staring upwards, skin turning thick and cold, but of course, they weren't there. A tide like last night would have carried them far away, and they'd be adrift in open water or nibbled by fish and floating down into the dark. If anyone did happen to see their bodies again, they'd be unrecognisable. Like Nellie. She closed her eyes. She didn't want to think of them far away from land all alone with their families unable to mourn them, no name on a gravestone, bodies dissolving somewhere between here and Holland.

She had to get the images out of her head. Looking down at the seaweed-strewn rocks, she concentrated on navigating them without slipping. A sudden gust blew long strands of hair over her face, and she drew them back.

"There's nowt I can do about it now," she told herself, looking at the scurry of waves tickling the shore. "Today is fresh. I'll not make any mistakes today."

Jonas was waiting where he always waited. She ran into his arms with such force he had to steady himself.

"I were worried when I heard," he said.

"Let's not talk about it." She held him tight. "I don't want to think about it."

"I've not long. I haven't rubbed Boy down yet, but I wanted to check you were all right."

"Better kiss me straight away, then," she said, pulling him towards the cliff.

The curve and crook of rock gnarled its fists into her back, and she shifted her weight. The wind caught her hair as it had before, and this time, Jonas brushed his hand over her head to catch the dark strands and hold them still. Cold air caressed her cheeks, but she felt warm. He nuzzled her neck. He were hers for the kissing.

The vast, charcoal sky still threatened. The chill of rain continued to lurk in the crevices and dampness of sand. A schooner, not yet a speck, sailed away from the coast.

Don't think about them. Jonas is here. Lips and tongues and heat.

His lips traced over her jaw, searching for her mouth. It tickled. She turned her head and pulled him in with her arms. Any minute and he'd press against her. That would make her want him more, and she'd soon forget everything else. She shifted her feet.

The wind swooped around the headland, ruttling seaweed across the sand. She smelt the sea, salty brine that mixed with the smell of hay on Jonas's skin. His tongue reached into her mouth. Spreading her hands on the curve at the base of his back, she held him to her. There it was. That movement.

Being with Jonas drowned out all thoughts of regret and questioning. Kissing him stopped her thinking. A dark blanket folded in her head, and her heart beat faster. She couldn't think about anything no more. Her cheeks glowed hot, and he moved like a piston up at alum mine. Ye gods, her brain was going to explode.

He shifted.

What is he doing? Don't let air in. Don't slow down. No, no.

"You can touch me," he whispered.

26

"Huh?" She couldn't speak. Couldn't breathe.

He nodded. The blanket in her head lifted, letting in light.

"Hold me there."

He touched her fingers, drew her hand down between them and placed it on his jigger. His massive jigger.

Wrenching free her arm, she pushed him back, and he staggered, flushed and bewildered.

"I were almost there," she said, her voice spitting each syllable. "Why did you do that?"

He meandered back, arms spread out as if he'd just woken up.

"I'm sorry," he said, tucking himself around her.

"Ger off."

He kissed her neck. "I'll make it come back."

"Too late, I'm off boil," she said, elbows and hips and knees sharp.

"No, you're not." He laughed, looking her direct in the eyes, his chin pressing her chin, his breath warm on her mouth as if it had magic charm.

She'd give him magic charm. She glared at him. He leaned against her.

"Is this all right?"

There wasn't a soul around. She tilted her head and ran her tongue over his lips.

"Stop it, Jiddy." He breathed heavy. "You know what that does to me."

He'd do it proper this time, she could tell by his expression, and she pulled him closer, hand grasping

27

his hair and her skin burning more fiery than furnaces. She didn't care about rough stone against her back or her skull or nowt but what was going on below.

And this time, she did explode like wood sorrel popping, and the relief in her body was worth it. He watched her cheeks cool, but they were too busy panting to speak. She could smile, though, and she did, big and wide.

"Ta," she said, kissing his freckled nose.

Jonas tucked in his shirt and adjusted his breeches while Jiddy checked her skirt hung down right and her chemise didn't fall too low. She turned around.

"Am I decent?"

He caught her waist, and she put her arms around his shoulders. Their lips fitted perfectly, and she curled into him and him into her. Breeze caressed them. Gulls called. Sea thrummed.

She pushed back his hair. "We've got to go," she said.

He gave her that cheeky grin that made his eyes sparkle. "Right you are."

She waved her hand. "Go get some work done."

"You don't know what the word means."

He scrambled up the cliff path before she could retaliate.

Clutching her skirts high to her knees, she leapt, jumped and twirled. Glancing up, she spotted him on the tops already, copper-brown hair against slate sky, off to pull cows' teats and fill buckets with warm milk. She smiled when he waved.

The causeway was in sight. Dropping her skirts, she put up her arms to an imaginary partner. Turning, she made the steps with her feet. Step, step, jump, step, step, jump. She still remembered the movements Mrs. Farsyde had taught her and that she'd danced with Captain Samuel Ryethorpe in Thorpe Hall ballroom. If only they'd remained strangers, she'd dance with him anytime. If only Jonas would learn, she'd be dancing with a partner she loved.

The gavotte was floating dancing. Spirit of air and water dancing. She could do it on the ground and feel six foot in the air. Round and around. Jump, step, step, jump, step, step. That was what it was, and she could do it with a partner or no. She twirled, sand sticking to her boots until she reached the rocks. Avoiding the bright-green strands as best she could and popping the small brown bladders, she slipped and scrambled to reach the causeway.

Granite clouds hung heavy over dappled grey sea. Once on the solid jetty, she swished past the half dozen cobles, their flat bottoms beached on dry land. Abe Storm, Silas and other fishermen handed out baskets with their catch. A couple of lasses busied themselves laying fish in boxes and covering them with salt.

"That's not sort of dancing we do round here, Jiddy Vardy."

Right at top of the causeway sat Betsie and Annie. Straddled across cut barrels, surrounded by boxes, they stared at her. Annie's grey eyes glowed round in awe, but Betsie's squinted hard as jet.

"I said, no-one dances like that," said Betsie.

Two preventives she'd never seen before stood at a short distance. Jiddy glanced at the fishermen. They were very quiet considering they'd got a catch in.

"They're replacement preventives," said Annie.

"They don't hang about."

"No, they don't, and they've already got their beady eyes on us," said Betsie. "And it's all clever Jiddy Vardy's fault."

CHAPTER FOUR

T he two new preventives had their eyes fixed on the fishing cobles. Keeping them in sight, Jiddy sashayed towards the two girls.

"Want me to teach you to dance, Betsie?"

Betsie gripped the glistening haddock on her lap. "Like heck."

Jiddy swayed to an imaginary tune, holding in the tingle of Jonas she still felt between her legs. What would they say if they knew? She couldn't help it. She smiled.

"Jiddy..." Annie broke in.

Betsie rose to her feet. "There's more important things than laiking about."

Jiddy glanced from Annie to Betsie. For a moment, she wished it was her old adversary, Nellie, not Betsie standing on the top of the causeway. She'd have relished the knife and nick of Nellie's wit. But then that feeling was gone, snatched away with gulls calling for a share of fish.

"Right then." With a small smile at Annie and a quicker wink, Jiddy swished past them, escaping the odour of fish and Betsie's bad mood.

"See you later, Annie." She waved a hand and, unable to resist, started spinning again, making a circle in the dock as if marking an open-air ballroom.

"Jiddy, wait!"

She paused, hands resting on her partner's imaginary shoulders.

"Stay." Annie nodded her head in the direction of the two preventives watching the cobles being unloaded. Straight away, Jiddy got it. This wasn't a huge trawl of fish in the boats; it was a haul much more precious. She glanced at wild-haired Abe Storm.

"You all right up there?" His voice bellowed too jovial while his cheeks twitched taut.

Jiddy returned towards them.

"Now then, lass," said gap-toothed Silas, all dribble and spit.

"Now then, Silas."

She turned her head. Betsie glared straight at her. Annie's pale face trembled. It was obvious, now she realised; folk were unusually quiet for when a catch like this was brought in. And these two new preventives, taking the places of Jimmy and Kenny, might see the entire load exposed. A great beginning for them in the Bay.

Busy straightening a canvas over the haul, Abe shouted at a scrawny lad. Immediately, Jiddy connected the schooner she'd spotted while canoodling Jonas, with the cobles and their catch. No wonder the process of salting and boxing up was awkward with two preventives watching their movements. Underneath the layer of fish, there'd be oilskin parcels of silk and lace, packs of tobacco, boxes of tea and spices, even kegs of brandy and gin. All of them could be caught red-handed. Why hadn't someone given the order to wait a few weeks after last night's disaster?

Betsie forced a laugh that sounded like a nag's whinny, and with one hand on her hip and waving her other arm, she began acting like a demented teapot. Preventives didn't know what to make of it, standing as they were, caught between dotty local lasses and surly fishermen.

Annie's eyes were begging Jiddy. Abe's silence weighed like an approaching squall. Her boots crunched louder than she imagined they could.

"Now then." She nodded at Abe. Betsie gestured even more. Preventives were having none of it, and Jiddy couldn't blame them. Desperation smelt pungent as fish. The taller of the uniformed men noticed her. She hardly had to do anything and they looked in her direction. Sometimes she couldn't bear it, but she was highly aware it was a useful gift. Nobody round here had shining black curls or large dark eyes that could lure a spider from its dinner. She lifted her chin and smiled. She knew what that smile and her long, thick lashes could do. Sauntering forward, she readied to take Betsie's place.

Annie's blotchy face and red-rimmed eyes gave her away. Sweet Annie were too nervous for this. She'd crumple any second. Jiddy caught Betsie's arm and pulled her in, slapping a hand flat against her back.

"Act up," Jiddy whispered in Betsie's ear. "Pretend you've not a care in the world."

Betsie's body stiffened, and she struggled to free herself, but Jiddy held her close, stepping wider to shift

33

Betsie's feet. Their faces were close, and Jiddy could tell that Betsie wanted to gob her. She turned Betsie swiftly.

"One, two, three, one, two, three." She measured steps, twirling away from the slipway, faster, spinning skirts. "Are they following?"

"No."

"Skip, skip, jump. Keep doing it."

Now they'd started, they had to keep going. They'd look daft if they stopped. Annie's face was a blur, the dock a huge space.

"What about now?"

"They're watching."

Holding Betsie closer, Jiddy steered towards the two men, swishing their skirts.

"Squire holds a ball every so often," she said in their direction. "Those that have a bit of style and know-how get invited."

Gazing from beneath the power of her lashes, she looked at the nearest preventive.

"Bet you know how to gavotte without any lessons," she said before twirling a surprised Betsie away again, across the dock, slower this time, giving them a chance to follow. "Best night of whole year!" she shouted.

Both preventives followed like rats. Betsie tightened even more in Jiddy's hold. Sensing the men at the boats shift, Jiddy hoped Annie would calm down. Glancing over her shoulder, she saw that the men followed.

"Who's Squire Farsyde?"

Jiddy feigned surprise. "I thought you'd know. Didn't others tell you? Newcomers always pay their respects to Squire Farsyde when they first arrive on duty. Captain Ryethorpe won't be too pleased if he hears you haven't been. I'd get myself up there right fast if I were you and claim your glass of port. Squire usually has it laid out on a tray for newcomers, but I'm guessing your fellow soldiers want to play a joke on you."

She waited, letting the words sink in. They all waited. Would they go on the fool's errand or stay and see the contraband Abe and Silas were so desperate to hide?

"Where is it, you say?"

"Top of bank, left up to Fylingthorpe and left again down to ford and Thorpe Hall. You'll see building from top of road. No missing it."

The red-faced one touched the hilt of a blade stuck in his belt, while the taller one looked over his shoulder at the men on the slipway. Annie stared into her barrel as if she'd like to sink into it. These new recruits bouldered heavy. Their faces hung tired and sceptical. Betsie breathed too loud. The anticipation they all felt speckled the atmosphere. A smile wouldn't work. They were going to remain in the dock and then…and then…

Jiddy kept her voice low and her offer humble.

"I can show you way if you'd like?"

CHAPTER FIVE

Relieved she only had to point the way for the soldiers—now eager, they could taste the port from the top of the bank—Jiddy jogged back down the hill and, bounding up the steps of Sunny Place, leapt through the open doorway. Gracie sat knitting. Mary was asleep, chin resting on her chest. She looked pale even with the heat of the fire. Helen Drake hovered around the table. Jiddy hated Helen hanging around with her predictions of gloom, and as soon as she saw Helen's magpie-sharp eyes, she couldn't stop herself.

"I sent two new preventives up to Thorpe Hall to demand their welcome drink," she said, strutting over to stand between Mary and Gracie. "Wish I'd gone with them to watch Squire Farsyde send 'em packing."

"What you on about now?" Gracie said with that softness to her voice.

Helen cut in before Jiddy could answer. "Being too clever by half, that's what she's on about."

Mary remained gently snoring.

"It got Abe Storm and Silas Biddick out of a scrape, so yes, it were clever," Jiddy said.

Helen Drake pulled that face of hers. Jiddy laughed.

"It were only a bit of fun to get rid of them. Abe Storm had more than fish in his boat."

"Your bit of fun will end in tears one day," said Helen. She glanced at Gracie. "I'll be stepping on. Tell Mary I'll check in tomorrow."

"Thanks, Helen."

"Thanks, Helen," Jiddy mocked as the door closed and they heard Helen's clogs on the step.

"Don't be rude," said Mary without opening her eyes.

Jiddy bent down and touched Mary's hands. "Were you faking sleep just to get rid of her?"

Mary's dull eyes snapped open. "She's right, you know. You're so sharp sometimes, you'll cut yourself."

"I don't mean to."

"Don't mean to indeed." Mary patted Jiddy's hand. "Let's go down to graveyard. I fancy a bit of fresh air, and we can have a word with Thomas at same time. Think you could do with a bit of his wisdom."

"I don't think it's a good idea, do you, Mary?" said Gracie, shaking her head at Jiddy. "You're not well enough, love, and day's getting on. Maybe tomorrow."

Mary pushed herself up. "Tomorrow might never happen."

"If you want to go, I'll take you," Jiddy said, hurrying to help.

"Now, Jiddy…"

"Thank you for thinking on me, Gracie," said Mary, "but this may be last time I'll be fit enough."

There was no way Jiddy could say no. She slipped one arm around Mary's back, and Gracie was on her feet straight away, tucking Mary's shawl around her face and an extra one for good measure. Jiddy busied, gathering cloths and a flask of water from the barrel she'd carried in the other day.

It took some time to walk the short way up to graveyard, and Jiddy tried to be patient, but it wasn't easy. They stopped at the slope to the main road, then again a few feet on, then again before mounting the steps. Just when she thought Mary couldn't walk any slower or stop any more times, they reached the rectangle of graves.

Jiddy knelt in front of Thomas's headstone. It was a rough piece of rock, but Robert Drake had chiselled Thomas's name and the date he'd died. Well wrapped in thick shawls, Mary sat on a three-legged stool while Jiddy gave the stone its ritual clean and wondered what wisdom Mary wanted Thomas to relate.

Mary pointed. "This bit, here."

Jiddy scrubbed the corner of stone. The activities of the previous night were beginning to take their toll, and her patience ebbed.

"And there."

If Mary pointed again, Jiddy would throw down the cloth, stand up and march off and leave her there. She knew she should be more patient, but it was so hard with someone telling her what to do. Even Mary. *Could be worse*, Jiddy reminded herself. At least she'd been brought up by Mary and not Helen horror-basket Drake or 'I hate Northerners' Signora Vardarelli.

Mary pointed again. Gulls crapped all day and seemed like every one of them had emptied their backsides on the graveyard with Thomas's grave their favourite target.

"I'm getting to it, give me time," Jiddy said, scrubbing hard at the crusted bird dirt.

Not that long ago, Mary would have retaliated, but she was a lot quieter nowadays. She'd developed a patience with Jiddy that was unsettling and which Jiddy didn't seem able to return. Mary was almost like one of the saints on the wall in the reverend's vestry—the one that looked into the distance as if watching for a ship to come in. This wasn't the Mary Jiddy had known all her life, the one who couldn't sit still for two moments together.

Jiddy glanced up at the rustling tall beeches. The wind hadn't yet settled, and grey clouds skittled overhead. Fronds of last year's blackberries clustered over the mossed cemetery walls, stripped now of their fruits and battered by last night's storm.

"You've done a grand job," Mary said in the monotone voice she'd developed of late. "Thank you."

Jiddy scrubbed a large white splodge. "Can't have Thomas covered in muck. He'll be back to haunt us, and we can't have that, can we?"

Mary smiled. Serene.

Fifteen minutes later, brushing down her skirt, Jiddy admired the clean headstone. It was rough Yorkshire stone, already weathered by seasons of rain and wind. The small graveyard stood almost full of graves, and as she always did, Jiddy wondered where they'd fit more corpses.

"When I die, I want to be put in a boat and set on fire and pushed out to sea like a Viking."

Mary smiled again, that angelic, listening smile, but her eyes struggled to connect. "I want to be lying here with Thomas, and I hope you will when your time comes."

A rush of tears swept through Jiddy, and she crouched at Mary's feet, clutching the motionless hands in the old woman's lap.

"Don't say that."

"It's what I want."

"But not yet."

It was hard keeping eye contact with someone who didn't seem as if they were looking at you.

"You don't think I were daft sending preventives up to Thorpe Hall, do you?" She hoped Mary would say *no, of course not, it was a clever, fun prank to play.* "It were to get them away from dock, that's all. If they'd stayed, they'd have seen contraband under fish, and they'd have arrested Abe and Silas and whole crew."

The serene expression on Mary's face didn't falter, but she said, "It'll make trouble of sorts."

Jiddy stood up. That wasn't what she wanted to hear. Bending again, she busied to pack the basket.

"When you've finished, I want you to lift up that white rock in top right corner by headstone."

Jiddy looked at the grave with its border of sandy stones. She'd always thought the white one odd, but Mary insisted it be there. *"It's an angel keeping eye on Thomas,"* Mary had always said.

Jiddy kneeled down. "This one?"

"Are there any other white ones?"

Mary'd lost none of her corners after all. Underneath the white stone, buried flat into the soil lay a small wooden box.

"Dig it out, then," said Mary. "And open it."

Inside, cradled in soft fabric, lay a diamond brooch. It shone dully, but even so, it was large and reflective in the day's thin light. Jiddy couldn't hide her astonishment. Mary held out her hand, and Jiddy passed over the box.

"Captain Pinkney gave it me," she said. "We didn't ask for anything. We were glad to take you, but he insisted." She looked at the jewel again. "He said it were for you. We kept it behind a loose stone in fireplace, but that always bothered me. I worried it would melt, so when Thomas died, I put it here."

"Aren't you worried someone will take it?"

"It's still here, isn't it?" Mary held it out. "You can put it back under stone for when you need it. I just wanted you to know where it were before…in case, you know, with me. Now, it's getting chill," she said. "Best be finishing up."

Footsteps caught Jiddy's attention. A girl approached, pink-faced and breathless, tripping up the cemetery steps in her hurry.

"It's Violet Ashner, Nellie's younger sister," Jiddy told Mary.

Weaving between the graves, lanky Violet Ashner stumbled over the uneven ground.

"You took some finding," she said, puffing out of breath. "It's Mrs. Farsyde. Says she needs you and nobody else'll do."

Violet's face scowled with effort. Jiddy bent to take Mary's arm.

"Missus says now," Violet said. "You don't want it spoken she's lost this baby cos Jiddy Vardy were too busy to come?"

"I'm taking Mary home first."

"I could tell squire it were you who sent those two nicky-ninnies up to hall."

Violet stopped speaking, catching sight of the open box in Jiddy's hand. Without a word, Jiddy closed it.

"Now then, Violet, how's family?" Mary asked, fixing her eyes on the colt-like girl.

"Da's still on whaling ship, Mrs. Waite," Violet said, her eyes lingering on the box.

"Help me up, girl." Mary reached for Violet's arm, and Violet had no choice but to help her walk along the path and not watch Jiddy replace the white stone at the side of Thomas's grave.

RUTH ESTEVEZ

CHAPTER SIX

Mrs. Farsyde made climbing stairs look worse than poor Gracie walking up Main Street. She gasped and panted and clung with both hands to the balustrade like it was a barrel keeping her afloat.

"D'you want hand?" Jiddy asked from where she stood at the bottom of the stairs.

Violet lingered near the door leading to the kitchens.

Mrs. Farsyde waved her away then gripped the balustrade again. Jiddy readied to leap forward at any moment. She knew the squire's wife hated being treated like an invalid and wouldn't thank her for fussing, but Violet had come to fetch her and made it sound urgent.

"Violet said you needed me."

"To see some lace."

Of course. Valenciennes lace that had come in last night. That had been brought up quick, and too right it had. Faster it was out with the gentry, less likely any in Bay would be caught.

"Right," Jiddy said, foot on the first step.

Mrs. Farsyde stopped, held her stomach and groaned. "Don't fuss."

Jiddy kept her mouth shut and remained on the bottom step. This being-with-child malarkey didn't look fun at all. It couldn't be good for you if it made you so sick,

43

and when you stopped being sick, weight of your belly started making your back ache. Who in God's world would choose that?

She waited. She hadn't been able to hide her shock at seeing how Mrs. Farsyde had bloated over the months since Jiddy had returned from the big city. It was horrific watching this graceful woman waddle around a room, hands supporting her back and moaning as if she'd broken it. Up close—unlike women of Bay, who didn't appear much different with child or not, they wore so many shawls—Mrs. Farsyde had turned into another person completely.

The squire's voice, loud as usual, blasted around the cracks of his study door. Whoever was with him had wound him up. His visitor spoke softer, but in their silence, waiting for Mrs. Farsyde to give her orders, Jiddy heard every word.

"I need your cooperation in obliterating the gangs," the other voice said. "I promise you, I will stamp them out with or without your help."

The squire was having none of it.

"I don't know what you mean, sir. What gangs might these be?"

"It's Captain Ryethorpe," said Violet. "He's up here all time, bothering either squire or..." She cast her eyes up the stairs. "Or her."

Damn. She'd been distracted, and Violet Ashner knew it. At least he'd not mentioned Nellie's body gone from the gibbet. Sounded like he'd more important plans for the villagers. Violet mustn't know either. Jiddy held the younger girl's stare, until, with that self-satisfied smile exactly like Nellie's, Violet broke her gaze and closed the servant's door behind her. Jiddy stepped on the second stair.

"Don't," Mrs. Farsyde said, waving a hand.

Fine. She wouldn't do anything, then, if it was all *don't do this, don't do that.* She waited where she was, distracted again by the men's voices.

"I am telling you, sir, I will root out each member of this smuggling ring if I have to question every man, woman and child in Robin Hood's Bay."

Jiddy waited for the squire to reply, but Mrs. Farsyde groaned again. It was too distracting, and she missed what the squire said. Surely, he wouldn't let every man, woman and child be questioned. He couldn't. Jiddy stared at her mistress, wondering how anyone had a baby on purpose. The men's voices became muffled. She'd have to find out later what they planned.

"Some women are stronger than others," Mary had said when Jiddy told her how much the squire's wife had blown up like a whale.

It couldn't be right, though. If it made you so haggard and exhausted by sicking up whatever you ate one minute and eating like a bull seal the next, there must be something wrong with the child. What was it babies knew about the world they were coming into if they refused to be born? No-one wanted to ask, not when the squire's wife had lost so many babies and this being the first to almost reach full-term. Jiddy didn't want to voice her doubts, not even to Annie, as to what the baby would be like when it made Mrs. Farsyde so sick. It must be some form of monster in her belly.

She had come to a standstill on the top stair, and Jiddy wondered why she didn't keep going now she'd got momentum up.

Thoughts swarmed through Jiddy's head. If the swollen woman fell backwards, she'd land on her and maybe Mrs. Farsyde would be all right, but she'd definitely crush Jiddy. *She must be heavier than a full tub of whale blubber.* Jiddy would have to bear it, though, because nothing bad must happen to that longed-for child.

The door behind opened then rapidly banged shut. Swift footsteps.

Samuel. Captain Ryethorpe rather. Pushing her aside, he bounded up the stairs, all righteousness and uniform. She'd like to see him try rushing up like that with a belly the size of Mrs. Farsyde's. Or even Squire Farsyde's. Typical officer, shoving his way through, showing off and taking over when no-one wanted him around. Jiddy would bet he was showing off in front of her as well. *"Look at me. This is what you could have had."* No way. No way, Mister Show-off who snogs like a wriggling kipper.

She couldn't believe it. He'd taken Mrs. Farsyde's arm and put his free one around her waist. Around her waist! And she let him, which was even worse. The squire had better not see that or Sam—*Captain Ryethorpe* would be chased off the premises by hounds, or even shot in the backside as he sprinted away down drive. She glanced at the closed study door, expecting it to be wrenched open.

"I think I'd best help," Jiddy said, climbing the next few steps, her heavy shoes loud on the oak boards.

The captain's face as he turned around could have halted a bull. He must hate her for telling him she couldn't marry him after all, but this was a reaction she'd not expected. His expression said he didn't want her within a hundred miles never mind in the same house. Well, stuff that. He'd no place at Thorpe Hall. He was an incomer and an officer on the other side of the law to them, and he was from the South to finish off that argument.

He'd turned back to Mrs. Farsyde, and he was saying something. How dare he bully a woman who could barely walk? And how ruddy dare he look at her as if she was a squashed beetle?

"Captain Ryethorpe?" Jiddy said good and loud, making sure the squire heard. Even she was impressed by her tone. She must have picked up some of Signora Vardarelli's lofty ways back in London.

He seemed merely annoyed this time. Worried, no doubt. However, the squire still didn't appear, and Samuel still moved his palm over Mrs. Farsyde's shoulder blades while she clung to his arm. That wasn't good. Jiddy took a few more steps towards them but stopped when she saw Mrs. Farsyde's face.

She had colour in her cheeks for the first time in weeks, and the look she'd given Samuel still hung on her features. She had the same dreamy expression Jonas had when Jiddy and he were full-on kissing, and for a moment, Samuel held the same hazy gaze when he looked at her.

They were in love. Watching them, even in that fraction of time, Jiddy knew. She'd seen their exchange, and they'd seen that she'd seen it.

Mrs. Farsyde looked terrified now. Too right. The squire would not want the captain of dragoons in love with his wife. Jiddy couldn't fight the other feeling that rose up her chest either. How dare Samuel replace her so quickly? And with someone who was married and chucking up each morning and waddling around the house as unwieldy as a calf-bearing heifer.

A noise made her turn around. The squire couldn't see them. He mustn't. But it wasn't the squire staring up at them. Caught in the doorway between the hall and the corridor leading down to the kitchen stood Violet, who stared at Samuel and Mrs. Farsyde with an unmistakable look of glee on her face.

CHAPTER SEVEN

The next morning, Jiddy found Violet around the back of the house in the yard, hanging out bedsheets. One, half-pegged, cracked wet in the wind, and Violet struggled as it wrapped around her.

"Let me help," Jiddy said, bending to pick up a couple of pegs.

"I don't need help."

The sheet slapped Violet again, enveloping her in its folds. Jiddy watched the shape inside, a moving ghost that was Violet, struggling to unwind herself. This wasn't a pleasant job. Jiddy knew well enough the smarting cuts of wind-dried knuckles and numbed fingers. Prising the sheet away, Jiddy scrambled for the edge. It fought back, intent on clinging to Violet, but Jiddy had battled with gale-whipped sheets before and she yanked hard.

"Peg it," she ordered.

Violet darted forward, nipping the top edge to the line. It tugged and snapped, but the pegs held.

"There's two more sheets to do," Violet said.

They lifted the next one out together, finding the edges and staying close.

"Got your pegs?" asked Jiddy.

Violet nodded. Funny. Jiddy had never thought they looked alike, but Violet did have a strong resemblance

49

to Nellie when you were up close. Same nose and mouth. It was an Ashner face. She grasped the sheet.

"Ready?"

They raised the bundle between them, and stepping apart, gripping tight, they opened out the bedlinen. The wind lifted it, almost dragging Violet off her feet. She screamed. Laughing, half with shock and half at the comedy, Jiddy nipped in her elbows, her muscles rounding as she gripped hard.

"I'll peg my end first," she said.

No answer. She couldn't see Violet with all the rippling fabric. How could anyone be expected to do this on their own? It made her angry, the thought of Mrs. Farsyde all fresh in clean sheets and Violet out here battling to pin them on the line to dry, and all after the struggle to wash out stains and wring the water from them.

She looked up at the first-floor windows. They'd not have a clue, her and Samuel, all doe-eyed and oblivious to what went on to make them so comfortable. *Jiddy, mend this. Violet, bring me some cake. Do this, take that away.*

"Jiddy!"

Violet's shouts were desperate. Jiddy fumbled with the pegs. One held, but she dropped the rest.

"Keep hold," she shouted against the cracking sheet.

Edging down, praying the one peg would hold, she grabbed the other two. A gust, and the sheet ballooned between them. Jiddy punched it back, pegged it down and traced the line to secure the second peg. Violet pulled taut her end until the sheet snatched but could not escape.

Violet stood panting, shoulders sagging and face drawn. She was exhausted, Jiddy could tell. Violet turned to the basket.

"I can manage now," she said.

"No, you can't."

Violet squatted by the basket.

"You all right?" Jiddy asked.

She saw the crown of Violet's head with its wide parting and white scalp. Violet had thin hair like Nellie. Winter brown and scratty as worn-out leaves. Jiddy knew the Ashner brood swelled like a rabbit warren and that Violet had lost three younger siblings in the long, drawn-out cold snap they'd had that February.

"Does Mrs. King give you leftovers to take home?"

Violet glanced up, her angular face smeared hungry. Hungry for more than this. She was nothing like Nellie in that regard. Nellie knew how to fight. Violet had to find other ways to get by. Sneaky ways.

Violet's lilac hands, reddened around the knuckles, clutched the sheet.

Jiddy crouched down. "It's none of our business what them in house get up to," she said. Violet stared, cold-eyed. "They're just people. They make mistakes. We're better than that. We make mistakes and we help each other get out of them."

Violet's eyes gave nothing away, but Jiddy knew that look. It was the look people had when they were too tired to think let alone speak.

"Last one," Jiddy said, rising to her feet.

51

The cotton clung to itself, making it heavier than the rest. Violet readjusted her hold and stumbled as she stood. It was even harder to control the last sheet. They were both tired and the wind determined to get the better of them.

"Do your side first," Jiddy said.

Violet didn't say a word as she grappled to keep hold, and she didn't drop a single peg as she wrestled with a cloud of white five times her size. Jiddy waited, hands numbed with wet and cold, taking longer to wriggle her pegs into position while still clutching the flapping sheet. Finally, breathing hard, they stood back to watch the sheets ripple in the wind. It was a grand sight. Large white flags like rolling white waves. Violet didn't linger. She walked back to the basket.

"Let's go beg some hot tea," Jiddy said.

Violet kneaded her hands together.

"It's bitter, Violet. We've earned it."

Violet's pinched face would have broken the toughest preventive. She lifted another item from the basket. White like the sheets but lace-edged and many times smaller. It was Mrs. Farsyde's nightgown, stained with small brown patches.

"Blood," said Violet. "I can't get it out."

"It'll need washing again," said Jiddy. "Why can't she be more careful?"

An explosion of gunshot sounded, and crows rose black and squawking from the elms.

"Flaming fires," said Jiddy. "Squire Farsyde's practising shooting someone. I'm half-hoping it'll be the captain, what d'you say?"

"We've got summat on captain with him being so sweet on Missus. If you make it so obvious, squire'll have to shoot him and we need this hold over them."

She shoved the nightgown into her hands, and Jiddy couldn't hide her surprise.

"That lot treated our Nellie like dirt and I'll not forget it!" Violet flung the words over her shoulder as she marched past. "Leave squire to me," she said. "I'll calm him down as long as you sort her upstairs out."

53

CHAPTER EIGHT

J onas pushed an armful of hay into the feeding trough
then, slapping the longhorn's back, pushed it aside.

"Violet's fourteen or fifteen at most," said Jiddy.
"Did you hear? Violet says she knows how to calm Squire
Farsyde down? You know what she means, don't you?
I can't believe she'd put herself through that, and it didn't
sound like the first time."

"Sounds like she's just going to flatter him to me."

"D'you think? I don't know, sounded a bit more than
that to me. How could Squire Farsyde? Yuck. It's horrible."

"Maybe she's more like Nellie than you think."

"It's Squire Farsyde who should be the grown-up in
this. He's married, and Mrs. Farsyde's having his baby.
What if she knows?"

"She probably does."

"What? That's worse."

"Have you not heard of gentry using their rights over
servants?"

"It isn't right. I don't think having more money than
someone else gives them any right to take advantage."

"Hard for a young lass to say no to a man like squire."

"Men should be strung high for it."

Jonas took an armful of hay, peppering the air
with dust.

"I like the squire," Jiddy said. "Rather, I did like him. I don't know, I thought he was a good man. Not now, oh, no, not anymore."

"This is why I worried about you working at hall in first place," said Jonas. "Lucky I know how you like to fight. Nobody can take advantage of you."

She glowered at Jonas. It was all right for him. He was a farmer. No-one told him what to do except his da and whoever was heading a run.

"I wish I were a man sometimes," she said. "You don't have to put up with any of this flattering and charming your way through life business."

Jonas carried a second armful and grinned. "Are you so sure we don't?"

"I feel so sorry for Violet," she said, ignoring him. "I'm going to do something to help her if nobody else will."

"She won't thank you."

"I don't need her to. This is for all lasses who work up at hall. All lasses in Bay, in fact."

"Did Nellie ever thank you for adding your pennyworth?"

"Are you saying I'm meddling?"

"Do you take kindly when someone tells you what to do?"

Jiddy folded her arms.

"I think Violet can handle herself," he continued. "She's an Ashner, isn't she? Knowing squire, he'll be kind to her, and if not, give me a shout and I'll set Rex on him."

Jiddy sat on an upturned bucket. *Kind.* That seemed a word with many meanings. It didn't sound kind if he needed young girls to flatter him. And he wasn't kind to Mrs. Farsyde if she thought about it. Squire was off a lot with his meetings and such. He left his wife alone in that big house for days. Was any of that kind?

"What about Captain Ryethorpe and Mrs. Farsyde? That isn't right, is it?" she said. "Maybe Squire Farsyde suspects. What d'you think if I tell Mrs. Farsyde we all know? She'll have to put an end to it with Captain Ryethorpe if she thinks they're in danger of being found out, and squire'll settle down and stop firing pistol out of window and Violet'll stop thinking she needs to calm him down. That's what'd be best, wouldn't it? Should I do that? What d'you think?"

Jonas gave the beast a shove. "How did other night go?"

"You never answer me."

"I listened. Do what you said and see what happens."

Jiddy watched him moving between the animals. He was so different when he had farm work to do. Well, she'd answer his questions even if he gave her offhand answers in return. She'd think of a plan all on her own.

"You heard about Jimmy Dowd and Kenny McLean?" she asked.

His head disappeared behind the longhorn. "Whole of Yorkshire knows."

"Some are saying there'll be price to pay and Captain Ryethorpe is on warpath. He were up at hall talking to

56

Squire Farsyde." Jiddy flicked a piece of straw at the animal's back.

Jonas didn't answer.

"Did you hear? I said, some are saying—"

"I heard." He reappeared, pushing towards her again. "Those in charge don't care about two preventives going missing. That Captain Ryethorpe'll just bring in more thugs to replace them."

Sometimes, just sometimes, Jiddy wished he was a bit less sure of everything.

"He sounds determined to put an end to smuggling ring because of it."

"You seem to have heard a lot of what Captain Ryethorpe is up to when you're supposed to be caring for Mrs. Farsyde."

Typical Jonas, seeing what she wanted to hide.

"I take care of her. I know birth bed can be as much a danger as sea."

Jonas laughed. "You come out with some rubbish at times. Shows how they gentrified you in London."

"They did not!"

"They did. Stop contradicting."

"I'm not."

He looked at her. That eleven-year-old boy talking down to her eight-year-old self. She tossed her hair.

"It's nowt to do with gentrified. It's how I talk, and I'll not change for no haystack lad."

"Budge." He dumped another armful of hay into the trough, holding the white-backed cow away with his shoulder.

She watched, wondering if she could find a way to tell him about Samuel's exchange with the squire's wife without letting on how jealous it had made her feel. It was so strange. She didn't care about Samuel anymore, but she didn't like the thought of him liking someone else as much as he'd liked her. It wasn't fair when Mrs. Farsyde was married and childbearing even if the squire did neglect her.

Jonas stood still, a faraway look on his face. He was good-looking without realising it, though the gaggle of lasses that would swoon when he passed should have given him some hint. Too busy ranting about government and laws to notice, he said. Too busy putting right all the mischief she caused, he insisted. It was moments like that when her heart yearned to hold him.

She waved the piece of straw at him. "What you thinking?"

"What a pain in the backside you are when a person's got work to do. Why don't you bugger off and teach hens some of that spinning stuff you were doing on beach."

"You saw me? You were watching?"

"I saw you thinking you were as hoity as gentry."

"I don't know," she said. "You just can't keep your eyes off me."

"Like a blind man."

"I remember you spying on me at hall, when Missus were teaching me to dance. Bet you're going to deny it, aren't you? But I saw you. I know."

"I don't need to deny it. I were coming to give you a lift out of goodness of my heart, and you came out with your hair all curled and too full of yourself to bother wanting to kiss me as you'd promised."

He pushed his way between the longhorns again.

Jiddy remembered the exact moment he was talking about. She had been excited. She loved the way her hair had bounced, and she'd wanted to show him. And the dancing with Samuel, guided by Mrs. Farsyde, had been scary but such, such fun.

"I did want to kiss you. I had to force you to stop Boy, and we went into woods, and we leaned against a tree, and oh—Rebecca spotted us. It's you that don't remember anything." She trailed away at the thought of Rebecca.

"'Course I remember. You were a right little frisky mare. I notice everything, like when you're mad at me like you were two seconds ago or when you want me to hold you, like three seconds ago, or like when you've been wearing one of Mrs. Farsyde's dresses and you don't want to take it off. I know when you've been up to put flowers on Thomas's grave and when you've had a bad night with Mary. So don't tell me I don't see nowt."

He bent low, stuffing hay into the feeding basket. Jonas never told her things like this. He had noticed that she wanted to hold him before she properly realised it herself.

"I remember I wanted to teach you what I learned about dancing," she said.

"I don't remember any teaching." Jonas's voice came out muffled as he bent to check an animal's hooves.

"You're not jealous, are you?" she asked.

Jonas studied the cow's hoof for some time. He straightened up and patted its rump.

"Jonas? Were you jealous?"

"Why should I be jealous? You're my lass, aren't you?"

His eyes looked unsure. A rare moment. He pushed the animal aside. Taking his arm, she pulled it around her waist and kissed his cheek, but he still looked wary.

"Are you sure you're lad enough for me?" With a grand gesture, she kissed his hand. He pulled it away before brushing past.

"Can't you see I'm busy? I haven't time for soppiness right now."

She grabbed his arm and pulled him to snuggle close against the animal's warm flank. "You were the one that started it."

"Shift, Jiddy."

She squared up. He patted the longhorn's neck and rested his hand. He wouldn't catch her eye.

"What's up?" she asked. "I can read you too, you know. I can tell what you want to do next."

He sighed one of his big, heavy sighs. "No you can't tell. You can't tell that I hate it when you talk about Captain Ryethorpe. If you knew that, you wouldn't bring up his

60

name and talk about dancing and stuff you did with him. I don't like it, all right?"

She rested her face on his jacket. She hadn't expected that. "I'm your lass," she said, "and you brought it up first."

He edged her away. "I can't tell what you're saying when you mumble. I don't know why you have to keep bringing him up, that's all."

He avoided looking at her, so she grabbed his chin and made him. His grey eyes did look hurt.

"It's all in your head," she said. "Not that there's much in there."

He pulled her in to kiss her, and she laughed. The heat of the animals and noise of them made the barn cosy. Whatever misunderstandings, they didn't matter because if they stood close, their bodies spoke loudest.

"I'm sorry. I don't mean to make you jealous. I worry you've not forgiven me for going off to London, that's all. But you know I had to leave Bay, even for a short time. I only mention the captain because he were kind to me, and I didn't know anyone in London, and Signora Vardarelli were that mean."

He forced a laugh. "Some mother she turned out to be, didn't she?"

She loved his ruddy freckles and his thick eyebrows and hair and the way he didn't let her get away with anything. He kept her on her toes. Kept her sharp. That made it seem as if he cared. Every other lad she could run rings around, but not Jonas. Jonas gave as good as he got. She pulled his head down to meet her.

61

"Let's forget cows and captains," she said.

She traced the line between his lips with her tongue. His mouth broadened in a smile. She loved the sound they made when they kissed. With the animals shifting, the feel of life around them, it all made what Jonas and she wanted to do to each other a natural thing and not something they should wait to do. One day, they wouldn't be able to stop, and what would happen then? She didn't care. Right now, kissing Jonas, she didn't care if they weren't married. She curved her body, and his grip tightened. He'd begun to stiffen. She lifted his hand and slid it over her breast. His touch was light, fingers sliding. They were so, so warm. Any moment, they'd cup her buttocks, and then who knew what would happen? Behind her, the cow moved, and the curve of its belly held her. She felt its muscles press. Jonas slid his hands down her arms and held her elbows. He dropped his head. Held her still. His breath came out wanting.

"Jiddy, I can't. I haven't finished, and Da will be in, wondering what's taking so long."

He pressed her away, sliding towards the stack of hay. She closed her eyes.

"We can't keep stopping like this," she said.

He looked at her as he adjusted himself.

"Want me to help?"

"Get on with you." He turned away.

She straightened her chemise, cradling a hand in the dip between her breasts. It was more than she could bear.

"Are you going to take over farm from your da?" she asked.

"I'd rather farm than owt else."

"Rather than what you do with me?"

He patted one of the animals. "As well as."

"Farmer Jonas?"

"That name'll do me."

"Haven't they enough hay?"

"One more."

"There's a raid on this Friday. The ship's coming from France, and Abe says there's no turning it back."

"I know."

She waited for him to say more, but he wasn't Mr. Talkative. He really had turned back into Farmer Jonas.

"I heard you're not taking cart out?" she said. "Is there something wrong with it?"

"I told Abe I need Boy more than usual at moment on farm, and I've still last load to shift if you remember. So, Stan Mason agreed to use his."

"Stan Mason's farm is miles away—"

"D'you know what, Jiddy?" Jonas interrupted. "I'd be happy never to do another run in my life."

"And what? Lend out your cart every time? Thought you hated others handling Boy."

"I mean it. I've got enough on with farm. I don't want to be up half night then knackered when I've got jobs to do next day. I'll not need to lend out Boy and cart if Stan's happy to do it. I want none of it anymore. Me and Da can get by without."

"What about salt for preserving meat through winter? And tea? We all need our cups of tea."

"I'll pay for it. We can sell logs from bottom wood."

"Jonas, tax on tea is more than cost of a few trees."

"I'm tired of it, Jiddy."

She waited, but he kept his face turned away.

"Ah, deedums," she said. "Does poor Farmer Chaplow need his beauty sleep?"

Jonas grabbed a broom and began giving short sweeps and making a pile of stalks and dust. "D'you see yourself out smuggling every night 'til you're fifty or so?"

"Yes!" Jiddy didn't hesitate. "I'd have stopped in London if I wanted a boring life. Maybe you should go down to London if you're so soft you can't keep your eyes open after a few hours on clifftop."

Jonas gave her feet a swift shove with the broom, and she jumped out of the way. Something was brewing. Maybe she shouldn't have mentioned London again.

"Did you only come back because you were bored?" he asked.

He gave gentler jabs. It made her smile. She did know him so well. He wanted to hear that she'd come back for him.

"Stand still a minute," she said. Your da won't mind." She clasped his face.

Pressing his lips made them squidge, reminding her how plump they were. Without releasing his face, she gazed into his eyes.

Throwing down the brush, he pulled her in. Thank heavens they had this. Words flew out the window when they got this close. Kissing Jonas was the best thing in the world. She must have lost all her sense ever thinking Samuel and his thin lips were worth considering. She'd tell Jonas that. Another day.

"M-m-mmm." She made the noise playfully.

Hands on her waist, he shook her, and she cupped his neck, holding her mouth to his. This was it. Life was back to how it should be. She wanted to do what they'd done yesterday, have that feeling again that made her more dizzy than running up a hill too fast and gulping in air too quick. She couldn't stop thinking about it. What if they flung themselves down in the hay? Could she resist sliding her hands under his shirt and feeling his warm ribs? She'd be desperate to undo her buttons and guide his hands onto her back and belly and maybe higher. *Oh, lordy.* This temptation was too much and her brain couldn't take it and she couldn't think and she didn't want to think.

"I love you, Jonas." The words foamed out of her mouth, a mixture of kiss and breath.

"Huh?" The noise sounded at the back of his throat.

"Mmm..."

Kiss, kiss, kiss, kiss, kiss. She wanted a better word. A softer word, warmer, wetter, a sound rather than a word so that they could speak it without it escaping into the air.

His hands moved, rucking over her jacket and up her back. She draped her arms over his shoulders, allowing space between their bodies. *Touch me*, she willed.

RUTH ESTEVEZ

Touch my breast. Instead, he drew his mouth over her lips and kissed her nose, then her cheek. She rubbed her skull against his.

"We could make this our life, Jiddy," he said, his voice drowsy.

She kissed the curve below his shoulder. "I'd be happy doing this all day, week after week."

"I'm serious." He leaned back.

She smiled at him. "So am I."

She reached to draw in his lips again, plump and juicy and pressing, but he held her at arm's length.

"Hey!" she protested, pushing at his rigid arms. "Let me kiss you."

"I were thinking about it all time you were away," he said, freeing himself and walking to lean against the wall.

She followed. "Don't think about it, let's do it."

"I don't want to hide anymore. You being away showed me that."

Jiddy stopped. He sounded serious. This could only mean one thing. Well, why not? She were seventeen now. Mary would be pleased, and that would mean they didn't need to hold back anymore. But if they did it, that might mean a baby. *Yuck.* She couldn't bear the thought of a mewling, red-faced infant.

"D'you mean you want to wed soon?" she asked.

Pushing himself from the wall, he walked to meet her. "I think most already know about us, so they won't be surprised."

66

"I don't think they know *all* about us." She smiled, touching his chest. "They might be surprised to know how close we've come."

"Well, we'd best not tell 'em everything." His eyes fixed on hers. She smiled, and he kissed her nose. "When we have kiddies, though, I want them to know I'm a farmer and nowt else."

"You are a farmer," she said. "Grumpy Farmer Jonas."

"*Only* a farmer, I said."

"And I'll only be a seamstress."

"I don't want to lie."

"What's there to lie about? We'll be married. Nothing to hide then." She snuggled closer, arms woven around him again.

"I don't want to carry on with the smuggling business," he said. "We have to lie about it, and I don't want to hide anything anymore. I mean, anything. I want to be me, honestly me, and I want to bring our bairns up being honest too."

"We don't have to tell them 'til they're old enough to understand," she said.

"If I have to explain it, it can't be right, can it?"

Ever since they'd been children, he'd been able to stump her with his way of thinking, and he stumped her now. She studied him instead of answering. His cheeks were flushed, and he had that face like when he was talking about taxes and government and who made up the laws that they lived by. She understood those now, they'd been rammed into her often enough. Plus, she'd seen what they meant for herself.

But this was different. This was going against what they'd always done together. This was starting new. This would be them cast adrift from the smuggling ring. This was what Jonas had been thinking about; a different future to the one she saw and not an easy one hereabout.

"I don't want to lend my cart and horse for carrying smugglers' goods anymore," he said.

"Your da gets a barrel of brandy for it."

"I want to have only what I earn from farming."

"But everyone does it."

"Everyone doing something don't make it right."

"Brandy and extra stuff is payment for doing a job. It's not different."

"It's not a job I can talk about to all farmers I meet at market, is it? Did you tell your mother and that Lord Ryethorpe you were a smuggler by night? Did you tell them you're a thief?"

"We're not thieves. And we can all help each other keep our mouths shut." She nuzzled his neck, but he wasn't having any of it.

"If we wed and I have kiddies with you, I want to tell them about everything I do that puts food in their bellies and clothes on their backs."

"Kiddies can know about it. I were smuggling at eight years old," Jiddy said, posing with her hands on her hips. "Captain Pinkney made me youngest smuggler in Robin Hood's Bay. Ever."

"He had no right."

"Were you jealous?"

Jonas raised an eyebrow. There it was again. That word kept rearing up. It was so odd. She'd never thought of Jonas as being jealous, and at times, she'd been desperate for him to be, but it had always been her. Jealous when he spoke to Nellie, then when Nellie flirted with him. When Betsie and Annie laughed with him. Jealous that he had a da and he'd had a mam and that his family had always lived at Meadow Bank Farm and that the whole of Yorkshire knew who the Chaplows were. He'd been above jealousy, but since Samuel had arrived in Bay, he fired up quick as dry kindling.

"What about salt?" she said. "No-one can pay for all salt we need. What about when you need to slaughter your animals?"

"We can smoke meat."

"And we dry fish in sun when there is sun, but we need salt for packing up crates of fish and sending them inland."

"We'll manage."

"Mmm." Funny how you could make the same noise and it sound so different. "Only way we could stop is if government gives up slapping taxes on everything we need."

"We can't wait for that," he said. "Might never happen. Why don't you give up, Jiddy? After next run, let's both give up on smuggling."

He was serious, and when Jonas was serious, there was no persuading him otherwise. She understood he worried about Boy going lame in the dark traversing the moor at night with a cartload of barrels or whatever, but to give up completely was a different matter.

"Jonas," she said. "I get it about not wanting to use Boy, but come with me and see what it's like in village when there's a run on. It's different to being on tops and having to be on delivering side. You don't get to see the cleverness of the way goods are delivered to houses. Once you've been on that side, then decide if you want to give up on being part of it or not."

"I don't know, Jiddy..."

"It's hard for you, always on your own, being a carrier, but if you come to Bay when run is on, see how folk are all part of it, the entire community, then make up your mind, hey? Please, Jonas, then stop if that's what you really want."

She waited for him to agree, but he had that thinking look on his face again.

CHAPTER NINE

A haddock lay cold and heavy in her palms, eyes unseeing, scales flaking. Over the next few days, there was so much fish to be washed, stored and layered in salt before rot set in that there was no time to head up to the farm. Jonas couldn't argue against this. They needed salt, and taxes on it were too high for them to pay. Salt had to be smuggled in because without salt, fish would go off and they'd have to burn them, and what a waste of good haddock. A waste Jonas had always railed against, from that first burning pyre on the beach she'd seen, to winters of near starvation. How could he give up smuggling in salt when it stopped fish going off? She couldn't stop smuggling. It would bring death to the Bay, and she wasn't prepared to die. She'd tell him that.

She'd make his participation during the Friday night run as involving as possible, and then he'd see what a community affair it was. He'd see it for himself and realise he wanted to play his part.

That night, Jiddy pulled her stool closer to the fire, rubbing fat on her sore, chapped hands. Mary sat, a pile of blankets with a face.

"D'you think government know how hard it is up here?" Jiddy asked. "Sometimes I think whole of Bay should go down to London and tell them how their stupid taxes make us suffer. They might understand then why we have to...you know."

Mary fumbled with the corners of the thick shawl around her shoulders. Her papery, thin fingers couldn't get a hold.

"I'll do it," Jiddy said.

"What, love?"

With the tips of her fingers, so as not to spread fat on the shawl, Jiddy eased Mary's hands away. She tried to loosen the knot, but her hands slipped. She laughed and held them up. Mary tutted and fiddled with the knot herself until it eased open.

"I were cold last night," she said.

"You've extra blankets now, and I'm sorry about the sticky mess."

Mary made a dismissive gesture. "It's not first time anyone's done that." She wiped her hands on the edge of the blanket covering her knees. "Is fire well stoked?"

"I can put more in, but you'll be in bed soon, so it'll be a waste."

Maybe if Mary ate the soup and fell asleep, Jiddy could pop up to the farm and let Jonas know the final plans for tomorrow night. She ladled a bowlful from the big pot over the fire.

"A couple of spoonfuls," she encouraged. "We need to build your strength up." She held the spoon to Mary's clenched lips. "Please. It'll slip down easy."

Mary's gloamy eyes lifted to look at Jiddy. "I'm not hungry."

"Please eat. You'll feel better. You always fed me with soup when I weren't well."

Unable to bear Mary's unflinching gaze, she focused on the spoon and soup and tried to stem her frustration. It were only soup; it weren't as if she were asking Mary to chew a pork chop.

Mary opened her mouth and Jiddy slipped in the spoon. Dipping it into the bowl again, she redirected it to Mary's lips. Mary stared ahead. A black, grainy sludge smeared down her chin and onto the shawl.

Jiddy dropped the spoon before putting down the bowl. Grabbing a cloth, she wiped Mary's chin and dabbed the wool, but the stain clung. Mary turned her head, eyes bewildered.

"I'm sorry, I'm sorry." Jiddy wiped the shawl again. "You said you weren't hungry. I'm sorry."

She wished Gracie or even Helen Drake was there and would know what to do and what this horrible stuff was. What was it? It looked like tea leaves all smushed up in the bottom of the pot. Finer. More like that coffee Mrs. Farsyde served on special occasions when the best of the county were visiting. That was it. It was like mushed-up coffee grains. But why was Mary spewing mushed-up coffee when she'd not had a cup of coffee in her life?

"I'm going to fetch Gracie," Jiddy said. She was shaking. Mary would see her hands shaking. She put down the cloth and touched Mary's cold knuckles. "I won't be long. I'll not be a minute. I need to fetch Gracie, that's all."

She was gone before Mary had the chance to say a word, not that she seemed to want to. *It's shock*, Jiddy thought. *I shouldn't have given her the soup.*

Gracie and Helen both came back with her, plus Helen's sister, Dottie. Mary hadn't moved from where Jiddy had left her.

"Now then," said Gracie, "what you been up to, Mary?"

"I've made a mess," Mary said.

No, Jiddy thought, tears springing to her eyes, *I've made the mess.* The stains on Mary's shawl were her fault. She was a terrible nurse and a terrible person. She could tell from Gracie's face that it was serious. Something about Mary had changed, and although they didn't say anything, Jiddy knew it wasn't a change for the better.

CHAPTER TEN

There'd been no time to talk to Jonas with Mary taking a turn for the worse and plans for the raid to be made. Jiddy hated that he hadn't sent word, but she hoped he'd come down to Bay anyway. She waited anxiously for him, gauging the noises trickling down the ginnels and over the rooftops until he appeared at the last moment, restless and nervy as a rabbit.

"Couldn't find you," he said.

"Shh."

Footsteps crept from Shell Hill. Intermittent creaks of leather made Jonas jump at each step. Jiddy gestured for him to stand still. It sounded as if soldiers were crawling over the entire Bay.

"Let's hide in someone's outhouse," she whispered, her heart beating so fast she was sure the soldiers would hear. Jonas nodded.

She led the way down a long flight of steps. If a soldier appeared, they'd be caught unless they could run back up the flight faster than their pursuer could follow. *Boots.* They squeezed into a nook between cottages, holding their breath. Jiddy sensed Jonas's fear. He didn't know Baytown like she did. She fought down her anger that he'd refused to take his cart out. Obstinate beggar. If he'd stuck to what he knew, she'd not have suggested he join her in Bay, and she'd be well out of it by now instead of having to keep an eye on him. This wasn't what she'd planned; it was each man for himself, not community together at all.

She peered from the top end of the yard, listening as hard as she could. The preventives must all have been out, as these weren't giving up. She hated this feeling of isolation even though there'd be someone behind almost every door, dismantling belts holding pigskins of brandy, rolling barrels away, sliding flat packages under mattresses. They were on their own, to escape or be caught. It was the way it was at this point of the game.

"Ready?" she asked.

He nodded, and she decided to go for it. Tapping his hand, she slipped out of their hiding place.

"Down there." The preventive's voice sounded nearby.

Boots, faster, louder. Closer.

"Stick with me," she said.

She scrambled up on a coal house roof, and they lay flat. She breathed as quietly as she could, but Jonas was out of breath. *Please don't hear us. Please don't look up.*

"We need some arrests tonight," a Scottish accent said, too near for comfort.

"*Quick,*" she mouthed, stressing each word so he'd understand. "*Straight on Brig Garth and up Jim Bell's Stile.*"

"*I don't know where you mean.*"

Ye gods. How could Jonas not know his way around the Bay?

"Don't lag behind then," she whispered, slipping off the roof.

She had an idea. She knew a place preventives wouldn't dream of searching.

Jonas was so close behind, his boots scraped her heels, and she realised it wasn't going to be so easy. The exposed path was long, and they could be trapped at any minute. Jonas was a liability. He'd slackened off and was several paces behind. He was panting hard and too loud, and that wasn't good in the clear air of night when sounds travelled easily.

She glanced over her shoulder. Jonas caught her eye. She'd never leave him; that was certain. She couldn't abandon him to get lost and caught, he must know that. Holding out her hand, she listened again. It was silent except for their breath. Where were the beggars?

Jonas caught her hand. She wriggled her fingers in his palm, then set off. The sliver of orange moon lit the slope of Fisherhead. Scrambling over the fence, she ran across the grass, half doubled over to keep low.

Reaching the top of the field, she held Jonas still. The light sweat from running made her chill in the cold of night, and she shivered. Jonas was jumpy. He was never jumpy on the clifftop or riding with a cart full of contraband, but the Bay was a maze to him. She should have realised, and now it was too late. Carrying goods across the moor was nothing to the dangers of dodging preventives in alleys and snickets.

Gesturing with a nod, she released his hand, and they skirted the top side of Fisherhead. They could head off over the tops, but it was too far to Meadow Bank Farm, and if the dragoons were out on horseback, they'd easily be outrun. No. Her first idea was best.

Running her fingers over the top of the door, she found the key. Jonas glanced right and left. The door unlocked and she fell into the room as Jonas shuffled behind. The relief when he pressed the door closed and turned the key made Jiddy laugh. She caught Jonas's arm and pulled him away from the door.

"We made it," she said.

"I can't believe we're in Captain Pinkney's house." He eyed the range, table and all the ship paraphernalia.

"No-one'll think to search for us here."

After a moment, both burst out laughing before Jonas looked again at the heavy door. "We'd best be quiet."

Jiddy smiled. "Bet you wish you'd stuck to your cart."

"Shush."

Outside, boots approached. They were trying to be quiet but failing. The boots stopped. Started moving again. Stopped. The silence went on and on, and the strain of listening made Jiddy's throat dry to a cough. She swallowed. Jonas's face had turned so pale she thought he'd be sick.

She pulled him towards the fireplace, pointing where to move so as not to knock into any of the chairs or the table.

"Let's hide to make sure," she whispered.

She eased down a hook, and the saucepan hanging from it slipped. Fell. Luckily, Jonas caught it in both hands. They stared at each other, and then, with a click, the wooden panel opened to reveal a concealed room. Easing the saucepan from Jonas's hands, Jiddy nodded towards the cupboard.

She waited for him to creep inside before restoring the saucepan to the hook and gently pulling the door closed as she shuffled in next to him. The door clicked into place, and they waited. The saucepan held.

Leaning against the back wall of the tiny space, Jiddy shifted her feet. Jonas, close beside, kicked her foot.

"Well, you shift," she whispered.

Wiggling to adjust her position, she pressed her palms on the rough wood at her back.

"Shush."

"There's no-one here. This is for your benefit."

"Listen."

Jiddy strained to hear what Jonas must have heard. They'd made a narrow escape from that bunch trundling all over Shell Hill with their muskets and trapping intentions. It had been a flash of inspiration coming here, and now she wanted to relax.

They were crushed together, taut, in the hidden cupboard. The dark was too thick to see, and her ears crackled with imagined sounds. Jonas was breathing in all the air in the tight space, and she felt stifled. She gasped, filling her lungs with whatever she could gulp in, filling the imagined noise with her breath.

"Shurrup."

"I can't breathe." She raised one arm, knocking his. With her other hand, she tugged at her bodice. "We don't really need to stay in here."

Jonas didn't answer. That fateful stomp of boots they all dreaded reached the path leading along Fisherhead.

"They won't come into an empty house," she said.

"It's not empty though, is it?" said Jonas.

"They think it is. They'll go past."

"Any reason to sack Captain Pinkney's place, they'll be on it."

"But he isn't here."

"We effing are. Why did I listen to you?"

"Cos they'd have caught us on Briggate."

He'd no answer for that. It was so uncomfortable, him prickling with embarrassment that he didn't know Bay like she did and she prickling, knowing it was true. She nudged him in the ribs.

"Doing this together isn't so bad, is it? Keen to stay a smuggler now?"

He shuffled his feet. Stubborn Jonas. He wasn't going to admit anything.

"You'll be glad to take Boy out rather than this."

"Futtocks, Jiddy. Is smuggling all that keeps you in Bay?"

His words sounded bitter, and they fired her up. How could he say that, after all they'd done in the long grass and leaning against trees? Pressing against each other wherever they could?

"Is that what you think?"

"I think you're still hankering after things them in London can offer. You need to keep smuggling so you can surround yourself in silk and lace."

That was it. She'd had enough of his snide comments. Fine, yes, she liked pretty things. Why shouldn't she? And maybe she shouldn't have kissed Samuel and fallen for him a little bit, but flaming hell, she and Jonas hadn't been promised to each other, and Mary had said make sure. So she had made sure. Jonas should thank her for that. Samuel had been right there in front of her in London, all smart and charming and caring, and Jonas had been so... what had he been? Small. He'd been a typical, mistrusting Baytowner, and what was worse, he'd mistrusted her and nothing had changed.

"'Course I'm hankering after things smuggling can get me," she said. "And you should be hankering after those things too. Don't say a word. Smuggling does keep me in Bay because I'm good at it, and according to Mister Misery Guts here, I'm incapable of having any other reason."

Silence. *Great. You think about that, Farmer Shitty Pants.*

"Ryethorpe's up at hall a lot."

"What you on about?"

"You're at hall a lot too."

Oh, for Christ's sake.

"I'm altering Mrs. Farsyde's clothes all the time as she gets bigger. And making baby gowns. Where else am I supposed to do that?"

"At home?"

If they weren't in such a tight space, she'd have walloped him.

"I thought you were supposed to be the clever one, Jonas Chaplow, and you come up with rubbish like that?"

"How do I know you aren't prancing around in that ballroom each afternoon like you used to?"

Is he serious?

"You only dare say that because we're in dark and I can't move to kick you to ground. Where on earth did that come from?"

"Are you?"

She found his arm with her fist.

"Ow."

"Well, grow up. He likes Mrs. Farsyde, not me. I told you, and I asked you if I should tell squire. Have you forgotten that?" Now she had to think about that again. Bloody Jonas. "You can be a right pain in the arse at times."

"Only in the arse?"

"I have a large arse, so that's a lot of pain."

He mumbled something.

"What did you say?"

"I said, nice arse."

"I hope you appreciate it."

"Steady on."

"Don't you tell me to steady on."

"You're shouting."

"I am not shouting!"

She was, though. He fell silent again. She giggled. Jonas laughed, and they subsided, laughing and giggling together until they started listening. They couldn't hear a noise inside the house or outside. Had the preventives heard?

"Mary's not so good," she said. He shifted. "She were sick today."

"You said."

"Not normal sick. It were black."

He tried to turn, but he couldn't. It made her smile. He wasn't the little lad anymore who could wriggle in any space. Nor could she, if she was honest.

"I were that shocked," she said. "Mary were shocked too. And she were sad and right frail. I didn't know what to do, so I left her to get help. I know I shouldn't, but I had to fetch Gracie. Helen came too." She could feel tears welling. What was that about? One minute laughing, next crying. She squeezed them away. "Trust Helen Drake to have to come."

She closed her lips tight. She was tired, and she wanted to be home.

"Why were it black?" Jonas asked. "What did you feed her?"

Jiddy shrugged. She didn't want to talk anymore.

Shouts. From outside. What were they shouting? Why were they shouting? Stupid preventives, announcing they were coming. It was a relief, though. She didn't have to think what had turned Mary's sick black.

"Stand still!"

"There!"

"See that?"

83

"Keep moving."

Then nothing. The immediate silence after the bustle of voices was one of their tactics too. Let you think they'd passed by. *Relax. Come out of your hidey holes.* Jonas gripped her hand so tight it hurt. She tried to move her fingers, inch her knuckles a little, but he held tight. Moving her feet to ease the ache in her legs, her wool dress scraped over the rough wood. Jonas snapped his grip tighter. She elbowed him. He elbowed back. They stood still, side by side, taking shallow breaths, rigid in the dark.

Somebody moved outside the front door. It was barely a transfer of weight, but she heard it. *Walk on,* she willed. Her sleeve touched Jonas's. She felt the muscle and bone of his arm against hers. What could she do? They could start kissing, and then, if preventives found them, they'd think they were lovers snuck away from prying eyes and leave them be, and maybe then they'd carry on kissing because confined spaces and the dark did that to you.

Jonas squeezed her fist. They'd gone. They could relax. Maybe kiss to celebrate.

Crack. Jiddy jumped; she couldn't help it. His arm, rigid, pulled her closer.

Thwack. Bang. It was the outside door. Tools, weapons, gun butts were at it, hacking and splintering the wood. The door had solid bolts and hinges. Captain Pinkney had built it to keep preventives out, but they weren't even trying to kick it in. It was axes they were using and hammers that knocked in fence posts. They wanted in for a purpose.

84

"Jiddy?"

"Keep still."

The noise was tremendous, filling the room and the cupboard and Jiddy's entire body. She couldn't hear anything but the bashing and crashing. She couldn't think about anything but the noise.

Bam! They were in, stamping their boots, bringing with them injustice and their version of the law. She pressed back, hard on the back wall of the cupboard, and felt over the rough wood. Jonas hadn't moved. Light glowed through cracks in the door. Preventives had brought in lanterns. A couple of soldiers, metal gleaming, strode around the room. A couple more piled in, pulling at drawers, stomping upstairs, bashing above, kicking and prodding and poking around the room on the other side of the door. Thankfully, she and Jonas were in the dark, and the cupboard door had no handle, making it seem like part of the panelling beside the fire, with a few hooks, dangling ladles and pans as camouflage. They were safe if they kept quiet. If they didn't panic.

The nearest soldier prodded around, so close they could hear him breathe. It sounded like he was sifting through embers, but the last fire in that grate had gone out months ago when the captain had made his moonlit flit.

She traced her fingers on the rear panel, searching for a lever to open it. It must be there, but she mustn't make a noise while they were tipping and kicking his furniture and belongings because they'd be listening for the slightest different sound. They were smashing chairs if the sound were anything to go by. Rough beggars. How would they like someone coming in and damaging their home? If only she could open the back panel, but she couldn't find a lever. She tapped gently, praying Silas was on the other side to open it.

It was like waiting for harvest. She clenched Jonas's hand, willing him to realise they could escape into the house next door if only she could find the latch. She held tight. A face—a nose and eye rather—so close it blocked out the light as it passed over the cracks in front of them. It moved again. Had it seen them? A fragment of warm candle haloed around it. She held her breath. An eye focused on her.

"Someone behind this!"

"Over here!"

The eye disappeared. Flares of light flickered, followed by the clanging of ladles and skittle being flung to the floor, hands, fingers, grasping for a way to open the cupboard. Then kicking.

Jiddy banged on the panel behind.

"Look for a lever," she ordered.

"Break it down!" The voice made them hold still.

The soldiers would have the panelling down in seconds. They should have kissed, pretended to be lovers, but it was too late now. Her heart pounded so hard it hurt. Streams of light sliced strips over the back panelling, her arms and Jonas. *Swoosh*. A door behind them began to slide.

Jonas, taken unawares, stumbled backwards into the gap, a mass of arms and legs, crumpling into Silas Biddick, who sagged to the floor.

Crack! The false door in Captain Pinkney's splintered.

"Jiddy!"

Jonas reached out from where he lay on the floor of next door's cottage, scrambling to untangle himself from Silas. She shook her head. It was too late. They couldn't all be caught or give away the Bay's secret escape routes. Sliding her hands, she drew the panel back into place.

"No!"

The second the panel closed, a hammer blasted through Pinkney's false door. Caught in the full glare of their lanterns, Jiddy breathed into the red, rough faces of two preventives.

CHAPTER ELEVEN

It was like they'd never known each other. Never talked before, never travelled in a carriage to London or shared that disgusting kiss that for some reason he'd thought wondrous. To think, she'd even thought of a life with him, and now she stood in the Whitby jail and he looked at her as if she were a scrap of mutton.

"No one likes to be scorned," Mary had said when Jiddy returned from London to the Bay. "'Specially a privileged man. You'd best stay clear of Captain Samuel Ryethorpe from now on."

Jiddy thought he'd leave Yorkshire after she and the other Baytowners had run rings around him and his men, but there he sat at the table in front of her, pristine and smug, eyeing her like he was waiting for her to talk and say something incriminating, but she wasn't falling for that one. Everyone knew if you opened your gob first, you were on a losing track, but Jiddy never found keeping her mouth shut easy.

The soldier standing by the door shifted his feet. The movement jolted her out of her thoughts and back to the stone floor of the unknown room. She refused to speak first. She wouldn't beg to be let go even though she was worried sick how Mary would be fretting about her and what Jonas would be planning.

Don't ask him anything. Don't give him satisfaction. Best concentrate on Mary. Mary'll be at home. Think about home. Neighbours'll be round. Gracie'll be making it all warm and cheery. Mary won't be sicking up coffee grounds anymore.

His hat sat on the corner of the table, casually discarded as if they were going to have some sort of friendly chat. He was taking his time, pretending to write something important. Well, she was having none of his tactics. She determined to call him Samuel and not uppity Captain, at least in her head.

He moved. Flicked his hand to send the other soldier out of the room. The door opened. Closed. It was only the two of them now. Before she'd rejected him, he'd have tried to hold her hand. Hold her closer. Hold her. But that was before. Before she'd rejected him and before she'd almost killed him in the marshes up on Whitemoor. She'd saved him and his men on horseback, though, even if he didn't know it was her that had done it. He wouldn't be so quiet and self-contained if he knew who she truly was.

The soldier remained outside the door, listening in, no doubt. She glanced at the window and at Samuel again, scribbling something else in that big book, trying to seem important, trying to seem cleverer than her because he could write more than his name. She wasn't having any of that either. Writing didn't make you clever, it just meant you knew how to trap the things you said on paper so that they could be brought up later and used against you. Well, he wasn't going to trap any of her words because she wasn't going to give him any.

"Why were you hiding in the cupboard in Captain Pinkney's cottage on Fisherhead?" Samuel's voice, now he eventually spoke, startled her.

Say nowt. Say nowt. Damn him, he still wrote something down in his book.

He looked up, his bright eyes hard as January ice.

"Jiddy? May I call you that?"

The rope around her wrists rubbed. No way was she going to let on how it chafed her skin. He could call her what he liked, she'd not answer him. They were left with a long, aching pause.

"You were found in a known smuggler's house. You were found hiding in a secret room. How did you know that hidden room existed?"

"It's a cupboard." *Blast. Keep quiet.*

He wrote in his book. She shouldn't have opened her mouth. Now she'd admitted it, it was in writing.

"And it's not hidden," she said.

"My men said they had to break in."

"If you pull the hook, it opens." Great. She was giving away all Bay's secrets.

"Why isn't there a door handle?"

"Why would there be, when one contraption does two jobs?"

He held her gaze. She refused to look away. No-one could argue with that.

He scribbled again. She should break his pen. Trouble was, with hands tied, she'd not do a proper job. Nothing like a proper job of snapping and crushing.

90

They were playing that waiting game again, that's what it was. She'd not answer this time.

She concentrated on the window. There was only one. Shutters, thick wood. Once closed, it would be a pitch-dark cell. With that and the door locked, it'd be a prison. She stepped from right foot to left. Wriggled her shoulders.

"I can't stand around here all day," she said. "I've got to be getting on."

"This is no laughing matter."

"I'm being serious."

"What are you involved in, Jiddy?"

"Nowt."

"I can't protect you, even for Signora Vardarelli's sake."

"I'm not asking you to, and why would she care, anyroad?"

He sighed loudly, like he was making a point. She sighed in response and tucked her nails into her palms. Her boots had traces of mud from the soft earth as they'd come down from the tops. Her skirt hung ragged around the hem. What a contrast to the gown she'd worn when she'd last seen the perfectly dressed Signora Vardarelli. The resemblance between her and her real mother must have disappeared with the finery.

"I need to go," she said. "Mary's ill and she needs me, and Mary's more a mother than any wealthy woman who abandons her child."

"I can't let you go, Jiddy. As it stands right now, you are a criminal."

91

The word inflamed her. Criminal meant Nellie Ashner turning black on the gibbet up at Buttercross and James Lanskill on a prison ship sent to Australia and pompous judges judging them on laws that had no meaning when you were scraping to keep from starving.

"What were you doing there?" Samuel asked again.

"Hiding from you."

"I'm on official duty," he said. He put down the quill. "You were different in London, Jiddy. Something has changed."

A torrent of words bubbled up from her stomach. Changed? Of course she had changed. She was back home. She was back doing what she was meant to do with people she was meant to be with instead of prancing around in silk and diamonds for some woman who hated her. Changed? She'd give him changed. Words were in her chest. Surging up her throat. She opened her mouth.

"You've no reason to hold me," she said, calm as sea at low tide. "Don't punish me because I live with fisher folk and work as a seamstress and because I talk different to you."

His expression changed.

"Have you forgotten what happened the night we returned from London?" he said. "In York, at the inn, while we were waiting for our horses?"

"I were only sixteen then. I'm seventeen now."

"You misled me."

There it was, in the iron of his voice; all his pent-up rage. She could retaliate. She could mention his slobbery and slippery kiss. That the nearer she got to the Bay and Jonas the more Samuel made her cringe.

"I were misled," she said. "You made me think I belonged in your world, and that's the last place I belong."

She wished he'd bring in the other soldier, anything but make her admit the truth out loud. Their different worlds had nothing to do with it. The point was, if his kiss had been different, at that point, right there and then, if they hadn't been on the way to Robin Hood's Bay, if they'd been on the terrace at the ball with the music and candles and that beautiful tight dress, maybe she could have chosen him and been happy, but that kiss had happened on the road to Robin Hood's Bay and she could smell the moors and sea air, and she had all her memories of Jonas wrapped up in the woods and bracken. If she was really honest, that had stirred something deeper in her than the slather of lips. That wind blowing, fresh and familiar, reached down into her belly, and no fancy dance or mouth-watering jelly could draw out the feeling she'd had as she neared home. The moors and sea called her then. Jonas called her. Warm, rounded voices that called a spade a shovel. It was Jiddy, not Jianna, that called loudest then.

"Are you part of the smugglers' world, Jiddy?"

She kept her mouth shut.

Samuel repeated the question, drawing out the words as if speaking to a two-year-old. Her heart thumped so loud he must've heard it. Her throat dry, she forced down a swallow. *So loud, too loud.*

"Well?"

She must be clever. She was known for being clever. She licked her lips, held them still. She was tired, of course she was, after being up all night, but she must shake her wits out of the dull fog settling in her head. She lifted her chin.

"Were you alone in that hidden room, Jiddy? What were you doing there?"

"I told you. Hiding. And it's a cupboard, not a hidden room, whatever that might be."

"People hide when they've done something wrong."

His eyes strayed to the door then back to the book on the table then back to Jiddy.

He'd better not say 'well?' again. The pauses between their exchanges were growing longer and more brittle. The presence of the soldier outside the door grew increasingly silent.

"Well? I asked if you were alone in that hidden room?"

If she was anyone else, if he was anyone else, she'd splinter and shatter that table he hid behind with one mighty kick.

"I told you it were a cupboard," she said instead. "And 'course I were alone. They didn't find anyone else, did they?"

"No."

No. They didn't find Jonas, but where was he now? He'd be coming to fight for her, wouldn't he? Maybe Big Isaac had convinced him to lie low. That would frustrate Jonas no end. He was probably on his way right now to kick down the door. Then he'd be booting up trouble like a fox amongst chickens.

"I were hiding from smugglers," she said. "They still don't trust me after I left Robin Hood's Bay with you. Baytowners don't forgive, and they sure as hell don't forget. Certain people would rather I were dead than be back in Bay. I were hiding at Captain Pinkney's because I knew no smuggler would go in there when the captain weren't at home. I thought I'd be safe."

He stared at her. She couldn't look away. If she did, he'd think she was lying, and she was lying, so she definitely couldn't stop staring back. She stared so hard his face blurred. So hard she thought she was swaying. The room turned into a boat on waves. He was shifting. She was rocking. He really was moving, rising up, walking around the table. And then he stood right in front of her, his face so close she smelt his clean skin.

"You were kind to me," she said. "I remember that."

"Yes," he said. She watched the sharp lump in his throat move. "I was kind to you, Jiddy." He was still staring. She didn't know where to look. "I was very kind to you."

She couldn't avoid looking at him. He did look kind. Gentle even, and she'd given it up, that gentle, easy life, but that kiss of his—she kept coming back to it and shivered at the memory.

He swallowed again, and as if he read her mind, the tender look disappeared. "I cannot be kind to everyone, or for always."

His eyes softened. His buttons sparkled. Next minute, he untied her wrists with careful, gentle hands and studied the red marks. His face blurred. He smelt sweet. Fresh. Clean. He took her elbow.

"Do you want to sit?"

She shook her head.

"I'm sorry it had to go this far," he said. "Let us put an end to this and put it down to wrong time, wrong place. You may go."

He walked back to the desk and closed the book. The pen rested by its side. She couldn't believe it. Was it a trick? He gestured to the door.

"I can go?"

"I have no more questions."

She left the room without looking back and walked past the soldier loitering in the hall. The call of gulls beckoned. She kept walking towards the front entrance with its door wide open and the smell of sea air and taste of light breeze. It was a dream. Samuel was still Samuel underneath. She was still Jiddy. She'd been right to care about him. He did have a heart. Even though exhausted, eyes beginning to burn from lack of sleep, steps a little unsure, she sighed with relief. The bustle of Whitby streets spread below; blue sky and white clouds billowed into the distance.

Hearing a noise coming from the doorway to her left, she took a step backwards to peer inside. At the far end of the room, two preventives struggled to keep a man in his chair. Preventives were useless, Jiddy thought. Unable between two of them to keep one man tied down.

The smaller preventive punched the man. Jiddy couldn't see his face, but a punch like that would mean a livid bruise in a few hours.

"Ger off me," the man said.

Jiddy knew that voice. She stepped into the room, crossed the floor and surprised the nearest preventive by grabbing his arm. A figure bent over. Jonas.

"This man must be one of those smugglers you were hiding from," said Samuel from the doorway. "Luckily for you, he'll either be hanged or soon be on a ship bound for Australia, and you'll never have to hide from the likes of him again."

She swung around.

"I did warn you," he said. "I can't be kind to everyone."

CHAPTER TWELVE

Jonas rattled his chains, only to be shoved back into his seat. This time, Jiddy didn't hold back. She marched back to the doorway to confront Samuel.

"You lily liver! Let him go!"

Samuel retreated into the corridor, and another soldier stepped into the room, taking a stance between them.

"Get Mr. Chaplow down to the dock," Samuel said from the safety of his position behind the soldier. "I want him on the next ship for Australia."

"You can't do that!" Jiddy pushed against the rigid chest of the soldier, who raised his arm to hold her back.

"Get off her!" Jonas, on his feet, shoved against the two preventives grappling to hold him down.

Jiddy struggled to turn around, to see Jonas and to free herself. Red-faced with veins on neck bulging, Jonas heaved his weight forward, dragging the soldiers, slipping and sliding towards Jiddy.

"Let go!" She yanked and kicked but couldn't reach him. Hands gripped her arms, painfully tight, and she twisted and squirmed.

If she could get her arms around him, they'd be all right. Shake this brute off. Punch and shove the swines holding Jonas and together battle their way out. She stretched towards him, grazing his sleeve with her fingertips, the thick linen rough under her touch. She tried again, twining the fabric around her fingers. She had his jacket and eased him closer, but they were hauling him out of reach. At the same time, the other soldier yanked her, and she bashed into him, flinching at the foul whiff of meat breath. She pushed herself away, but he grasped her wrist, twisting her arm and making her cry out in pain.

Jonas barged them, bashing his shoulders into his captors and stamping his boots into their shins trying to reach her.

"He's done nowt wrong!" she shouted, turning to face Samuel, but he'd gone, left in a smear of cowardice. She yelled in the nearest soldier's face before turning to the other. "Your captain is a shag-bag! It'll be you that suffers for this, not him."

Jonas head-butted the biggest soldier. The sledge-hammer sound of two skulls cracking made them all freeze for a moment before the big soldier fell back, shaking his head. A second later, he ploughed his fist into Jonas's stomach and the three of them clattered over a chair, toppling the table and ending on the floor in a thrashing tumble of arms and legs.

"You can't pack country folk in the hold of a ship," Jiddy argued, her arms now restrained behind her, rough hands on her shoulders. "Let go, you lobcocks! You can't do it."

All reason had fled. Saving herself had been easy; her words had flown with logic, but Samuel had tricked her. Jonas had been next door all the time, and Samuel knew it. She hated the weasel. She'd seen their friend,

James Lanskill, being marched onto a prison ship. She couldn't let that happen to Jonas.

"This is what criminal is!" she shouted. "It's you breaking our laws!"

They'd got Jonas on his feet. Dazed, he teetered sideways.

"Hold the wild cat back while we get him out of here," the bigger soldier said.

She hurled forward, stretching, reaching, and she almost touched him. He was almost touching her, his reddened eyes firing with desperation. He strained his entire body. Another inch and they'd touch. Chin, mouth, it didn't matter, something, some part of each other. At the same time, their captors heaved them apart.

"He'll not survive!" Jiddy writhed until a swift strike to her shins sent her crumpling down, shooting pain through her knees as she fell to the hard stone floor.

"Jiddy!"

Another fist to his skull and Jonas slumped. His boots scraped the floor as they hauled him out of the room, leaving her lying on the cold flags.

Her limbs wouldn't move. The floor sucked her down. Movement caught the tail of her eye, and she looked at a pair of clean, shining boots. Twisting her head, she saw pristine breeches and a red jacket with shining buttons. She turned to see his face, and they held each other's gaze. Samuel looked at a loss, but he didn't help her up. She pushed herself onto her haunches, willing him to be afraid. They'd called her a wild cat, and she readied her dirty, rough claws. She could scratch and bite, and she could bring him to his knees. A noise outside changed Samuel's expression. A clatter of boots made him turn around.

"Where's Jiddy Vardy? I need to see Jiddy Vardy."

Sleeve torn, joints burning, she put one hand on the wall, and catching her breath, she struggled to her feet.

Squire Farsyde's flushed, familiar face loomed at Samuel's side.

"What on earth has been going on?" Squire Farsyde demanded, pushing into the room. "Jiddy? My God, man, fetch a doctor."

"Arrests had to be made," Samuel said. "Miss Vardy fought back, and unfortunately—"

The squire put his arm around her. "I am taking you home. We'll call Doctor Newburn to come to the hall."

"Sir, I must—"

"Sir. You are no gentleman," interrupted the squire.

"We've got to go to the dock," Jiddy said, breathing in the squire's rich aroma. "Jonas is going to be forced on a prison ship. We have to hurry."

Samuel blocked their way by resting his hand on the doorframe.

"We arrested Mr. Chaplow, Squire Farsyde, because he has contraband on his property, and you know as well as anyone what the law demands as punishment for avoiding the payment of taxes."

The squire looked at Jiddy, but she continued to stare at the captain. She was tired, bone-deep tired. "What are you on about?" she said. "You've arrested him because you've a grudge against me, that's truth of it."

"Move aside, sir," the squire said. He glanced at the captain before tightening his grip on Jiddy's arm.

Samuel's face didn't express any feeling, and he didn't budge.

"A ream of silk was found in Mr. Chaplow's hayloft," he said. "What would a farmer be doing with a ream of purple silk, I ask? I must insist, with the law to back me up. Anyone who smuggles goods into the country without declaring them deserves to be on a prison ship bound for Australia. Jonas Chaplow will be banished to that outpost. He will pay the price for breaking the law of this land."

CHAPTER THIRTEEN

It took a moment for Jiddy to take in Samuel's words. *A ream of silk. At the farm. Purple silk.* Then it all came back. She, at eight years old, finding the bundle in the cave on the beach, winding it around herself as she'd seen Dottie do, and struggling along the beach like a trussed-up chicken. Jonas angry, shielding her as she tottered up King Street, unwinding her and then taking the silk away so that preventives wouldn't find it at Sunny Place and punish Mary. How she'd kicked and screamed and yelled names at him, but he'd taken it all the same. She couldn't believe she'd forgotten about it. Jonas had taken the silk and hidden it to save Mary from being found with stolen goods. As always, it was her fault. Helen Drake's words came back.

"There'll be someone to pay."

She brushed past the squire and squared up to Samuel. "That's my ream of silk. It's nothing to do with Jonas, and you know it."

Samuel had what he wanted. She'd not been able to keep her gob shut. He had them both, one for possession, one for ownership, but she'd fight until they both swung side by side at Buttercross if she had to.

"You have no right to retain Jiddy," Squire Farsyde said. "Let us both pass."

"I am sorry, sir, but that is not possible now that Miss Vardy has confessed to the silk being her property." Samuel looked satisfied now. Calm.

"He's holding you up on purpose," Jiddy said, grabbing the squire's arm and dragging him to the doorway. "Please, go down to dock?"

"I'm not leaving you here," said the squire. He turned to Samuel. "You must call a doctor. You have a doctor on hand, I take it?"

"Don't worry about me," Jiddy said, shoving him so that he stumbled into corridor. "Please find Jonas. That's the important point. Insist he be tried here. You can come back for me after."

Squire Farsyde didn't budge, and she realised by the expression on his face that she'd overstepped the mark, but what else could she do? Silk or no silk, if anyone could stop this nightmare, it was the squire. He would gather all the important men in Whitby and haul Jonas to safety if need be.

"Please," she begged. "You have to use your influence to stop the ship sailing with Jonas on it. There's no time to argue with anyone. Please will you go?"

He looked at Samuel. "A postponement, I trust we can agree on that?"

"Tell the officer in charge you have my word," said Samuel.

The squire nodded before turning to Jiddy.

"You can take my carriage to Robin Hood's Bay then send it back for me." The squire turned his attention once more to Samuel. "I can assure you, Jiddy won't disappear and will be available for you to speak to, but she will not stay in this knocked-up prison. Now I suggest you see that your men accompany her and make sure she is safe, otherwise, I will have to return and further use my influence if you understand me, Captain?"

"Escort her to Thorpe Hall in Fylingthorpe and stay there," Samuel ordered straight away, beckoning to one of the soldiers. "Sir," he looked at the squire, "I will come with you."

"Don't trust him," Jiddy said. "Would you hurry, please, Squire Farsyde?"

She yanked her shoulder free and faced Samuel. She could spit in his cold, blue eyes. She could bite his thin, hard lips. Instead, she raised her chin. Her face was so close to his, she could snog the words out of him. She could sink her long fingers into the flesh of his neck and retch up his remorse.

"Do you really mean it?"

The muscles on Samuel's cheeks twitched, and his eyes didn't leave hers. It was as if he hated her, thought she wasn't human, below a dog or cat, a tick or a dead cockle—nothing he would touch, yet he was unwilling to let her go. She willed him to admit he was doing this terrible thing because she loved Jonas and not him, and when he admitted that, maybe he'd give them both release.

But he admitted nothing and left, sweeping the squire ahead of him and beckoning the remaining soldiers to follow. The door slammed, and Jiddy stood alone in the cell-like room. The sound of a bolt smashing into place made her jolt.

"Hey!" She ran to the door, grabbing the bars. She couldn't see anyone. The door to the outside, where she'd snatched a sight of the sky and the bustle of Whitby town, had been closed. "Let me out!" she shouted. "You said I could go!"

She yanked the bars until her arms ached and she rested her forehead against the iron bars. No-one had come. He had tricked her. Tricked the squire. He had no intention of taking her to Thorpe Hall.

She couldn't shout anymore. She no longer had the strength to thump or punch. Throat ripped sore and arms and shoulders aching, she slumped to the floor. Light from the window shot glimmers of yellow and orange over the lilac. It was as if the contraband silk were taunting her. The blanket that had covered it, spiked with snatches of straw and dry husks from a hay loft, lay crumpled on the floor. Jiddy touched her neck. She felt hot, cold and sick. Exhausted, she closed her eyes.

"If I can't see it, it isn't there. If I can't see this room, I aren't here. If I wish hard enough, the silk will be a dress I stitched years ago, and Mrs. Farsyde will be wearing it and Jonas will be free, and he and me will be romping over moors without a worry in our heads."

She waited. Voices trembled in from the street. Boots shifted, dry on a stone floor. A seagull pierced her hopes, and she opened her eyes.

The dusty blanket still crouched on the floor. Sunshine still drew copper and gold from the purple threads. Nobody in their right mind would think the silk belonged to Jonas. It didn't matter she'd said it was her silk; Samuel wanted to punish her in the cruellest manner he could. The squire would delay the inevitable at best. Samuel was so smug with his good fortune at finding the silk at the farm, he would not let his prey go now he had proof of Jonas's involvement with smugglers. Samuel would not let go a weapon to hurt her, but through all that, an idea pricked her brain.

Hearing a noise in the corridor, she crawled to the door, pulling herself up and grabbing hold of the iron bars that formed a window.

"If the captain's still here, I want to see him," she said to the guard.

She stepped back, reminding herself that she must use her wits. She stepped back further from the door.

"Tell the captain I want to talk. I want to confess to everything I've done."

If she was clever, if she played the game, he might succumb. She'd seen the look in his eyes when they stood close, and she could bear anything for Jonas. She brushed down her hair, straightened her jacket and waited.

He didn't come. Of course he didn't, but another officer entered the room instead. She recognised him as Staincliffe, the deputy who made it his business to speak to the folk of Baytown as if he were their mate.

"Captain Ryethorpe is down by the ships," he said. "Besides, you've already confessed."

"I've something else I want to tell captain, and then I can tell it in front of the courts. For all to hear, but he must hear what I have to say first."

"That changes nothing for Mr. Chaplow," he said, "Or Captain Ryethorpe."

Jiddy couldn't hold back any longer. She stood so close to him, he put one hand on his belt where the pistol lay.

"That silk don't belong to Jonas Chaplow," she said when he seemed incapable of speech.

"We know that."

"I hid it in his barn, he knew nowt about it. You can't punish him for something he didn't know."

"Mr. Chaplow knows who it belongs to and he won't tell us."

"You know it belongs to me. I told you!"

"No, it doesn't belong to you. It belongs to the king's government, and the local smuggling ring stole it. You are not that important. We want the name of the head of this smuggling ring. That is the important name we require from you."

So that was it. This was a bigger trap than Samuel had let on. Jiddy broke away and, walking to the window, she stared out, marvelling at the normality of the street. Air wafted fresh on her face. Warm sunshine. The screeching gulls sharpened her brain. She turned to Staincliffe again, knowing she'd be a silhouette to him, curves of her outline, curls of her hair.

"It's my silk, nothing to do with anyone else," she said. "I found it on the beach, years ago."

"For all to see?"

"It were in a cave. I were picking up shells and pebbles as you do…"

"Not as I'd do," he said. He wasn't going to give any leeway.

Jiddy touched the cold of the stone wall.

"I found it in a cave, and it's been in the Chaplow barn ever since. You know Jonas Chaplow is sweet on me. I ordered him to keep it there, and he couldn't say no. There's no head of any smuggling ring telling me what to do with something I found."

She waited. He didn't say anything. They might arrest her again for the eight-year-old she was, not for who she'd turned out to be. They'd have to admit then that Jonas was an accessory at most. She strode up to him.

"I found it and no-one claimed it. Take it if you want, but neither Jonas nor me are guilty of a crime. Nobody is. Finders keepers is what the law says in Robin Hood's Bay."

The silk glowed in the sunshine as if determined to be seen after so many years hidden. If only she hadn't forgotten Jonas was storing it for her. If only it hadn't been found. Soldiers had been drawn to its beauty, stamped across the farmyard, climbed the wooden steps and found it. It was her fault. She should have taken it to Thorpe Hall and cut and stitched a dress for Mrs. Farsyde if not for herself.

"Will Captain Ryethorpe give him a chance?" she asked.

"He has been found with contraband on his property."

"Will you tell him what I've said?"

"Mr. Chaplow is hiding goods at Meadow Bank Farm that should have been declared. That's the end to it. There's no point arguing over a fact."

She moved forward, and he stepped back again, hand to belt. She was desperate. This was unfair, too unfair to think it more than a joke.

"But we were bairns and it were a prank we forgot about," she said.

"Crime must be paid for."

"But who says it's a crime? As far as anyone round here is concerned, it ain't no crime. Silk were just lying there."

She stepped forward again. He couldn't go anywhere else but stood with his back pressed to the wall.

"Silk has a tax to be paid on it," he said, so close she saw the gleam on his teeth. "This silk has not been paid for and someone needs to pay for hiding it from the revenue."

"I told you, we were kiddies, ignorant kiddies. We're not educated. We can't read good or write proper. How could we know about taxes? We fished in rock pools and made swords out of sticks. If you punish a dog an hour after it's bitten you, it don't know what the kick is for. Crime's past, Deputy Staincliffe, you know that. Tell your captain that."

Finally, after so much repetition, she had him. She knew she did. He couldn't argue with her reasoning. He pushed back his shoulders and straightened his belt.

"Guard?" he shouted, twisting around her for the door.

When a tall uniform appeared, he forced his way past.

"Give her something to eat and drink, but don't let her go."

"No! Tell Captain Ryethorpe! Stop him putting Jonas on that ship!"

Jiddy rushed to follow him, but a guard blocked her way. Staincliffe half-turned and eyed her up and down.

"I advise you to sit back down and contemplate how you want the rest of your life to pan out, Miss Vardy," he said before the guard shoved her back into the room. "Bring some pie," he called over his shoulder. "And ale."

"What d'you mean? Come back!" Jiddy struggled to edge past the guard.

"Bring the grub!" Staincliffe shouted.

The thoughts in her head only made it worse. Meadow Bank Farm belonged to Jonas's da, not Jonas. By rights, it was Mr. Chaplow hiding silk in his barn, not Jonas, but she couldn't say that. Mr. Chaplow was old and too frail for a journey to Australia. Besides, Samuel didn't care who owned the farm or the barn or the silk. Samuel made up his own rules and laws because he wore a uniform and acted in the name of the king and his government. He was rich and they were poor. He was the law and they'd broken his law.

Staincliffe's voice battered through the door grille. "And that squire of yours is dining too. When Captain Ryethorpe asked him why he was so interested in rescuing a known smuggler, he seemed less keen to go down to the dock. He didn't say no to some pie, though.

So, when you've both eaten, you might both want to discuss whether it's a good decision to go down to the water to see if that ship is still there or not."

She flung herself against the bars. "Let me out!"

"All in good time. You don't need to worry your pretty head. The captain convinced your squire that he'd sort out all misunderstandings."

He stood back as she bashed the door again. "Squire Farsyde!" she shouted. "Squire Farsyde? Where are you?"

CHAPTER FOURTEEN

Lord Ryethorpe studied the jostling crowd. He couldn't believe Samuel wanted to prolong his posting in a god-forsaken place like the Yorkshire coastal village of Robin Hood's Bay. They avoided parts of London for the very reason that they stank as Whitby dock stank. Mongrel dogs barked. Men, women and dirty children all spoke words he didn't recognise, words that ran short and round and fast. Sentences blurred one into the next, and he marvelled how anyone communicated.

Lifting his handkerchief, he covered his nostrils. The air was rank with whale blubber, fish and stale body odour. He watched the line of men shuffling up the gangway to the prison ship, so close to each other he couldn't tell if they were manacled or not. Crates and barrels stacked on the dockside swung both into the hold and on deck. It seemed chaotic, but he realised, as the ship filled with cargo and humans, that there was an approximation of order. They were all leaving England.

He glanced at Samuel, pristine in his uniform, buttons gleaming, white breeches immaculate. Samuel seemed to be the sole motionless figure in the seething mass that teemed over the quayside. Even those standing still gesticulated with jerking limbs.

"This ship is heading for Australia," Samuel said. "The voyage will take months, as you know, and not all on board will survive. If they hit rough seas, which I am sure they will, the sickness will be unbearable."

"Many will die?"

"I expect those not used to the sea will perish."

Samuel moved without warning, striding forward, graceful yet authoritative. He spoke to three soldiers, one struggling to hold back a bloodhound while the other two held bayonetted rifles like shining pinnacles rising from their shoulders. When Samuel walked back, he revealed no emotion, which made Lord Ryethorpe wonder what had been the reason for Samuel's swift action. He felt he no longer knew his son. He definitely wasn't the same man as the one who had left London with Signora Vardarelli's daughter Jianna. Letters had been sparse and factual, which was the main reason he had come north. All he knew was that there had been no formal engagement between Jianna and Samuel. *Jiddy*, he corrected himself, a name he still struggled to say.

Even so, Signora Vardarelli's—*Maria's*—relief and rapid dismissal of the news had shocked him. He had tried to elicit Jiddy's side of the story, but Maria pointed out that a Northerner would hardly put quill to paper when she could barely strangle a decipherable vowel out of her mouth.

So he had travelled north to York alone, across that bleak moor that went on forever, and arrived in Whitby by the sea. He had decided against revisiting Robin

Hood's Bay. From what Samuel said, there were not many inns to stay, and the best was only suitable for a deputy and his men.

He looked up at the hill. In spite of the stench, Whitby was impressive. The ruined abbey silhouetted against the sky for one. The number of merchants and goods being traded was outstanding for a small town on the eastern coast. Whitby was as full of wealth as he had heard, yet it was still an affront to the senses. The wealth was based not only on its famous whaling trade, but also on the illegal trade of smuggling. To think his friend Gregory and his family had holidayed hereabouts. As a child, he'd been disappointed his family never let him join the Hartshorns' August sojourn. Now, seeing all the illegal goings-on and breathing in the stink of fish and the stench of the alum mines, he fully understood why.

Once again, his eyes were drawn to the line of dishevelled men shifting towards the entrance of the ship's hull. *Too bad*, he thought, *but they should not have broken the law.* Maybe others witnessing this punishment of banishment would see that smuggling did not commend itself. He pressed the handkerchief again to his nose. There was only so much punishment a gentleman could stomach to witness.

"I'm going to take a stroll," he said to Samuel. "I will see you for supper?"

"It may be late," said Samuel. "We have a full cargo today and more prisoners than usual."

115

Lord Ryethorpe took a last glance at the motley assortment of old and young. They looked beaten. His son was right. Many would not survive the long journey.

A commotion caught his attention. The three soldiers that Samuel had been talking to earlier were pushing a group of men and women towards the gangway, and a dog, sniffing at a woman's skirt, barked loudly. One of the soldiers grabbed the woman's wrist and hauled her out of the line. Her face contorted with fear.

"What has that young woman done?" he said.

"She is hiding brandy under her skirt," said Samuel, still watching the vista of the dock. "They hide contraband under their clothes. Stupid of her to think we wouldn't find it."

Lord Ryethorpe studied the girl. She could be no more than thirteen years old. If she survived the trip, she would get a new start in Australia, and by the look of her, she might be glad of it.

"No!" she cried, her words sucked into the tears. "Don't let it bite me."

Of course, the dog. The soldier yanked its lead but the animal growled through bared teeth.

"Hold it back, you bully."

A man's voice, rough and round, bellowed out. A ruddy-haired man with a bruised cheekbone and darkening eye lunged forward. Lord Ryethorpe watched the soldier with the dog taken off guard. The dog leapt at the man, and the other two soldiers fumbled with their rifles.

People around pulled back; whether afraid of being bitten or shot, Lord Ryethorpe couldn't determine.

The man who'd shouted grabbed the girl's arm and pulled her with him as he pushed into the crowd. The soldiers pointed their rifles, but the man and girl were already disappearing into the seething mass. Surely, they wouldn't fire at random? Lord Ryethorpe glanced at Samuel, who was already striding after them, unleashing his pistol as he did so.

Looking at the crowd, Lord Ryethorpe calculated if this would turn into a battle, but as far as he could tell, the common folk were unarmed. Samuel was in no danger unless they mobbed him.

"Get back!" Samuel shouted.

The dog barked, showing his teeth.

"Steady!"

Men on the gangway had stopped moving and were turning around. Uniforms gathered from all sides. Samuel raised his voice louder.

"Do not make matters worse," he warned. "Stop where you are, Jonas Chaplow!"

The man's head reappeared as the crowd pulled back to reveal him and the girl. *So much for loyalty to each other*, Lord Ryethorpe thought.

"Hold your dog back," the man said. "Why d'you need weapons when we don't have any to protect ourselves?"

Thick accents rang out. Lord Ryethorpe took a step closer. It wasn't his place, he didn't have any authority, but he couldn't stand and do nothing. Soldiers hauled the pair towards him, and Samuel rested his hand on the girl's shoulder. She wiped her tear-stained face with the back of one sleeve but didn't struggle. The young man faced Samuel. He was taller, broader and altogether rougher, and Lord Ryethorpe realised that in a fair fight, the Yorkshireman would win. To his relief, two of the soldiers took the man's arms and shouldered him into a vice-like hold.

Taking a moment to study his battered face, Lord Ryethorpe realised the man seemed familiar. He took a step closer. Even under the bruising, this man reminded him of someone. The copper-brown curls and intense dark-grey eyes set off a memory. He moved even closer. There was an expression on the man's face that he'd seen before. He tried to puzzle where, and then Samuel's voice rang out and broke his concentration.

"Lawbreakers don't have rights! This girl has been caught with contraband brandy on her person, and she has to pay the consequences for that just as you have to pay the consequences for having contraband silk in your barn."

"This lass is only doing what she must so as not to starve," the man said.

"Stealing, for whatever reason, is a crime," replied Samuel.

More shouts. Screams. The girl bent her head. Samuel beckoned to several soldiers, and they shoved the pair towards the gangway where prisoners had started to move once more. Lord Ryethorpe knew there was something wrong in the situation; this couldn't be right. He pushed his way through to Samuel and touched his arm. Swinging around, Samuel readied to strike. Lord Ryethorpe straightened his shoulders, appearing even taller than his six-foot frame.

"It's me," he said, holding up his palms.

Samuel couldn't hide his agitation. "You should go. This isn't a peaceful process."

Lord Ryethorpe walked up to the copper-haired man facing them. His eyes had that same intensity as someone he hadn't seen for a long time.

"Tell me your name?" he said.

Jonas stared at the tall man with the gentle voice but before he could answer, Samuel put out his arm.

"It doesn't matter what the farmer's name is," he said. "His destiny is on that ship."

CHAPTER FIFTEEN

The ship would soon be leaving the dock, and Samuel wished Lord Ryethorpe would take himself off, but instead, his father had led him to one side. The noise of voices, feet, shouts from the ship and gulls wheeling for scraps made it difficult to hear.

"What do you mean, you think you know him?" Samuel asked, glancing down to where his father gripped his arm.

Lord Ryethorpe released him. "Right now, you need to get him off the street and back to where you hold your prisoners, and we need to talk."

"I don't understand your interest, Father. He's a criminal. If people see that some prisoners get special treatment, we'll have a full-scale mutiny on our hands."

"I'm not saying you set him free, but there are ways and means. Now let us go and discuss this somewhere more private, but for God's sake, do not put him or the girl on that prison ship."

Samuel squeezed the hilt of his sword before nodding to the soldiers. "Take him back," he ordered.

The dog continued barking. One of the soldiers tapped Jonas with his stick. "Come on. You're a lucky beggar."

"Huh?"

"You're not going on this one."

"What about her?"

"Just you."

Dragging the girl in his wake, Jonas forced his way to stand in front of Samuel.

"Lass stays as well," he said.

"I beg your pardon?"

"If that young lass goes on ship, I'm going too. Up to you, but make your minds up because I'm sick of being pushed one way then t'other."

"See?" Lord Ryethorpe murmured close to Samuel's ear. "They aren't all for themselves, these locals."

"You sound as if you admire him, Father."

"He's offering his chance of freedom for a scrap of a girl." He looked at Samuel.

Samuel sighed and gestured to the soldier. "Get them out of here, but wait to release her when there's no-one about to see."

Samuel and his father walked swiftly away, once the soldiers had escorted the local man and the local girl out of sight of the dock.

"I wish I'd suggested you went off riding or visiting the alum mines today," Samuel said.

"I'm glad I was here."

Samuel guided the way through the crowded streets, hand ready on his sword and repeatedly checking his father followed. They didn't speak again until they were alone and ensconced in a private room at the White Horse and Griffin on Church Street.

Lord Ryethorpe took off his hat and placed it on a table. Samuel did likewise.

"Would you like some?" Samuel raised a jug of wine that had been brought in.

His father nodded and strode to the window, taking off his cloak. The room, even on a sunny day, would be dark, but the grey sky made it even darker, and the candles struggled to brighten the solid blackness of the wood that surrounded them.

Samuel dragged out a chair from under the table. It had been a long day, and all he wanted was to eat and then sleep. Taking a sip of red wine, he waited. No-one could rush his father, who was well known for measuring every word and gesture. What he'd done on the dock had been completely out of character. All Samuel could think was that his father must have his own intentions for Jonas Chaplow. He took a gulp of wine and wished his father would get on with it.

Lord Ryethorpe returned and picked up his wine. "People here don't care about the war in France, do they?"

He caught Samuel off guard. "They think what happens on the battlefield won't affect them."

"What do they care about?"

Samuel shrugged. Sighed. "I don't know. A good catch. Showing off their whale bones. Defying the law."

"I think you're wrong. I think they care about extremely important matters. To them, that is."

"Fine, but what has this to do with us?"

"Everything. If they realise smuggling means that all their strapping young men are packed off on prison ships or forced to fight for the king, then maybe they'll change their minds about this illicit trade? And if that is the case, we'll have our taxes back and our armies well catered for."

"They know that already, and they know they're stealing from our soldiers. They just don't care. Few are caught, and our soldiers are out of sight in another country," Samuel said. "You are well intentioned, Father, but that is not how they think. They don't look ahead or outwardly. They're not capable. They cannot see beyond their own backyards."

"There must be men from here who have fought in the America wars and are fighting now in France?"

"Yorkshire is a long way from London, let alone France and America. All this talk of helping our soldiers fight the enemy by raising taxes to pay for their weapons and uniforms means nothing to them. They know, but they don't see the point. And one or two strapping young men, as you put it, will not change their minds."

"Then appeal to their fears. Don't they see the dangers of our enemies? I take it they have heard of the French revolution and the guillotine?"

"The press-gangs take local men for soldiering as well as for manning ships, so they will have heard something but we've found if men do return, they speak of the rotten Frenchies who've overthrown the king with their guillotine not as heroes but as wrecking working men's lives. We don't have to worry they want a revolution here, nor are they tempted to fight against it. As I said, they see it as a Southerners' war."

123

"That's grand," said Lord Ryethorpe. "They don't want the French ideas here any more than we do. They see that their own lives will be ruined if revolution comes here, but they're not prepared to support us."

"You have it. All they want is to avoid paying taxes. The French might as well live on the other side of the world, all the worry they feel about them invading our coasts. These people steal, kill and lie. They don't listen to reason. In fact, they are like the Frenchies if only in their defiance. You have to understand, like them, they corrupt others, so we need to carry on dealing with them the way we're doing until we've either packed every last one of them off to Australia, thrown them in jail or strung them from a gibbet. I can't have you doing what you did today with Jonas Chaplow."

"Is it working, what you're doing?"

Samuel put down his wine. "No, it isn't entirely working. Sometimes we do intercept contraband, and on occasion, a fair few are press-ganged, but some hardliners, particularly those of Robin Hood's Bay, seem adept at avoiding arrest and dispersing any contraband. It doesn't help that the houses are built on a steep hill, and they're packed together with narrow alleys and flights of steps making a maze of the entire place. We know there are hidden tunnels. We've uncovered some, but the place is riddled with secret passageways."

He paused. Saying it aloud made him see the madness of it all. They were in enemy terrain, and they didn't know all the places where these people hid. Tunnels and caves and who knew what secret passageways ran like a rabbit warren under the streets. Trust his father to spot his Achilles' heel.

"Father, tell me why you did what you did. This Jonas Chaplow you wanted to save is a key figure, and the best message to send out is that the punishment for smuggling is to be put on a prison ship and never see family again."

His father rested his hands on the table. That was what he always did when he was going to say something unpleasant. Samuel took another drink, knowing that he would have to eat soon or he'd not be able to converse with any coherence.

He clutched the almost empty goblet. He'd been pleased to see a familiar face when his father had arrived but not when he discovered the reason for the visit was to find out why he and Jiddy Vardy weren't married. He still didn't understand himself what had happened. What rankled more was that no-one he knew here seemed to think it was a complete breach of trust. He'd call it illegal, but Squire Farsyde had merely seen it as a young girl's change of heart and with no vows formally traded, their romance was nipped in the bud.

This was a strange place, he could see that, but he had thought the squire decent until this point. He thought Jiddy's guardian, the old woman, Mary Waite, who had helped them escape the mob, at least would have seen the good fortune that had brought him to ask Jiddy to be his wife.

"I'd like to know what has caught a farmer up in this smuggling business," Lord Ryethorpe said.

"Sometimes I think it is sheer bloody-mindedness. They think it is us against them, and that is good enough reason."

"Yes, yes, but this Jonas Chaplow. Why is he involved? He seems an upright young man, standing up for the girl who had contraband hidden under her skirt."

Samuel downed the remains of his wine. "So what do you have in mind for him, seeing as you undermined me in front of my men and everyone on the entire dock?"

Lord Ryethorpe took a drink himself before pulling up his chair next to Samuel.

"My apologies," he said, "but I think I know something of this young man. I think this man is the son of my closest friend."

Samuel spluttered. After wiping his mouth, he spat out his words, "You've only seen him once, father and briefly at that. What has brought this on? Is it Signora Vardarelli? Is she looking for children all over the country?"

"Do not be rude, Samuel. I taught you better than that. And I am not mistaken."

"I apologise, but he's a farm worker, Father. He's the son of a very lowly farmer. I don't think any Chaplow can be a friend of yours."

"I am certain. Jonas Chaplow may be a farm worker now, but I'm positive he is related to my old friend Gregory Hartshorn in some way. He has the exact same hair, eyes, even his skin tone. His face is the same.

His demeanour. It was like seeing a ghost. Believe me, he is the embodiment of Gregory Hartshorn."

"Who is Gregory Hartshorn?"

"Viscount Gregory Hartshorn. My childhood friend who drowned off this coast eighteen years ago. You've heard me speak of him. I know I've spoken about him."

Samuel refilled his glass. "Not to me. You've never mentioned him to me before."

"You haven't listened, that's all. That's your trouble, Samuel. You only take notice when someone is standing in front of you."

"That's unfair, Father."

Lord Ryethorpe picked up his wine again. "It doesn't matter. What matters is your Jonas Chaplow is Viscount Gregory Hartshorn's son."

"Viscount? Are you going to tell this man? I'm sure he won't thank you."

"I can't tell him, that's the problem. My friend is dead, and his family deny all responsibility."

"Will you tell the mother then?"

"I don't know the mother or her family, but I'm guessing she is a local woman."

"Yes, and so is his father. This place has obviously upset you by resurrecting long-buried memories."

"The Hartshorns have been visiting Yorkshire for as long as I remember. I don't know who the so-called father is you talk of, but his mother must definitely be a local woman. We must speak to her."

"I believe Jonas Chaplow's mother is dead," said Samuel. "Even so, I don't think you should say anything to anyone. It's in the past, and there's no point in firing up scandal."

Lord Ryethorpe drained the goblet. "You're right, of course. It is in the past, and his living relations might not want to know. They certainly didn't when Signora Vardarelli went to them, so why should they about this bastard child? But I feel it's my duty. I must do something."

Samuel felt a wave of alcohol sweep over him. He didn't want this Jonas Chaplow turning into a nobleman. He reached for the jug, but his father caught his arm.

"Samuel," he said, and the tone of his voice held Samuel still. "My friend, my good friend Gregory was with me on the ship when pirates boarded. They threw him into the sea before I could do anything. Then they pushed Signorina Vardarelli and me overboard. You were at home with your mother in London. Gregory and I were returning to England on leave. We had met Signorina Vardarelli when we first arrived in France, almost a year earlier. Gregory and she fell in love. She was travelling with a companion, but unfortunately, her companion died almost as soon as we boarded the ship for home. It was our duty to care for her. The baby she carried was born early, Samuel. She gave birth on board the ship. It was a baby girl. Gregory's daughter."

Samuel's head swam. He didn't comprehend how Jonas Chaplow fitted into the scenario. Maybe his father was confused. The scene on the dock had not been pleasant.

"Samuel, Maria called the baby Jianna. Ji-anna. Don't you understand? My friend Gregory is Jianna's father." He waited. Samuel frowned.

"Yes, Jianna is Jiddy."

Lord Ryethorpe stressed his words. "Gregory is not only Jiddy's father, but I believe he is Jonas Chaplow's father too." He waited for it to sink in, but Samuel still appeared confused. "I must act on what I know, and all you've told me is that Jiddy and some farmer are, well, what we all hoped you and she would become. I'm taking that this farmer and Jonas Chaplow are the same?"

Samuel nodded.

"Well, then. That confirms it. We cannot let that happen, Samuel. It would be incest, and incest is unthinkable. It is against all God teaches, and I cannot stand by and let Signora Vardarelli's daughter fall into that sin. I am positive Jiddy and Jonas Chaplow are brother and sister."

"Then why did you stop me putting him on the prison ship? That would have solved both our dilemmas."

"*My* dilemma is that he's my closest friend's son, and I cannot let Gregory's sole heir die on a ship in the middle of the Atlantic Ocean. For God's sake, Samuel, it's clear for me, but please, be with me on this one! Yes, you have to prevent them ever being together and committing the abomination of incest, but on the other hand, please, you cannot send him, the last in his line, to his death."

CHAPTER SIXTEEN

Jiddy watched the ship grow smaller and smaller until it merged into the line where sea met sky. People nudged her as they jostled past, but she didn't shift. She couldn't. Her arms hung leaden by her sides. Her jaw set closed. This had happened because she'd forced Jonas into joining her last night. She'd forced him when he'd wanted to stay at home and give up smuggling. She might as well have pointed at him in plain daylight and shouted, "Take him! He's a smuggler and you need to pack him off in one of your prison ships!" She might as well have tripped him up and manacled him herself and chucked him on board and yelled, "Cast off!"

She couldn't take her eyes off the speck on the horizon. Perhaps, if she fell in the water, plunged into the depths, she'd wake up to find it was all a nightmare. The panic, the cold, the desire to live would stir in her limbs if she found she were drowning. But she was drowning, right here on the dry dock, and she was already so numb she could scarcely breathe.

Deputy Staincliffe had let her go too late. Samuel must have known when he left without Squire Farsyde that it would be too late, and by the time she got there, the ship would already have set sail. And Squire Farsyde had believed him because he was a captain, a man of authority.

There was no anger left, nothing to feel because she was empty. Maybe, equally empty, Jonas held the side, gazing at the dock and searching for her. Maybe he was blaming her. Maybe if she had been able to persuade Deputy Staincliffe sooner, better. Maybe if she'd fought harder. Maybe if she hadn't goaded Jonas into one last night of dodging the preventives.

Jonas liked the solid feel of the ground under his feet. He liked hills of wind-blown wheat and long grass. He'd never been surrounded by heaving troughs of grey sea. Thoughts silted up her head. Heavy. Dull. No more emotion left to feel. She crossed her arms over her belly. The North Sea rippled. Waves licked the dock wall. Taunting, relentless, they filled her vision. Water. Waves and nothing more. Somebody nudged her elbow. She wanted the world to go away.

"Jiddy?"

"Leave me be."

"Jiddy? Come away."

Squire Farsyde's firm grip held her elbow. His words grabbed at her eyes.

"It's gone," he said. "Let's return to Robin Hood's Bay."

She shook him off and turned back to the sea. He didn't move. "Go away," she willed. "Let me alone."

Waiting. The word came in through the bones that guarded her heart. She'd wait. She'd wait for his thoughtful eyes and freckled cheeks and beautiful lips. She'd wait for his stubborn jaw and hands that were so much wider than her own. She'd wait until he came back. She waited until a voice filtered in.

"My mam went on a ship like that."

Jiddy lowered her eyes to a boy standing at her side. He lingered for her to say something back.

"So you live with other relations?" Squire Farsyde's voice cut in. "Or do you live with your father, young man?"

He isn't a man, Jiddy thought. *He's a boy. A small boy.* The small boy avoided the squire's question.

"Run along, then, lad," the squire said.

She wanted everyone to run along. Except Jonas. She wanted Jonas to run back. She stepped towards the sea. Her skirt brushed the small boy, and he tilted his chin, his hungry eyes seeping into her peripheral vision, the presence of the squire at her other side. Boxed in, her only route was straight ahead. She stepped, a shuffle, and the boy scuffed forward. The squire breathed heavy.

This is something, she thought. *Something, something.* The pull of the ship and the sea. One step. The boy shuffled as if attached to her skirt. Small head, scruffy hair, large eyes and sharp-boned cheeks. With each step, she saw more of him, but she didn't want to stop. She wanted to walk over water and pick up that tiny boat and peer down through windows into the husk of wood and see Jonas, sun-dappled, russet-apple-cheeked Jonas, held safe in that shell of a boat in her fingertips. She stepped forward.

"No!" Squire Farsyde grabbed Jiddy's arm. "Help me, someone."

People always helped the squire. Other hands held her, dragged her back from the edge. Tried to soothe. Cursed. Placated. She didn't want their help if they couldn't bring Jonas back; nor could drowning bring him back. So she let the squire lead her away from the dock and through the streets. Let him raise her into the carriage. Let the door close. The whip crack. The horses clatter their hooves and the carriage jolt.

The squire banged his stick. Through the window, Jiddy watched Whitby streets stream past, crowds moving, until she looked at the trees and the fresh green of late spring.

She thought about the landscape as she watched moorland open out. That great ship in the massive North Sea, heading towards the Atlantic all the way to the Cape of Good Hope. Heading towards a name and a colony. They'd want Jonas to farm when they got to Australia, and Jonas would want to farm after months cramped in a ship's hull. She couldn't allow that. Jonas's farm was in England. He didn't belong anywhere else.

"Who do we need to talk to?" she asked, jolting the squire out of his reverie. "Is it magistrate or someone higher? Who's higher than magistrate? Do you know who it is?"

The squire couldn't hide his surprise.

"Jiddy, love, ease up," he said. "What's all this talk of the magistrate? A good supper and a night's sleep are what you need."

She leaned forward, toppling sideways and landing at the squire's feet with a bump. He shuffled in his seat, swaying as the carriage rocked over potholes. "Have you hurt yourself?"

"No, no, I'm fine," she said, even though her hip hurt. She grasped his hands. "We need a plan, that's what we need. What are we going to do?"

He smiled. "As I said, food and sleep. I don't know about you, but I'll think and make better decisions after that."

"I'm not tired. We need to—"

"Let's get you back on your seat." He tried to lift her, but she pulled back.

"We can't eat and sleep," she said. "We can't keep Jonas waiting a moment longer than we have to."

"I know, I know, but first thing's first."

"Doesn't Magistrate Avery live in York? You'll have to tell Billy to turn at Buttercross."

"He lives in Scarborough, Jiddy."

"Then tell him to keep going to Scarborough."

"I'll not wake Magistrate Avery tonight. He'll not thank us for that."

"But the sooner we can stop the ship—"

"Stop the ship?"

"With Jonas on it." Jiddy shifted back onto her seat and clung to its edge. "If we can get word to stop the ship in Hull or London or wherever it stops next, we can get Jonas off and bring him back safe and—"

"Jiddy," the squire interrupted, placing a stubby hand on hers. "It's not quite so easy as that."

"I know we can't do that but magistrate can. It's all nonsense anyway. He'll see that and give Captain Ryethorpe a right rollicking."

The squire sat back. His hat shaded his face in the dwindling light. "Let me have a think," he said.

She leaned against the leather. Her hip did ache where she'd banged down on the floor. Her body ached, bruised by the tight fingers and hard floors. She was tired, but she couldn't rest, not until they'd talked to Magistrate Avery and she knew that the ship would be stopped.

The carriage creaked every time it rocked, but she was glad to be out of Whitby and away from Samuel. She couldn't bear to be near him anymore. It didn't seem real now they were quiet in the carriage, listening to the horses' hooves clopping and wheels chattering through the ruts and stones of the road. But they'd formed a plan, a plan of their own.

"Squire?" she said, shifting forward again. "We mustn't tell Mr. Chaplow about Jonas. I can say he's doing some favour for a farm up coast. He'll catch it when he's back, but better than worrying his da for no reason."

Pleased she'd thought of that, she sat back again, cradling her hands in her lap and feeling the line of each finger. The squire remained quiet, and she wondered if he'd fallen asleep. Jonas wouldn't be asleep. He'd be wondering how she'd manage to get him back. He'd be relying on it, and that'd get him through the night.

"Jiddy?" The squire broke into her thoughts.

"Yes, sir?"

"You're a good lass," he said. "I know you want to help Jonas."

"He'll be relying on us to sort it."

"That's just it." He paused. The sound of wheels bumping and horses' hooves pounding didn't seem comforting anymore. "I'll go myself to see the magistrate first light tomorrow," he said. "Not tonight. Tomorrow."

She grasped his hands, fumbling for them in the folds of his cloak. "I have to come as well. I'll sleep in here. I won't get out. I'll be ready."

"No, no, you mustn't Jiddy. I'll be best going on my own. I know Avery, and it will come across better that way."

"But I know Jonas best. I can—"

"I know Avery. He does not like to be told what to do by females. Especially young females."

It was her turn to pause. She knew the likes of men like Magistrate Avery. They'd rather let a man die than listen to a young woman who knew their business better than they did themselves. What could she do instead? She could check there was nothing else hidden on the farm or in the barn or hen hut. Not give Samuel any reason. Or she could go back to Whitby. She could go back to Whitby and have it out with him.

"Jiddy!"

"Yes?"

"I don't want you getting your hopes raised too high."

"They're not," she said. "I only want it fair. Magistrate will see injustice. Are you sure you don't need me to come? I can tell him about when I found that silk and I made Jonas help me. It's true, I'm not just saying it."

"It's all right, I'll explain it all," said Squire Farsyde, "but you must keep it in mind that the ship has sailed, and a ship is very hard to stop. You will promise you'll bear that in mind, won't you?"

"But it has to stop at ports on the way," she said. "Jonas can get off at one of the ports."

The squire rearranged the folds of his cloak. "He'll need a reprieve, Jiddy. I can ask Magistrate Avery to give him that, but I can only ask."

"That's what we need. With magistrate's reprieve, no-one can keep him on prison ship."

"If he'd still been on the dock or in the prison cell, but he's sailing on the open sea, Jiddy. Down through the Atlantic Ocean, on a ship laden with cargo."

"Not cargo, they're innocent men and women."

"These ships don't stop, Jiddy."

"There'll be kiddies on board."

"They will make new lives if they can't return."

"No," she said. "No. Jonas won't. He'll hate it. His home is here. He wants to stay here. His da needs him. Don't that count for anything that there's only him and his da to run farm and his da is old? He needs Jonas. Jonas needs to come back."

"As I said, we will try."

"Please will you go tonight?"

The carriage swayed. Squire Farsyde steadied himself, hand on the ceiling, scraping his wide thigh against hers as he clumsily sat beside her and put a firm arm around her shoulders.

He was expecting her to cry, so she turned her head away instead and looked at the darkening sky. They were nearing the Bay. In the distance, Ravenscar brooded, the same hump as always, and houses jiggled towards them.

She wouldn't give up hope. Tonight, they had a chance. Magistrates were important, and their dealings went all the way to London. Anything was possible if the right person put their mind to it and they acted quickly. The carriage jolted.

"Not so fast, Billy."

Jiddy slid along the seat of the carriage as they veered sharply.

"I said, slow down!"

The carriage slowed, wheels quietening as they rolled up the drive to the house.

"Go to the kitchen and tell Cook to pack a basket for you, Jiddy," the squire said. "Take something back for you and Mrs. Waite. Billy, attend here. I'll be back in fifteen minutes."

He stepped down before the horses stopped shifting their hooves. He held out his hand to help her down. His fingers were spongy, but she took his hand, eyes on Violet Ashner as she ran out to meet them.

"Mrs. Farsyde's had a fall," Violet said, words scrambled together in her haste. "Hurry, sir. Doctor's here. We've been right worried where you were and no word and Missus screaming like a stuck cow."

Violet looked Jiddy up and down. The squire dropped her hand and hastened up the steps, propelled by waving arms and a slipped wig. A high scream made him stop, and the sneer on Violet's face disappeared.

"Jiddy, come!" Squire Farsyde ordered.

Jiddy hurried after the squire, followed by Violet.

The noise of bustle and screams from upstairs met them in the hall. Mounting the stairs, all a tumble, they heard another sound. Rapid footsteps. The squire halted. A door opened. A man's voice. They turned the half-landing side by side.

"Will Missus want tea?" Violet panted behind Jiddy. "Or something stronger? Shall I bring a glass of wine?"

"Nothing right now," snapped Jiddy. "Go back down. You'll not be needed."

"And you are?"

"I'm Mrs. Farsyde's companion," Jiddy flashed, her arm barring Violet's path. "Why don't you make yourself useful and go back to the kitchen and warm some milk."

"I'll not take orders from you."

All three turned to mount the final few stairs but stumbled to a standstill behind the squire.

Two of the housemaids walked out of the bedroom, eyes to the floor and bundled sheets in their arms. The squire froze. Violet gasped. Jiddy stared at the bloodied sheet. Doctor Newburn stepped towards them, while behind him, the bedchamber resounded with silence.

CHAPTER SEVENTEEN

The sky blanched silver. Dew whitened the grass and darkened the trees. The chattering dawn chorus had already quietened, and the only sounds were her boots as she dragged herself down the driveway. The basket of bread, cheese and dishes Mrs. King had given her weighed heavy. Jiddy tried to remember when she'd last slept. It felt like years, and she craved the solitude of her bed.

She tried not to think about what she'd seen. Mrs. Farsyde, whom everyone thought would have expired at the first sign of pain, sat up against plumped pillows, twisting her small hands and darting her eyes to the view of trees as if wanting to be out climbing them. She'd fallen, lost blood, but not lost the baby. The doctor said the patient had to stay in bed until her time came. It sounded like too much of a sacrifice. She'd never be able to stay in bed for months on end, and the squire had upped and offed at dawn. She was relieved to see him go, to remember his promise even when his wife was so fragile, but she couldn't celebrate when it meant so much conflict. Mrs. Farsyde probably wouldn't notice, but it didn't seem right that he'd gone even if it was to help Jonas. Helen Drake's words kept coming back. "There'll be someone to pay." She never expected it to be Jonas.

An image of him hung in her mind, Jonas under a blazing sun, with his shirt abandoned. Him swinging a scythe alongside a line of men. Waving grass stretched over plains. Jonas turned his face towards her and grinned.

She tightened her grip on the basket handle. Mrs. King had rammed it full. There was even a jelly to tempt Mary. That was something to concentrate on. A lick of that jelly to savour on the tongue. She was desperate to quench her thirst, but she restrained herself. Maybe Mary would give her a spoonful. A soothing cup of tea. Sleep. She pictured steam rising from the hot liquid and pulling back the sheets on her bed. Anything but think of Jonas happy in Australia.

She stopped. Two figures sat on the wall at the bottom of the drive. Their faces sharpened. It was Annie and Betsie.

"Jiddy?" Annie jumped down.

Betsie didn't budge but watched, unsmiling.

"How are you?" Annie linked arms. "Violet told us about Jonas when we came for word about you, so we waited."

"Mrs. King sent us away from house. That's why we're hanging about down here," said Betsie.

"They'll want it quiet," Jiddy said. "Mrs. Farsyde isn't so good and has to be kept peaceful."

"What's happened? Has she lost baby?"

Jiddy shook her head. "No, but she has to stay in bed until she's ready."

They remained silent for a moment until Betsie piped up, "We couldn't get much out of Violet other than Jonas were on a prison ship. We really want to know about Jonas, not her up at house." She lowered herself from the wall. "Maybe he'll meet James in Australia."

"Betsie!" Annie cried out.

"It's all right. It's being sorted," said Jiddy, setting off. "Squire's talking to magistrate in Scarborough. He'll get Jonas a reprieve."

"You don't need to pretend with us," said Betsie, nudging Annie aside to take Jiddy's arm. "I know how you feel, so you can cry on my shoulder. Lads are numbskulls getting themselves into pickles."

"James chose to go, Betsie. Jonas would never choose to leave Jiddy," said Annie.

Betsie's arm tightened. Jiddy closed her eyes for a moment. She wanted to go home. Feed Mary the jelly. Sleep. She didn't want to argue that Jonas may never reach Australia or that he'd be home in a week or never or that he'd be happy in a hot, sunny country. James would never come back. She couldn't think that about Jonas.

"You're right, he might meet James," Jiddy said. "They'll have a grand time getting lost in all that big land."

"But they'll find other lasses to wed and forget about us. Don't that wrench your heart, Jiddy? Don't it make you want to weep?" Betsie's voice rose higher with each word.

Jiddy put down the basket and in so doing released herself from Betsie's hold. Annie bounded to her side.

"Jonas would never forget you. He'll never court anybody else. He loves you. And James were a nobbit, Betsie. Don't you remember how mean he were? Besides, you weren't sweethearts the way—"

"No, I don't want to weep," Jiddy interrupted. "Jonas will soon be back. You never know, magistrate might be able to do something for James as well if you ask."

"Don't patronise me, Jiddy Vardy. My James has been away a lot longer than Jonas. He were desperate to stay with me, but if he hadn't gone, he'd be dead now, and what's use of a dead sweetheart? I'm glad he went. You should let Jonas be and not bother magistrate. That's what proper love is, you see. Not selfish. Thinking of other person is what counts and not wanting them dead. Proves how much I love James."

"You were cursing his name for leaving you to become an old maid!" said Annie.

"That were grief talking. And we all talk different when we're grieving. You can say whatever you want, Jiddy, to us. I won't judge you."

"Nor will I!" Annie grasped Jiddy's arm and glared at Betsie. "I'll take care of you."

Jiddy bent to pick up the basket.

"Thanks, girls," she said. "But I'm wiped out. I'm sure Mrs. King'll give you a slice of bread and dripping if you go and give your best wishes for Mrs. Farsyde's continued health."

"Ooh," said Annie. "You don't think they'll mind?"

"Who cares?" said Betsie, placing herself in Jiddy's way. "What I want to know is why you're not more upset?"

"I'm getting bored of this," Jiddy said without breaking eye contact. "I've told you. Jonas is coming home."

Betsie folded her arms over her stout frame.

Annie clapped her hands, her eyes resting on the house. "I hope it's going to be a girl. I mean, it's always boys. Boys inherit. Boys get to ride and shout louder and carry a pistol."

"Girls can do that too," said Jiddy.

"I know," Annie agreed. "I know, it's just—"

"No they can't," snapped Betsie. "Be honest about it, Jiddy. Boys can do whatever they want, and wealthy boys can do it more than anyone, and when we wed, they take everything we own on top of all their own stuff. They take our hearts, our babies and our dresses. They can even take our underclothes if they want."

"They can't!"

"Sorry, Annie, they can," said Jiddy. "But I'd like to see a lad try that with me!"

"Even you can't escape the fact," said Betsie. "I think it's good James and Jonas are gone, right for that reason. They've done us a favour. Now we don't have to worry about a husband being in charge of us and telling us what to think and be and what we can have."

"You're a surprise, Betsie," said Jiddy. "I always thought you were desperate to be wed."

Betsie's lips stayed tight.

"My mam and da aren't like that," said Annie. "Ma bosses Da about. She tells him what to do."

"Mary and Thomas weren't like that either, Betsie. Your mam and da are same."

"That's because they're poor," Betsie butted in. "I bet Mrs. Farsyde don't tell squire what to do. I bet she don't get to say that she'd rather not have bairns because there's a chance she'll die having them."

Betsie halted. Her round face sagged and her mouth dropped. Annie, always nervous, fingers playing with her skirt, trembled. Jiddy let out a long breath.

"How close were you and James, Betsie?"

"I told you, we were going to wed."

"Had you done it?"

"Done what?"

"Were you ever scared you'd have a bairn?"

"Jiddy!" Annie gasped. "Betsie? You didn't, did you?"

"No, we did not," said Betsie. "I'm no fool."

"Jonas and me talked about getting wed," Jiddy said, "but Jonas and I've not done it proper either. To be honest, if I don't do it proper soon, I'm going to shrivel up. I don't think having a bairn will be in my head at that point."

A second later, they all broke out laughing. Annie blushed bright pink.

"I thought you already had done it," she said. "You seem so touchy together, you know, like he knows you."

"Stop being so coy," said Betsie. "What have you done? You have to tell now, and don't miss anything out."

Jiddy looked at their eager, innocent faces. They were starved. Not only of the right food but information. More than that. Tenderness. Excitement. A life bigger than the life offered in Robin Hood's Bay.

"You sure you're ready for this?" she said.

Annie nodded.

All three looked back at the hall to see if anyone appeared to tell them to keep down the noise, but the house remained quiet. Jiddy leaned closer, and Betsie and Annie bent in to hear.

"We've done it with our clothes on," she said and waited for their response.

Annie frowned. Betsie pulled a face. Jiddy realised how little experience they had of boys.

"Completely dressed," she said. "We've made each other..." She reached for the right word.

"What?" said Annie.

Jiddy remembered Jonas moving against her and how it made her feel.

"Jiddy! What?"

She couldn't bear the thought of not having that feeling. He had to come back, he had to. She really would wither away if she couldn't feel that again.

"Let's get off," she said.

With Annie and Betsie on either side, they passed through the gate and headed up the incline towards the main track to the Bay.

"Come on, tell us what you've done," said Betsie.

"What did you do? How? I don't understand!" said Annie.

How to explain? It made her miss him too much. They nudged her. Peered into her face. There was nothing for it.

"He keeps his britches on, and I keep..."

She remembered his hands rucking up her wool skirt and his fingers scrambling through her petticoat and up her thigh.

"We have our clothes on," she said, "but we can feel each other."

Betsie inched closer.

"You're not going to have a baby are you?"

Jiddy let out a relieved laugh. "No!" she said. "That's why we do it that way."

Annie stopped, forcing the others to halt.

"I mean, we wouldn't anyway, not really," Jiddy continued. "I don't think we would, but Betsie, Annie..." She turned to Betsie. "Betsie, you'll know. The kissing, it's so good, isn't it?"

Betsie nodded.

"Annie, you need to kiss Billy Hardcastle."

Annie put her hands to her face. "How do you know about Billy Hardcastle."

"Have you two kissed?"

Annie giggled. "Not yet."

"Make sure you do," said Jiddy. "If he don't kiss right, you get rid of him, you hear? A bad kiss isn't worth sticking with. That's what Mary's always told me, and she were right."

She set off again, and they eagerly followed, nipping at her heels like newborn puppies.

"What do you mean, Jiddy?" said Betsie. "Has Jonas ever kissed bad?"

"Jonas is a perfect kisser," said Jiddy. "Perfect." She must never mention kissing Samuel Ryethorpe. Not to anyone. Betsie were like a frog leaping on any snatch of betrayal.

"Tell us," said Annie. "Tell us what it's like kissing Jonas."

"Betsie knows what it's like from kissing James, don't you, Betsie? I'm sure that were as good for you. You tell Annie what it's like. I've done my bit with the rutting business."

"Jiddy!"

"Stop shouting my name!"

"But it's so rude."

"Oh, give over. It's natural. All animals do it, and we're no different."

"But it sounds so…"

"Animal. Well, like animals, I prefer it outdoors than in some uncomfortable, narrow bed."

"Jiddy!"

"Mary would have a fit."

"Mary doesn't know."

Annie studied her chest. "I don't think I want a lad to touch these," she said.

"He'd have a job finding anything," said Betsie.

"They're growing," said Annie, running her hands over her chest before looking at Jiddy.

"What?"

Betsie and Annie laughed, united.

"Oh." Jiddy smiled at the curves of her own breasts.

"If either of us had what you have," said Betsie, "we'd not be so behind-hand."

"I've got to use what nature gave me," Jiddy said, pushing out her chest. She smiled. "They come in handy for all sorts."

"We don't want to know," said Annie, blushing again.

"Yes, we do."

"I give in," said Annie. "I do want to know."

Jiddy swung the basket. "Flirting, that's all," she said.

Annie and Betsie settled. The seriousness of what Jiddy meant by flirting quietened them. Jiddy got information out of preventives, and her canny words were well-matched by her figure.

"Right," said Jiddy, "stop dawdling. I need to go home, I've not seen Mary since yesterday morning, and I've not slept since night before."

"Oh dear," said Annie, "let us carry your basket."

Betsie grimaced. "You mean, I will."

"I'll carry it," said Jiddy.

The sound of approaching hooves caught their attention, and they waited to see who rode in such haste.

It was an elegant horse and rider. Jiddy jumped back onto the verge, pulling Annie with her in time to get out of the way as it galloped past, spraying dry dust.

"Weren't that...?" said Betsie.

"Yes, it flaming well was," said Jiddy.

Leaving a stunned Betsie and Annie with the basket and instructions to take it straight to Sunny Place and give it to Gracie or whoever was there, and with further orders to feed Mary the jelly, she hauled up her skirt and ran back towards Thorpe Hall.

CHAPTER EIGHTEEN

The kitchen beat with activity. Everyone was busy baking or banging around or chattering and gossiping in hushed tones, so that Jiddy hurried past without being questioned. Finding the hallway empty, she ran unhindered into the main house in search of Samuel. He wasn't in the morning or dining room. Listening at Squire Farsyde's study door, she rounded her hand over the handle. Dare she? She tapped. No response. She pushed open the door.

Samuel strode up and down in front of the far window. He turned his head, but his expression wasn't what she expected. He strode towards her, rippling with anxiety.

"How is she?"

"She? You mean me? I'm furious, that's what I am. You expect—"

"Mrs. Farsyde? How is Mrs. Farsyde?"

He walked to the doorway, peered into the hallway then strode back again.

"Where is Squire Farsyde?" he asked.

His face came close to hers, and she smelt the whiff of stale breath. She pulled back. His clothing was dishevelled. His hat lay sideways, discarded on the desk. This wasn't the captain they all knew.

"He's in Scarborough," she said. "He's gone to see Magistrate Avery to sort this rubbish with Jonas's return."

"Good," he said. "Good."

He walked back to the window. *Good? What does he mean by good?* She wasn't going to forgive him, if that's what he thought. He'd tricked her and put Jonas on that ship for Australia, and now the squire had to be off trying to sort the mess when he should be with his wife.

"Why were you in such a hurry riding here? Are you going to sort Jonas's return? If you follow squire to Scarborough, you could be in time."

Samuel stared at her as if she was an apparition.

"Is it possible to see her?"

"What? No! You should go. You should—hey!"

Samuel pushed past her but stopped at the door and turned back. "Is the physician here?"

It was Jiddy's turn to be confused. "He went an hour or so ago. Why do you want to see him? Are you injured? I hope so. You deserve to be."

His skin gleamed pink yet sweaty pale at the same time. His eyes darted, unfocused, screaming consumption or blood-poisoned fever. He definitely didn't look right; she could see that now.

"I can send word," she said. "If you're not well."

He didn't seem to understand. He paced past her again, then approached. "How is she?"

She'd never seen him like this before. Always so neat, so controlled, and here he stood, not having slept or bathed or cared to correct his attire.

"I'll ask doctor to be called," she said. "I doubt it'll be Doctor Newburn. He'll be worn out after the night here with Mrs. Farsyde."

Samuel gripped her arms so tight it hurt. "Tell me how she is doing? Is she going to be all right?"

"Let go. You're hurting." Jiddy pulled herself free, but he grasped out at her, catching hold of her wrist.

"Is the child…" His eyes searching the staircase. "Is all well?"

"It's none of your business."

"You're sure the squire isn't here?"

"No, I said, he's—" It clicked. "Why do you want to see Mrs. Farsyde?"

His eyes loomed too large for his face. The lump in his throat leaped. "She didn't die and…and the baby?"

"There is no need for concern."

He lit up like a buttercup. "Is it born?" he said. "Is it a boy?"

"It's not the time yet," she said. "Mrs. Farsyde had a fall, and everyone were worried, but she's fine now."

"I must see her for myself."

"What? No!"

He was already through the door, halfway across the hall, reaching for the stairs. She hurried after him and caught his sleeve.

"You can't. She'll be sleeping."

She became aware of their voices in the quiet house. There was that look again of bewilderment and desperation.

"Mrs. Farsyde is exhausted," she said, pulling him towards the room they had just left.

This was what the scene on the stairs the other day had been about. Samuel was in love with Mrs. Farsyde and she with him. It were more than a fancy. He was out of his mind, but she couldn't let him go upstairs. For Mrs. Farsyde's sake, for the squire's. For their child.

And how dare he? He'd been in love with her only a few months ago. How dare he replace her so fast? She took his arm and dragged him back to the study, even though he kept looking over his shoulder at the stairs.

"You can't see Mrs. Farsyde in her bedchamber," she said. "It wouldn't be right."

Samuel's face as they went back into the study shocked her. He had been in Mrs. Farsyde's bedchamber before, and for more than a brief visit. That's what that expression said. That touch of his on Mrs. Farsyde's waist when they'd stood on the stairwell told her that. It told her they'd kissed, and Mrs. Farsyde hadn't been repelled as Jiddy had been. Even though her anger at his recent actions simmered, the worry he now showed made her soften.

"Samuel," she said, "you can't do this to Mrs. Farsyde. It will ruin her."

His expression changed to disdain, making her drop her hand.

"I am Captain Ryethorpe, and I will do as I please. I have rights. The child..." He didn't finish the sentence, but the word hung between them.

"Don't speak to me like that," she said.

"I'll speak to you however I want."

"You asked me to marry you."

She hated it. Hated this feeling of being so small and pathetic. The fact he had power over them. She didn't want him but had thought he must still want her if he was prepared to punish her. She'd put it down to jealousy. Thwarted love. Not scorn. Not what she saw in his eyes.

"That is a different matter," he said. He started to say something else, then stopped. "I do not have to explain myself to you."

That word, *you*. He made it sound like the lowest thing anyone could be. *You*. The disgust in such a small word.

It was enough for Jiddy. She slammed the door, and the bang reverberated around the house. She didn't care who came running or if Mrs. Farsyde woke and screamed with terror at the sound.

"Open that door."

Slap. His cheek bloomed red. He raised his hand to his face.

"You were in love wi' me, and you bedded Mrs. Farsyde at same time? You're a piss pot, do you hear me? A stinking fish. A rotten puffcock!"

Shocked at her own words, she stamped hard on his nearest foot.

Yelping, he hobbled sideways and caught hold of a chair back. "How dare you—"

"You seduced me. I didn't go after you," she interrupted. "Don't you remember how you were so infatuated with me, you sucked blood from my neck in chapel when I fainted? I woke up, and you were at me like a bee to honeysuckle. And it were you that were stuck on courting me, you kissed me. I didn't kiss you, and it were awful. Worst slobbering kiss I've ever had."

His scorched cheek twitched. His hands flexed. He shifted his feet towards her, and she readied to deflect his blow and strike back.

So he wouldn't hit her. He wouldn't even touch her with his precious gloves, but she could tell her words angered him more than the slap. Well, she knew how to use words as well as her fists. It wasn't only upper-crusters that thought they had words to wound.

"Bet Mrs. Farsyde finds your wet gob as disgusting as I did, only she's too polite to say. D'you want to find out? Fine. Go up. Ask her. Then see if she wants you visiting her in her bedchamber."

The door hitting her shoulder blades took away her breath. Samuel stepped back, horror on his face.

"S'all right," she said. "We're tough round here. Whatever you can do to me, I can do a hundred times worse to you."

Pain forced the air out of her lungs, but she tried not to let it show. Strength. That's what she had, and she'd use it, if it meant she collapsed later.

"You discarded me," he said, "and I offered you all I had. That is your loss. I thought it was mine. I hoped, our parents hoped, but no. You showed me who you truly

156

are by choosing to come back here and align yourself to some farmer."

The final words came out bitter as rancid milk.

"You were bedding Mrs. Farsyde!" she said. "Don't you dare cast me as one that did wrong."

"Did you tell your farmer that you said you would wed me?"

Words. Words, the promise of rotten words.

"You're jealous of him!" she said. "That's why you've packed him off. Can you blame me for choosing him over you when your type are vengeful and sneaky and vile as dog turd?"

She watched his face change again, gathering up his breeding and aloofness and refusing to retaliate. Jiddy couldn't bear it.

"If only you knew." He smirked.

That was it.

"You cannot see Mrs. Farsyde," she said again. "Only her husband may visit until she's had child, and whatever you say, it belongs here. Squire'll never give it up."

Anger simmered in him, but he couldn't do anything. If Violet was in the kitchen, she'd be down the hall faster than a hare across a hillock, to see what was going on. Samuel must have realised too. He straightened his jacket.

"Squire Farsyde will not be able to bring Jonas Chaplow back, whatever you say," he said. "And if you are not careful, I will send you to the opposite side of

157

the world on any prison ship or tug or rowing boat I choose. Do I make myself clear? Do you understand?"

Yes, she understood. Did he think she'd not heard those words before? Being poor and a woman, she had the double chance of being asked if she understood, and if he knew how those words rankled, he'd never dream of saying them. She held out her hand. *Go then. Go up the stairs to the lady of the house's bedchamber. Go where you want because you are wealthy and a man. In broad daylight and in the squire's manor house, you're a king, but wait for nightfall, and in the Bay's ginnels, I'll be the one in charge. I'll be king there, my lad.*

"Don't forget your hat."

He walked back to the table. She opened the door.

"Lead the way."

Despite the noise she'd made banging the door and their raised voices, Violet hadn't appeared. The squire would be gone for hours. She'd done her best, it was up to the mistress of the house now.

Jiddy led the way without saying a word. She was so tense with anger herself, she had to keep her back to him. Her belly knotted and twisted, ached and stiffened, and she yearned to lash out. Yes, it was stupid, yes, she hadn't wanted to punch anyone so much since Nellie Ashner, but she couldn't bear his composure and his threats. He'd lied and cheated her, and how dare he? The fact that Mrs. Farsyde's baby was his had made it too much. It couldn't be his. Maybe he was lying about it to hurt her. That was it. He'd been hurt or embarrassed or whatever it was he wanted to call it, and he wanted to strike back.

She stopped. Turned. Barred the way. In the dark of the stairs, he lost his arrogance.

"Is it your baby?" she said.

For a moment, only a moment, she thought he was going to admit it, but he gestured to the stairs.

"May we continue?"

From the doorway, Jiddy watched as he strode across the room, pulled up a chair and took Mrs. Farsyde's hands. In return, she beamed at him. The pair of them made an entire field of buttercups, never mind one.

"You've come," she said. "You've come back."

Propped by pillows, in lace cap and gown, hair over her shoulders, she radiated happiness.

"I love you," she said. "I'm sorry, but I cannot hide it anymore. I love you, Samuel."

He cupped her face in his hands and planted kisses on her cheek, nose, other cheek, all over and then gently and slowly kissed her mouth. They remained, lips together. Jiddy couldn't believe it. They loved each other. Her him, him her. And this wasn't a kiss like she and Jonas did as they pressed to be inside each other. This kiss didn't move. It was tender and sweet and quiet. He'd not done that with her. He'd slobbered all over her mouth and chin. She had to stop herself crying out. He was treating Mrs. Farsyde like a lady, and he'd treated her like she was a piece of stock he owned.

Jiddy touched her skirt. A trickle of liquid squirmed in her lower belly, and her back ached. She pressed her hands to her groin. How could she not have read the signs when they happened every month? She'd have to leave them together. She couldn't help them now, even if she wanted to. If she didn't fix herself up fast, this time, it would be her blood all over the floor.

CHAPTER NINETEEN

The rags she took from the sewing room helped to mop up the stream of blood down her legs. Tying a silk cradle for them seemed a waste of good material, but she'd wash them and anyhow, she liked the act of defiance of using Mrs. Farsyde's silk.

She told a surprised Violet that she was going and not to disturb Mrs. Farsyde but to check on her in an hour's time. Give Samuel and her time for whatever soft words and light kisses they wanted to offer each other. It was a relief to get away from Thorpe Hall, to have an excuse, if she was honest, not to have to be near. She shouldn't have turned back to follow him. She should have let Betsie or Annie carry the basket, and she'd have been home now. Mary would have had the jelly. She could be asleep in her bed. Nothing would make her turn around a second time, even if the squire drove past waving Jonas's parchment of reprieve.

It seemed to take forever before she viewed the jumble of rooftops of the Bay. Mary's bedroom was cramped but so much more comforting than Mrs. Farsyde's rooms. Mary, frail and old, was so different in her bed to Mrs. Farsyde with her big pillows and covers, all bright and white and with *him*. But Jiddy felt safe with Mary, cocooned from what was going on out there. She sat on the little stool and pressed the woollen bag holding a hot stone against her belly. How come she was always unprepared? Every blooming time.

"Is this what you did?" Jiddy asked.

"Is it helping?"

"Not much." Jiddy leaned forward, pressing her belly harder against the stone. "I hate this."

"Means you're a woman."

"I don't want to be a woman."

"You want bairns, don't you?"

"Never."

Mary smiled. "Maybe when Jonas comes back."

Jiddy couldn't believe the things Mary came out with sometimes.

"I don't care. This isn't worth it. My back's hurting. My legs and my belly are killing me, and I feel sick."

"First day is always worst."

"This happens each month."

"You're not only one. We've all been through it, and others will too. It'll get easier."

"When?"

Mary remained quiet. She did that sometimes, and Jiddy couldn't make her talk when it happened. It didn't matter. The silence was fine when she felt like this. At least this meant she didn't have to explain her aches and pains and her arrest. All the business of being a woman eclipsed the actions of men.

Mary broke the quiet. "Tell me what's happening with Jonas."

Jiddy closed her eyes. They hurt as though she'd been crying for a week.

"I don't know," she said.

She wanted to be rocked by the sea. A warm sea. A hot bath of a sea. A buoyant and soothing sea. No clothes to drag her down, a body with scales like a fish so she could swim away from everyone and everything.

"I thought Squire Farsyde were going to talk to Magistrate Avery in Scarborough."

"He's not back yet."

"I would've thought you'd have waited. Gracie would've stayed with me. You didn't need to hurry back."

"I started *bleeding*! And Mrs. Farsyde didn't need me."

Of course Mrs. Farsyde didn't need her. She had Samuel sloppy-chops Ryethorpe. She hadn't noticed Jiddy hobble down the stairs. She'd been too happy all right. Jiddy had to admit she'd looked pretty too, even after nearly miscarrying. Mrs. Farsyde should have been looking like she was two shakes from a corpse, yet she'd glowed like a bride. Love. She was in love. That would do it. But it was a shock Samuel glowed the same.

She tried to remember if Jonas gazed at her that way. She couldn't quite see it.

"I can't remember what Jonas looks like," she said. "Mary? What do I do? I can't remember."

Mary reached out her hand, and Jiddy leaned her head onto it.

"You've not forgotten."

"I have. I'm a horrible person."

163

"Sit up," Mary said. "You're all muffled, I can't hear you."

Jiddy sat up. "I'm a horrible person. My face is covered in ugly big spots and my belly's swollen and I've forgotten what Jonas looks like and you're poorly and you don't whinge and I'm moaning about a belly ache and turning into a woman...and I never want to have a baby." Jiddy wiped her tears with her sleeve. "And I'm always talking about me and having to say sorry." She snivelled.

"You've got to learn not to be so hard on yourself," said Mary. "Now let's think on something else, so you don't get maudlin on me. They've all been baking downstairs. Can you smell it? Gracie's left a pie, and Kitty and Helen have brought bread, and I know you've been bringing bits to tempt me from kind Mrs. King."

"All these spots will turn pus yellow, and I'll look like I have the plague."

"You have two spots."

"Four."

"Are Kitty and Helen still downstairs?"

"Whole of Bay's being kind," Jiddy said, wiping her face again. "They know I can't bake."

"It is kind, but I can't eat any of it, and you'll never get through it all."

"You might eat something," said Jiddy. "In a day or two."

"I'm not hungry for what they've brought. I fancy a tasty bit of haddock." She licked her lips.

"D'you want me to bring you some?"

"I'll have a nap," said Mary. "You take basket from hall up to Mr. Chaplow. He'll be pleased, and he'll appreciate it. Bit of comfort."

"But I can't go up—"

"Walk's good for your belly."

"I've not slept."

Mary had closed her eyes. That meant the conversation was over. Clutching the warm stone, Jiddy stood. The stool was getting uncomfortable anyroad, and she wasn't sure anymore if it was the stool making her back ache or the bleeding.

She slumped downstairs. Covered dishes filled the table. Mary was always right. There was too much food. Mary was sneaky too, keeping Jiddy busy so she didn't moan or dwell on Jonas.

She lifted the cloth off the basket. It was all untouched. Annie and Betsie hadn't even unpacked it. Picking up the little dish of jelly, she sat by the fire. The cool jelly slipped down her throat. Tea and bed and Mr. Chaplow forgotten, she fell asleep in the chair by the fire until Mary's voice woke her.

"Jiddy?" It crept soft down the stairs. "I'll have that jelly now."

CHAPTER TWENTY

Jonas tried to twist his hands, but they were bound tight. He swore he'd not say a word until they untied the wretched rope or he bust free. He'd not let on how it scraped his skin raw either. He was hungry too. Any minute, his belly would roar, but he didn't want this hoity man to have satisfaction on that either. He'd heard how you could be starved into submission, parched into saying untruths.

The tall man moved.

"My name is Lord Ryethorpe," he said, then waited, his face expectant.

Jonas shifted his weight.

"I believe your name is Jonas Chaplow. You own Meadow Bank Farm?"

"It's me da's farm."

"You work with him?"

Jonas nodded.

"Do you know why you were going to be sent to Australia?"

"Preventives and press-gangs put anyone they want on ships. Don't need no reason."

"Don't need no reason..." The man cleared his throat. "Do you have any questions?"

He had a thousand questions about rights and law and what they'd done to Jiddy and how unjust it all was, but this man didn't want a discussion man to man. He wanted a confession, and he'd wheedle it out of Jonas, make him admit to something he'd not done. If Jiddy was with him, she'd know what this man wanted and bat it right back.

Jonas held out his hands. "When are you going to take these off?"

The man was weighing him up. Jonas knew the questions that must be going through his head. *Will this thug attack me if his hands are free? Do I show him trust by releasing him and make him think he's my friend so that he spills his guts?*

He's wondering if he should call a soldier in to cut the rope and then stay in the room. But there'd be no alliance in that.

The man stepped forward. He was leaner than Jonas and taller, but he was older. A soldier. He had the air of someone who'd been battle bruised. If he attacked, could Jonas fight well enough with his hands tied?

Deftly, Lord Ryethorpe drew out a knife. The blade gleamed sharp. Jonas stepped back and stared the man out. The man studied Jonas's belly. If he cut there, Jonas would bleed like a stuck pig and it would be over before he'd had a chance to defend himself.

It all happened fast. Lord Ryethorpe moved fast, grabbing Jonas's arm with one hand then sliding the knife under the rope that bound his wrists. Jonas stepped back, studying the cut rope as he steadied his breath.

"Bring in some food," the man shouted.

Miraculously, the request was answered, and Jonas devoured the plate of mutton and bread and gulped down the mug of ale. He wasn't proud. He was ravenous and parched, and he was going to eat before they changed their minds and took the food away.

Ryethorpe watched. He didn't seem mean like the other soldiers or cold and haddock-eyed like his son.

Jonas ran his tongue over his teeth. Strands of meat caught in the cracks, and he tried to waggle them free. He took a final swallow of ale and whooshed it around his mouth. Ryethorpe was smiling. When did lords sit at a table with a farmer and smile?

"You'd make a good soldier," Lord Ryethorpe said. "Strong, determined and capable."

It didn't seem to warrant an answer, and Jonas put down the empty mug.

"Don't you want to fight for your country?"

"Why would I do that when there's folk relying on me here?"

"I understand that. You're a farmer."

"My da's farmer. I'm his farmhand."

"Your father relies on you?"

"Has to. He's getting on."

"I commend your loyalty."

"It ain't loyalty. He's my da. It's what we do in Yorkshire."

***

This young man was a different breed to those Ryethorpe was used to. For those who had seen the wounded returning from battle, an uncle or cousin perhaps, that made war less attractive a prospect. But for those who saw bright uniforms and heard tales of bravery and battles won, the call of glory beat strong. This young man fell into neither camp. His world revolved around a small farm in a remote northern village, working the land with his father. Generations of men before him had no doubt done the same thing and probably many planned to do that for generations to come. But Jonas Chaplow was not any man.

"Have you heard of the French Revolution?" Lord Ryethorpe asked.

"Them that killed their king?"

"Murdered him, yes, alongside his queen, plus noblemen and women and many common people too who disagreed with them."

"They must have done something wrong."

"Who has the right except the law to say what is right or wrong?"

"Men make laws, don't they?"

"Yes."

"Men are men. They make mistakes all time. Maybe they got the laws wrong and somebody noticed."

Ryethorpe studied the young man. He couldn't have been more than twenty. Probably couldn't read or write; not well, at least. Certainly had never travelled out of Yorkshire, not even to York. Yet he had a knack of seeing right to the heart of a dilemma and spearing the argument at its root.

"Right or wrong, we have to live by rules," Ryethorpe said.

It was Jonas's turn to study Ryethorpe.

"They're French rules," he said. "I'm not French. I'm not telling them how to live. I'd be better off heading to London. They've got rules I know for definite are a mistake."

This was incredible. It almost made Ryethorpe doubt that Gregory could be this young man's father. He loved Gregory as a brother, but even he couldn't say that Gregory was the brightest star in the night sky. He cleared his throat and touched the edge of the table.

"I knew your father," he said.

Jonas wiped his mouth.

"You've been up to farm, have you? What did me da say to you? He's not a man of many words."

Ryethorpe held up his hand as a barrier to the thought of Jonas's father.

***

Jonas sat up as straight as he could. "Farm's prosperous. Been in family for generations."

Ryethorpe dropped his head and turned over his hands so that the soft palms showed upwards before turning them back again. He was considering something, but Jonas couldn't tell what. Were they going to take the farm away? Keep Jonas away until his da, unable to keep up with all that needed to be done, lost the farm to some greedy, thieving landowner?

"I hear your mother died."

"Many go in childbirth."

"You never knew her?"

Jonas didn't know what to say. Southerners were far from sharp at times.

"My son says you don't look like your father," said Lord Ryethorpe.

Jonas pushed back the stool and glared at the older man, fists clenched.

"You'd have done better keeping that soldier in here rather than having him stand outside door."

Ryethorpe rose, placing his hands behind his back.

"I didn't mean to offend you or your father."

"You don't look like your son neither, but us Northerners don't insult with underhand comments," Jonas said.

"I don't mean to insult you."

"Then I'll be off. Ta for grub."

Jonas kicked back the stool and made for the door. Noises outside told him the soldier had heard.

"It's all right," Ryethorpe shouted. "I pushed over a chair. Stand to."

They'd been in the room for hours, and Jonas wanted out. He wanted to be riding back to the Bay and to put all the secrecy and lies behind him.

"Where's Jiddy?" he asked. "Me and Jiddy need to be getting back. We'll be missed. We've work to be doing if that's all right with you?"

"Mr. Chaplow? Please. I have one thing to say, and I offer you a choice—"

"A trap."

"Opportunity."

Jonas hovered at the door. He couldn't admit it aloud, he barely knew what it was himself, but when he thought he'd be put on that ship bound for the other side of the world, a tiny part of him wanted to go. To see. And then it had gone, relief taking its place that he'd return to the familiar, and he and Jiddy could build a life together. If Lord Ryethorpe was offering them an opportunity, he wanted to hear it.

"I believe you and this Jiddy Vardy are friends?" Lord Ryethorpe said.

There was something loaded in that question. Another trick, with carefully chosen words.

"Where is she?" Jonas asked again.

"Back in Robin Hood's Bay. She's probably going about her business. Captain Ryethorpe found no reason to hold her. She is a friend of yours?"

"What's that to you?"

There followed a silence. Jonas waited. His heart beat fast. There was more to the question than it seemed, and he didn't know how to answer. He could say she was his sweetheart. He could say he couldn't imagine a day without her. He'd thump the man if he suggested she marry his son.

"Aye, she's my friend," he said. "More than that. We've promised ourselves to each other."

He swelled his chest, readying to strike if necessary, but the lord looked like fighting was the last thing on his mind. He walked to the window then turned to face Jonas again.

"I hope you don't mind my asking if you resemble your father, Mr. Chaplow." The man cleared his throat. "Your real father, I mean."

"What you going on about?"

"The man you've been calling that name all these years is not your real father."

"Give over." Jonas turned to the door. "Ask guard to open this."

"Jonas? May I call you Jonas?"

Jonas put his hand on the door. It was thick oak. Unbreakable. He bashed it with his fist, but it didn't shut the man up.

"Your real father is Viscount Gregory Hartshorn. He was a brave solider, my closest friend. If he hadn't died, he'd have led a regiment and be fighting the French. I know for a fact he'd be proud if you joined the same regiment he served in and took up his sword. Your father is Viscount Gregory Hartshorn, Jonas, not a farmer. Not a Yorkshireman called Chaplow but a man of great wealth and standing from the south of England. A viscount. And a man you resemble with an indisputable likeness. It is uncanny. I knew as soon as I saw you. Anyone who saw you would know in an instant whose son you really are."

Jonas clenched his hands so tight together his knuckles hurt. His head was a jumble. What was this man going on about? His name was Jonas Chaplow. His da was William Chaplow. Always had been, always would be. What did he have to do with viscounts and men of standing? It was a trick to get him to join the army of his own volition. Well, no way was he doing that. It was always a trick when you talked to this lot. He shouldn't have stayed as long as he had. Get back to the farm, get back to what he knew. He would never fight for a cause he didn't believe in, however they tried to wrap it up.

"Are you going to open that door?"

***

He shoved his way through the crowded market, heading for the abbey steps. One hundred and ninety-nine. He'd counted them as a lad. Never believe what you're told without finding out the truth for yourself. One hundred and ninety-nine. He'd counted them on the way down and on the way back up.

Striding through the old graveyard, he headed for the coastal path. The breeze cleared his head, but the lord's words stuck in his mind. It wasn't a local name, that was for sure. Hartshorn. Sharp name. Hart meant stag and horn was a hill, wasn't it? Some bigwig thinking he was a stag. Well, that suited the beggar. No way was he calling a man like that his da. His real da was a quiet man. And he'd be worried. The farm was already too much for him, and Jonas had been away an entire week. He hoped his da had not been proud and had called in help. Knowing how stubborn he was, he'd probably be struggling to get it done himself. Maybe Jiddy had been up. That was the sort of thing she'd do.

174

He kicked through the long grass. There wasn't a ship or a boat in sight on the water. The thought of being in one made his stomach tilt. That had been a close call. Too close. He'd definitely tell Abe he'd not be lending his cart no more. He didn't care about extra tea and stuff. His da would understand. Better a son on the farm than an empty chair by the fire. It wouldn't be easy, though. Isaac wouldn't like it, and his da would miss rum on a cold night.

Grey clouds billowed menacingly. Better not rain. He wasn't in the mood for a soaking. He turned up his collar and quickened his step. Jiddy's face kept coming into his mind. Those crooked furrows on her forehead. Those black eyes. She'd be as worried as his da. That made another dilemma. Who should he see first? Jiddy, of course. It was always Jiddy who came first.

Now he'd thought about Jiddy's lips and breasts, his sugar stick hardened. He rubbed his groin.

"Keep moving," he said. "And you down there, behave yourself."

The wind blew chill. Damn and blast them preventives. Damn and blast that Captain Ryethorpe. Sod that nonsy lord.

Hartshorn. Hartshorn, Hartshorn. Bloody hell. The name wouldn't go away.

Jonas marched on. Wiping his forehead of sweat, he shook off the cold that couched his body. This was how you caught a chill. Bloody southern invaders. He'd go straight to the farm. That's what he must do. Jiddy would understand.

With that thought fixed in his head, he kept his eyes on the path, winding up and down, determined not to stop, catching his breath at the top of a rise and edging sideways, step by step, when the way became steep. At last, he saw smoke and the outline of rooftops of Robin Hood's Bay.

For the first time since he'd left Whitby, he allowed himself to stop. In Whitby, that Lord Ryethorpe had shouted after him to stop but he hadn't. Not once. He hadn't wanted to. He didn't want to hear what it meant if William Chaplow wasn't his real da.

CHAPTER TWENTY-ONE

Jiddy flung herself at Jonas, knocking him over so they fell against the kitchen table.

"Ow."

"You're back! You're back! That was so fast! Where were you? Scarborough? Not Hull? Tell me, tell me everything." She kissed him, gripping his face in her hands, so that he struggled to answer. "It don't matter, you're back. Thank the Lord, you're back. Squire's a saint! A true saint!"

He smiled when she leaned back and studied his face, touching the bruises along his cheekbone and gently tracing her fingers along his jaw.

"They hurt you," she said, running her palms down his arms and scooping up his hands to study. "I could bash them. They're bullies. Just because they wear uniforms and say they're acting for the law. They're not acting for the law, it's a stupid, cruel law that doesn't take care of us and help us..."

She caught Jonas's eyes staring at her. "They just make me so mad." She laughed. "You must've smelt all food I brought for your da. He doesn't know what happened. I haven't told him, so he's not been worried. Oh, here!"

She flung her arms around him, snuggling her dark head into the crook of his neck.

"Jiddy," he said, laughing awkwardly and pushing her away by her shoulders. "Let me look at you. They hurt you too, didn't they?"

She stepped back and held out her arms as she turned around.

"I'm fine but you have no idea how worried I've been." She caught his hands in hers. "How did Squire Farsyde do it? I can't believe how fast you've made it back. Where did the ship stop?"

"I weren't on a ship. I never left Whitby."

"You were here all time? But I saw the ship leave. The swine. He lied, Captain Ryethorpe lied to me."

"They're all liars," said Jonas, stroking her hair. "You can't believe a word they say."

"But they hurt you." She wriggled closer. "They're not after you, are they?"

"No."

"You sure? I know how to use a pistol. I'll send them on their way."

"They're not coming for me. They wanted me to be a soldier, but I told them, I'm a farmhand. I've got duties. I've got—"

"A lass to love!" Jiddy interrupted. She laughed, clasping his shoulders and kissing him.

He dropped his hands to her hips, holding her still. He couldn't last though. Soon, his hands were moving up her back and then they were kissing good and proper. She pulled his jacket, and he stumbled forward. The table edge hit her buttocks. A chair wobbled. She laughed again.

"What if your da comes in?"

He grabbed her hand and led her outside, where they looked around. Only chickens and muck. They crossed the yard. When they were inside the barn, he closed the door. Jiddy waited. It was quiet. They had the barn to themselves. Taking Jonas's hand, she towed him towards the ladder that led to the hay loft.

He followed as she climbed, the ladder creaking. Crawling across the rough wood, she rolled onto a mound of hay. It smelled of grain and dust. He fell beside her, gathering her in. She wrapped her arms around him, shuffling to free her legs from her skirt, wishing she'd taken it off so that it didn't get in the way and glad as hell that it wasn't last week when she couldn't have done any of this stuff.

Kissing was good with Jonas. Even so, he'd not seemed quite so desperate, kissing her so hard and fast she didn't have time to get comfy. Her mouth would be sore, and she could barely breathe. His hands wouldn't rest still either. It was too fast. Too much. The straw prickled. The floor gave her body no comfort. She didn't want this. It wasn't right.

"Jonas?" She foisted him back. Panting like a dog, his hands reached for her again. "Jonas!"

His eyes, bleary and unfocused, snapped open.

"Can't we go slow, for once?" she said. "No need to go at me like a fox in a rabbit warren."

"I'm sorry," he said. "You're always one dragging at me. I thought you liked it this way."

It was true, she did like it fast and frantic, but she'd not known you could kiss slow and gentle. Mrs. Farsyde and Samuel kissing so softly made her unsettled. She didn't know why, but their kiss looked special as if they had a secret only the two of them knew about.

"Can we kiss calm like?" she said.

Jonas reached out. "I thought that's what we were doing."

"And not touch?"

"How do we kiss and not touch?"

It was true. Kissing meant touching lips, then it was tongues, then it was hands and then it was, oh, surging tide, she'd soon be wanting to pop like jewelweed.

She held him back with both hands.

"Like when we were kiddies," she said.

He looked appalled.

"We never kissed as kiddies."

She laughed. "Do you remember when you were trying to get me to say that sea tasted of salt and I didn't know what you were getting at? I said sand, or grit, I can't remember, but I didn't guess salt."

"It were like pulling a rotten tooth."

"You said, 'Stick your tongue out,' and I did, and you touched my tongue with your tongue."

"You hated it."

"I guessed salt."

"You were always quick on uptake."

Jiddy hit his arm. But she remembered that day, sitting in the shallows. A sunshine day. A day of skittling clouds and goose pimples.

"Can we do that?" she said.

He put his arms around her.

"Thought that's what we were doing."

She eased herself back.

"Without the tongues," she said. Settling herself cross-legged, she pushed his knees, and he sat opposite in the same way, with an amused look on his face. "Now let's kiss slowly," she said. "No tongues. Just lips. And we're not allowed to touch each other. No hands, arms. Nothing.

It tickled. That first touch, and they sat back, embarrassed. It seemed so revealing. Vulnerable. Scary. It was hard to make eye contact. The silence of the barn boomed loud. They leaned towards each other again. It was unsettling. She didn't expect everything to home in on their lips with such intensity. They made a sound. Seaweed popping underfoot. Eyes closed, every part of her body disappeared until she was only lips. Floating lips. Lips dancing with other lips. She didn't know how long they sat, sensing each other through that small touch. It was like a wave rising over her body, salty, warm, and her heart felt so tender with care for him. Real care, real love, not frantic animals no more.

"Jonas?" a man's voice called from the barn below.

They stared into each other's eyes, spell as yet unbroken.

"Jonas? Are you in here?"

Neither of them moved.

Feet stamped, then the barn door made that familiar sound when it didn't quite close.

"Da's looking for me."

She couldn't speak. Mouth open, all she could do was breathe and stare. She couldn't explain it, she didn't have words. It was so deep inside she'd have to dive into a cave to explain it.

"Jiddy, I don't know what to say. That were…"

He felt the same. Jonas, who knew the answer to everything, couldn't explain it either.

She leaned forward and brushed his cheek with her lips. The soft hair of an early beard stirred under her touch. She leaned back. The rise and fall of his chest showed he was breathing heavily.

Jiddy smiled. "That were beautiful."

"Yes."

"We're not animals."

"No."

"I liked it."

Jonas nodded. He kissed her so lightly it was barely contact.

"I feel closer to you than I ever have, Jonas. I feel I know you more. I feel…"

Leaning in, she kissed his lips, lingering on them before releasing again.

"Marry me, Jiddy," he said. "Marry me tomorrow. Today. Right now!"

She smiled again. "I'll marry you any time of day or week or year, Jonas Chaplow."

They kissed again. Soft and warm. A little longer than before. A little more desire.

"Come down when you're ready," he said, pushing to his feet.

He was at the ladder when he turned.

"I've got to tell you something," he said.

"That you adore me?"

"Apart from that," he laughed. "We might have to invite some high-up people to our wedding."

"I don't want my mother there," Jiddy said. "Signora Vardarelli might as well be a stranger for all I care."

"Have you ever heard of a Viscount Gregory Hartshorn?"

"Of course I have," she said, shuffling to her feet, "but he won't be coming either. He died when I were born. She told me. I almost believed she had feelings when she said what had happened to him."

"How does your mother know him?"

"I told you. He was my father, apparently."

The happy grin vanished. "*Your* father?"

"He's dead, though," she said. "How do you know about him?"

She wandered over to the ladder. He climbed down a few rungs before looking up at her, his face drained of his usual pink.

"You should have told me," he said.

"But why? Why are you asking?"

He looked away. "Shit, Jiddy. Shit."

"What's matter?" Jiddy crouched down. "How'd you find out his name? She reached out her hand, but Jonas climbed down a few more rungs. "Were they lying to me?

I wouldn't put it past them. Is he alive? Did you meet him in Whitby? You don't need to worry. I won't want either of them at our wedding. I have to tell Mary straight away though, but other than Mary and your da…"

He descended a few more rungs before looking up, his face a mixture of embarrassment and fear.

"How did you know Signora Vardarelli was your real mother?"

"Why are you talking about her? Mary is more my mam than she is. I told you, I don't want her here when we wed."

"But you didn't doubt she is your blood?"

"What's matter, Jonas?"

"Tell me straight, how did you know for sure she were your mam? It can't be just because someone said so?"

Jiddy shook her head. "It were like looking in a mirror, only at me in future. Older. She were almost a twin."

The mop of his head obscured his face, and he continued to descend. Something was wrong. He never spoke about her mother or London or wanted to know what she'd done, or who she'd seen when she'd been away. "Jonas?" She waited. Boy shifted his feet, and the straw rustled. "Tell me."

His hands clung to the ladder, strong fingers, rounded knuckles.

"All women from Naples have dark hair and eyes, don't they?"

"I suppose."

"And the men?"

"I don't know. I've not met any gentlemen."

184

"It's got to be more than you look alike. You could look like every woman and bairn in Naples. I could look like every man in London—don't make them kin. Don't mean just because I don't look like anyone here…"

He dropped his head again and rested his forehead on the rung. She had to hold him, tell him whatever he was thinking or had been put into his head mustn't bother him. The threat of the prison ship had frightened him, that was all. She could make his worry go away.

"I'm coming down," she said, hoisting her skirt.

"I met someone who knew your da in Whitby."

She stopped. "Who?"

"He were his closest friend. He couldn't stop looking at me."

"Well, tell me about it. What did they say? Jonas, wait for me." She hooked one leg around the ladder and began to climb down. "Jonas? What's hurry? Wait!"

By the time Jiddy reached the bottom, Jonas had already gone.

CHAPTER TWENTY-TWO

Jonas marched into the farmhouse as Jiddy closed the barn door behind her. She ran across the yard, skipping over the odd dried cow pat and dodging a scurrying chicken.

"Da?" Jonas called.

They knocked into each other in the doorway as Jonas came out again. He sidled past and strode to the gate, which he leaned on to shout over.

"Da?"

Jiddy hurried after him. "Wait! Tell me what this man said. You can't leave it like this, I want to know if my da is really alive!"

Jonas opened the gate and walked along the path that led across the moor. She watched him turn about, looking in every direction. He brushed his thick hair out of his eyes and he turned his back, looking towards the woods. Peewits were calling and the wind rippled the grass, but no-one called back. The way he stood made her feel she couldn't approach. He was different. Angry.

"He'll be back soon," she said when he strolled back into the yard and closed the gate. She leaned next to him, following his gaze. It was no different to usual, chickens clucking around, mud caked dry where the cart had come in, yet Jonas seemed to have changed.

"What's up?" she said. "Who was it you met in Whitby? You started to tell me. You can't not finish."

She moved to stand in front of him and block his view, but his eyes wouldn't meet hers. She gripped his sleeves in her fists and gave a rough shake.

"Tell me all," she said. She waited but he didn't respond. "Are you listening?"

Jonas turned his back to look over the fields again, and she stepped to his side, trying to peer into his eye line.

"Don't you think it's like fate?" she asked. "That I were here when you came back? And that with your da not being here, we could have time together. And that I suggested kissing a bit different, just to see what it'd be like, and I'm glad we did. Aren't you? I like how we get carried away and we get so close to…well, you know. But this were special, don't you think? I felt nervous. Didn't you feel nervous?" He looked over her head, eyes fixed on the farmhouse door. "I'm rambling," she said. "Stop me rambling, won't you?"

She waited for him to say something, but he scuffed the ground with his boots then bent to stroke Rex, who lifted his head into the cup of Jonas's hand. Kneeling beside him, Jiddy stroked the dog, and immediately Jonas set off back to the house.

"Tell me what's wrong!" Jiddy shouted, running after him. "Don't be so rude. I were talking to you." She touched his arm. "What is wrong with you?"

He turned swiftly. His face looked pinched, like it did when he was fired up about something. His eyes were tinged dark and purple. He looked rough.

"I have to go," he said.

"Let me bathe your face."

"Got to sort something."

"But your da will be back soon enough, and we hardly get any time just two of us."

His body tensed, and he glanced over her shoulder at the yard again.

"What do you have to sort?"

"I meant I have to leave farm."

She laughed. "I'll come with you. D'you need to see squire?"

His slate eyes glinted granite.

"I'm going to France."

She laughed again. "Can't see Farmer Chaplow in France, somehow."

"I'm going to fight for the British Army."

"Stop it. Don't joke about things like that. Is Captain Ryethorpe forcing you to do that? He can't force you. No-one can force you to go off and fight."

"I can't wait for Da. Will you tell him I've gone?" Jonas asked, walking into the kitchen. Jiddy followed.

"No, I won't. You're not going. He can't make you. Squire Farsyde won't allow it. He's spoken to magistrate. You don't have to do what they say. Is that why you're keen to see your da?" Jonas shrugged. "He'll be against it too. Let's tell him we're to wed and forget this stupid business."

"He'll understand when I tell him," Jonas said. He wouldn't hold her gaze but scanned the room instead.

"What are you looking for?"

"This." Jonas picked up a sharp knife.

"Are you going to stab all the French to death?" Her voice sounded harsh, but she couldn't help it. She was so confused and angry too, at Jonas. What was he playing at? This wasn't like him at all.

"I'll organise help at farm," he said.

"Stop it, Jonas. This isn't funny. What's happened? We were all fine and talking about wedding. Didn't you mean it? You can't just say that to a lass, you know, and think you can brush it away. Jonas! What's wrong with you?"

"Nowt."

"Then why are you suddenly asking about Gregory Hartshorn and France and fighting? I told you, he's dead. Samuel Ryethorpe is making mischief, that's all. I'm not going off to London or anywhere—are you worried about that? You don't need to. Just don't listen to him, he's mean. He just wants—"

"I'm sorry, Jiddy. I got carried away. That kiss, it were… we shouldn't. I mean, we'll put wedding on hold, that's all. I don't want to start anything up when I'm going off."

"Too late for that, mister." She flung her arms around his waist, but he wrenched free, squaring up for a fight. Shocked, she stepped back. "What the heck is wrong with you?"

He folded his arms. "Nowt," he said. "Don't you have to be taking care of Mary?"

He wasn't going to give way, she could tell that. This was something outside her scope, and the stubbornness that was always in him had built a wall.

"I'm sitting with Mary later," she said. "Grace and Helen are with her at moment."

"I think you should be there now," he said.

"Don't tell me what to do. We're different now. We're closer. We couldn't get any closer. You love me. I love you. We've…"

She stopped talking when he avoided her eyes again. That was something she couldn't bear. She couldn't stand him not looking at her. She stepped right up to him, so close she stared up his nostrils. So close she saw the lines in his lips and the pores on his skin. He didn't flinch. Then, after what seemed like the longest silence between any two people, he turned away. Picking up a cloth bag hung on the back of the door, he dropped it on the table. He took a spoon from the table drawer and shoved it in the bag along with the knife.

"What's got into you? You never thought about such things before. It's the whole smuggling business, isn't it? And you getting arrested and nearly thrown on that ship. If it bothers you so much, we can stop our dealings with Isaac and Abe. We can be straight and work farm and—"

"You're right," he said. "It did shake me up. I think it's better to find out for myself how soldiers fare with us robbing them of their blankets and bullets and such. Then I'll know for sure I'm making right decision about stopping smuggling."

She couldn't believe it.

"You're not telling me everything." She grabbed his sleeve. "Why are you acting odd?" He busied himself, opened a table drawer and rooted inside. "Jonas! Look at me! Look me in the face."

Jonas pressed a blanket into the bag. He opened another drawer and riffled about. Closed it again. She pulled him to face her. His eyes glowered hard.

"They said to bring our own kit," he said. "Shortages."

"You're not going!" she shouted, grasping both his arms and staring into his face. "I won't let you. I won't let them take you."

"It's not up to you, Jiddy. I said I'd go, and I'm going."

This wasn't the Jonas she knew. Something had changed and suddenly. He was hiding something; she knew him too well not to realise that. Well, she'd have it out of him if she had to drag it up along with his guts.

"You can't leave, Jonas. We're going to wed and take care of farm for your da. Don't that matter to you? We love each other, and now you're acting like you're angry at me or something. Don't say it's because I didn't tell you my father's name. I didn't because it's not important. Gregory Hartshorn's nothing to me. Viscount or whatever he is. He's dead. That's all we need to know. Dead men can't do anything to me or you."

"He were a soldier. If he'd lived, he'd have led a regiment. It made me remember my duty, that's all."

He fumbled in the bag, pushing stuff down.

191

"So what if he were a soldier? Lots of men are soldiers. You've never been bothered before."

"I'm bothered now."

"But you don't know anything about him. How do you know what he'd be doing if he lived? Why would you care?"

"Stop mithering me, Jiddy. I've decided. I need to see more than this farm, don't I? You've been to London. I thought you'd understand a man needs to see the world."

"How do you know about him? How d'you know he were a soldier?" Jiddy grabbed his arm. "You said I never mentioned him, and I haven't." She tried to look in his face, but he turned away and began foraging in another drawer. "What did this man in Whitby say?" She followed him. "Were it Samuel? Is that why you wouldn't say who it were?"

Shrugging her off, he pulled the bag into his arms and held it tight.

"I'm sorry that silk got you into trouble," she said. "I tried to explain to them."

"It isn't the silk." He closed the bag and slung it over his shoulder.

"You're not going right now?"

"I told you. I have to."

He sounded so serious and sad. And something else too. Something she couldn't read. She flung her arms around him again. "I won't let you. You'll have to take me with you because I'm not letting go. Or tell me why so I can talk you out of it."

His fingers dug into her arms. They dug into her skin as he tried to prise her away, but she clung on tighter, wrapping herself around his torso and clinging like a limpet, her left cheek pressed hard against his jacket so that the buttons hurt her cheekbone.

"Let go, Jiddy."

She raised her chin. "Kiss me. Then you definitely won't want to go."

She was desperate, hoping that he wouldn't be able to go if they kissed. She was begging, but she didn't care. She knew his mind as well as she knew her own, and if they kissed, that heart-burning kissing again, then he wouldn't leave. He *couldn't* leave. She reached for his neck, but he dragged her hand roughly away and she fell back.

"What have they done to you?" She stepped forward again, arms ready to embrace. "I love you, Jonas. You love me. You know that. You know that in your stomach and heart and bones. We've proved it to each other. Please stop this. Please stop pretending you're going. What's happened? Tell me what's happened." Her throat strained. A heavy weight pressed in her chest. "Jonas? Talk to me, tell me what's wrong."

His eyes shone, but he didn't seem able to speak.

"Jonas," she said more gently. "What do you want me to do? Tell me. I'll do anything."

Suddenly, he pulled her to him, an arm around her shoulders, and she put her arms around his back, pressing close against him, wanting to melt like smelted copper into him. Neither of them moved, but for the first time,

193

RUTH ESTEVEZ

she didn't know what he wanted. His breathing was heavy. Was he crying? No. He couldn't be. Jonas never cried. What could she do? What did he want her to do? That was it. It was simple. He'd tried to get her to do it before, but she'd refused. But now, if she did it, now he'd stay.

Sliding her right hand around his ribs, stepping slightly away, making a gap between them, she ran her hand to his hip. Could she do this? Holding her breath, she slid her palm over his belly. She stretched out her fingers. His donger stirred. In one rapid movement, he pushed her away and they faced each other.

Her heart pounded. His cheeks flushed, his eyes looking everywhere but at her. He readjusted the bag over his shoulder.

"See? It won't work," he said. "I have to go."

He walked to the door while she held back the tears by focusing on the black beams dividing the low ceiling.

"Tell me what you want," she said.

"Bye, Rex." His voice rang out, then his boots crunched across the ground.

She ran to the door. He'd already reached the gate, Rex circling his legs.

"If you go, I'll hate you forever!" she shouted. "I hate you, Jonas Chaplow! I hate you!"

194

CHAPTER TWENTY-THREE

Jonas kept walking, Rex bounding by his side. He couldn't look back let alone walk back. He scuffed the grass as he strode downhill, praying Jiddy wouldn't follow.

"Go back, Rex, go back," he said, but Rex remained with him.

Jonas felt sick in his stomach. Angry. Embarrassed. Ashamed. He was sure of it now. The suspicion that had followed him along the clifftop shouted out it was true. He didn't know what had convinced him, but he was positive Viscount Gregory Hartshorn was his real blood-and-flesh da as much as he was Jiddy's. Only thing to do was to go away. He looked over his shoulder. She wasn't following or shouting after him. She must really hate him, and why not? He'd broken her heart without saying why. He had to cling to the fact that this way was less hurtful than telling her they were flesh and blood. And they'd come far too close to mingling their flesh and blood. He hated himself for what he'd just done, but it wasn't as bad as making her hate herself for loving a brother.

Brother and sister. They were brother and sister. They'd come so close, and what would they have done if they'd found out too late and been wed and properly bedded? What if he'd made Jiddy with child? He couldn't bear the thought. A voice rang in his head.

"What you've done numerous times is as close to ungodly as the full-on thing."

Their kisses had always been full-on. Pressing against each other had aroused them both. He'd even tried to get her to hold his sugar stick. But that last kiss, that gentle touching of their lips, had been more than he could have imagined. Tears welled up his throat, and he choked them down.

He loved her. He loved his sister. And he couldn't tell her that.

Bending over, he spat. Remaining with his hands on his knees, he focused on the yellowing grass. He had to banish her face. Banish her voice. Her lips. All thought of her beautiful hair and eyes and touch. All memory of her skin and breasts and her sitting astride his crotch on the clifftop in the long grass and the smell of the soil and the sound of the sea. Standing straight, he tilted his head back and closed his eyes. Rex licked his hand.

It seemed so obvious now, that his da wasn't his real da. He was too old for one thing, much older than his mam, from what folks said. He and his da looked nothing alike. They didn't even think the same way. He'd always thought he took after his mam; that's what everyone told him, so why didn't he believe that anymore? Even his da said it. Easy to say when you'd nothing to argue toss against.

Barking, Rex sped off downhill. Typical, when he couldn't bear the thought of seeing him, there he stood. Hearing the dog, Mr. Chaplow looked up, grey hair flapping in the breeze. The old man lifted a rock off the back of the cart and dropped it next to a couple of others. The wall was depleted. There'd been a spate of stone thieves, pinching top stones and whatever else they could load up onto a wagon. It was a filthy habit, stealing from those that couldn't afford to be stolen from.

"There you are," his da said.

"Beggars at it again?" Jonas said as he reached the cart.

He waited for his da to speak, but he only got a clicking of a tongue. He patted Boy's neck and waited a moment for the horse to nuzzle his hand. His da tried a second stone in a gap when he found the first wouldn't fit. That didn't fit either, and he looked at the cluster of stones on the grass. Jonas put down his bag. "Let me."

His da pushed him aside.

"I've managed all week without you," he said, heaving up the stone and edging it into the gap. He looked at the wall, catching his breath.

"I'll have it done in a trice," Jonas said.

His da nodded to the bag on the ground. "What's that?"

Rex sniffed at the bag. Obviously, he'd discovered the meat pie Jonas had found in the basket.

"I'm joining army," he said.

"You what?"

"I'm not stopping, Da. I came down to say goodbye and…"

He stopped. Could he ask? What if his da didn't know? The old man was thin and tired. *Don't feel sorry for him. He's a strong old goat.* Still, it was on the tip of his tongue to ask if Viscount Gregory Hartshorn was his real father.

"Da?"

"Thought you were off?"

Jonas lifted a stone and wedged it into the wall. He looked around and chose another. His da leaned on the back of the cart and uncorked a flask.

"I should be fighting in France, so I'm going to go."

He rammed in the stone and settled them against each other. He'd miss the touch of these rocks and his da's silences.

"I don't know when I'll be back."

"Hear that, Boy?" his da said. "Jonas is leaving you wi' me. Looks like I'll be taking up carrier's job for Big Isaac."

Jonas stood up, stone in his hands.

"That's not fair," he said.

"You're leaving, you say?"

Jonas nodded.

"Taking Boy with you?"

"No."

His da picked up a stone, straddled with it to the wall and dumped it, crashing and sending chips on top of the stone Jonas had just placed. It didn't sit tight, but Jonas kept quiet. His da went back to the cart. Rex lay on the ground, eyes and ears alert. Boy stood, head erect.

"Ideal world, you'd stop and help me on farm, but life's not fair. We can't all have what we want."

Too right, it wasn't fair. Jonas didn't want to be the son of a strange man or that man to be Jiddy's da. He wanted life back as it had been, Jiddy and him courting, him readying to take over the farm. All clean and honest and as it should be. As it was, he felt filthy for all he and Jiddy had done, dishonest that he had to keep the smuggling malarkey a secret and a coward that he couldn't ask his da if he were his flesh and blood. And that kiss with Jiddy. That gentle touch and flutter in his heart. He'd never have a kiss like that again. *It's kindness*, he told himself. *Kinder on everyone if I go away.*

He picked up his bag and slung it over his shoulder.

"Does lass know you're going?" his da said.

"Mary's dying. Jiddy's got enough on her plate."

"Mary's not going to last long, and then Jiddy'll be all on her own. Cottage is rented, you know. Can't see her being able to keep it."

"Ask her to stop here with you. I'm sure she'd say yes if you asked."

His da adjusted the stone, and it tumbled on the grass.

"Is there a reason she should?

"Mary's been like a mam to Jiddy, hasn't she?" Jonas said.

"And Thomas were like a da."

"Do I look like my mam?"

His da stood up and studied him. Jonas shrugged the bag to make it more comfortable. "I'll be off then," he said.

His da made a noise and turned back to the wall.

Jonas waited, but the old man kept busy. He was halfway back to the road when a shout reached him.

"Jonas! Stop!"

Rex barked. His da ambled over the field, Rex lolloping beside him. Jonas waited until the dog bounded around his legs and his da, short of breath, approached.

"You're in a hurry," he said.

"No point in dawdling."

Mr. Chaplow stood catching his breath. "Don't be a soldier, lad, it's not for you."

Jonas looked over his da's shoulder, then at Rex, flopped on the grass. "We all heard about that revolution thing, and how some in London want it here, Da. We can't have that. It'll only make things worse."

"Aye," his da agreed. "I'll give you that. Quality and thinking types want it, but squire says it won't work same here as it does over there with them Frenchies."

"I want a better way for us, Da, and I want to say I stood up for it."

"As long as you don't join East India Company's army. You'd not only be a soldier but you'd be joining biggest criminals in world if you did that."

"I won't do that, Da. It's British Army I'd be joining, and it's only to France I'll go."

"Fighting won't make it right, lad."

"I'm fed up being told what to do by everyone. I want to see more than this farm and folk round here."

"Better devil you know, son."

Jonas looked up at the sky. Clouds were scuttering fast. The weather was changing.

"I need to see somewhere else before it's too late," he said.

"You can do that without going to war."

He couldn't say the truth that was the crux of it. He couldn't say it was because he didn't care if he lived or died either. Too many questions in that statement. More and more things he couldn't say.

"Brave men do it," he said. "I want to prove I'm no coward."

"All sorts of ways of showing you're brave."

"It's because..." He looked up at the sky again. A lapwing circled. He looked at his da. He couldn't hurt this man who treated him like a son. He couldn't hurt the man who'd brought him up and taught him all he knew. He couldn't tell him that he knew he wasn't his son.

He bent to rub Rex's head. The dog's movement rubbed into his palm. Clouds scurried across the sky, the breeze, smell of soil and grass and muck filled his nostrils. His old man silently begging him to stay was too much.

"Let them in power do fighting," his da said. "Let them stick bayonets into other lads' bellies or blow their chests out. Give them a musket and some muddy ill-fitting boots, but not you, son, not you."

He couldn't listen to being called son any longer. This was it. He patted Rex's head again. Adjusted his bag another time. "I've got to go."

"Go to Scarborough or York. Durham if you want, but not France."

Jonas half-wished he'd kept walking. He couldn't stay in England. If he stayed in England, it'd be so much easier to seek Jiddy out. A day's ride away rather than a battlefield's march. His da's eyes had begun the first signs of that milky blindness. A day's ride away. If he said he was going to any of those places, his da would know he had a chance of staying alive. He nodded.

"I'll think on what you've said."

He turned and walked towards the track that led inland and tried not to look over his shoulder. He tried so hard his shoulders and head ached with the effort.

CHAPTER TWENTY-FOUR

Jiddy stood in her undergarments, her jacket and skirt discarded on the bed. Helen Drake's voice bled under the closed door from Mary's room across the landing. No way was she going to talk about Jonas to Mary with sharp-eared Helen Drake listening. Besides, she wasn't even sure she should bother Mary with this. Mary needed calm. Mary didn't need Jiddy shouting and stamping and throwing things to relieve the pain that coursed through her body. Calm and peace. That was the main thing, Gracie said.

"Leave her be. Let her rest."

"Don't get her wound up," Helen Drake said. *"Only tell her pleasant things."*

It was insulting. She'd never wind Mary up. Who did they think she was? A two-year-old? She could keep calm. She could keep the storm in her belly and not spew it all over Mary's bed. She rounded her fist. Unclenched. Picked up her jacket and threw it across the room. It slid down the wall. She hurled her skirt at the door, and it sank in a crumpled heap.

She clicked the cupboard latch and yanked open the door. There it was. Waiting. She pulled on the dress she'd hidden for too long. It fitted perfectly, and she stroked the material. No ordinary clothes. Not today. Skirt tight on her waist, she smoothed it down. Adjusted the bodice, pulled the cords. Perfect.

One eye on the closed door of Mary's bedroom, she snuck down the stairs. The fire rattled, but no-one sat about, and she breathed easy. Opening the front door, she stepped outside. Sunny Place stood empty, nobody to stop and ask what she thought she was wearing or who did she think she was or where she was heading. She hurried up the Stiles and through the woods, tramping the bottom way to Thorpe Hall, her mind reeling with thoughts and plans. Mrs. Farsyde would keep her busy. Busy altering clothing and making and mending. She'd not miss Jonas. She'd not think about him or talk about him or utter his name. She'd not think about anything at all. Then she'd spend the rest of her time with Mary. She'd barely sleep, she'd be so occupied. She wouldn't give herself a second to think about Jonas and false promises and how he'd broken her heart. She didn't need Jonas, she had Annie and Betsie. Lads were selfish and useless and only good for one thing, and even that she could manage herself if she had to.

Sod Jonas. Sod, sod, sod him.

Reaching Thorpe Hall, she strolled more slowly up the drive. The image of Mrs. Farsyde and Samuel came into her head. Samuel. It would be hard not to throttle him. He'd arrested Jonas and got his soldiers to beat him up. He'd threatened to put him on a ship for Australia. He was most likely the one who had told Jonas to go to war. What was she thinking? She couldn't give up on Jonas. That was what Samuel would want. It was all Samuel's fault. Jonas was putting on a brave face and saying he wanted to fight.

The hall glowered unwelcoming. Sulky rooms skulked behind mullion windows. Smoke wound from the chimneys, but that was the only sign there was life in the house. Washing hung limp and neglected in the yard. Even the stables were closed in with guilt. She pushed down the latch on the back door. It stuck as usual. No-one could sneak into this house unheard.

Kitchen, house and ground staff slouched lacklustre in the kitchen. As usual, nobody looked in her direction. She took off her cloak and hung it on the peg next to Violet's and those of the others who came up from the village. Annie's cloak hung there too.

Running her hands over the dark-red bodice of her dress, she fingered the gathers around her waist. The ochre skirt underneath glowed in the opening triangle of the overskirt. She'd not worn this dress since she'd returned from London. It felt good. Tight. She walked different in it. She was different.

She'd washed it so carefully and put it away after she and Jonas had escaped from the sea. Of course, she had glimpsed at it, checked that salt hadn't clung to its silk, and she'd run her fingers over the embossed pattern. But she'd not worn it again until today. If Jonas could put on a soldier's uniform, then so could she.

She glanced across the passage. Mrs. King and all of them would be gobsmacked if they saw her in such finery, it beat any of the dresses Mrs. Farsyde had given her to wear. The fact that she was out of her usual skirt, chemise and jacket would please her, and Jiddy wanted to do that. As for Samuel Ryethorpe, she'd show him he couldn't treat her like a scrap of potato peel.

She walked down the passage and through the door into the main house, where she listened for voices—movement, a dog whining, thumping its tail—anything. Sounds from the kitchen, trapped behind the heavy door, barely felt their way through. Voices, elusive as dust specks swirling in sunlight, reached for her fingertips, tantalisingly close yet playing hide-and-seek. She remained motionless, listening for a giveaway word or laugh.

She didn't like the quiet. She never had. This sort of quiet came before an ambush. This sort of quiet shouted that she didn't belong. Well, today she belonged more than any two-faced officer of the law. The paintings of old squires and their ladies surrounded her. She looked at their faces. They all knew exactly who they were and where they belonged. Her face didn't match any of theirs. Samuel's face would belong here. A pale face. A privileged face.

"I don't care!"

Her voice rang out, but nobody answered. *Fine.* Wealth didn't make you right. Wealth didn't mean you knew better, it just meant you thought different and behaved different and got away with it. Well, now she looked wealthy in her rich lady's dress.

She pushed the door open to the big room where the family usually sat at this time of day, but the room stood empty. Voices came from elsewhere. Footsteps.

A door closing. She hurried into the hall. The door to Squire Farsyde's study stood ajar. Good. It was right Squire Farsyde should be there. He'd get word out immediately to bring Jonas back for good. And he'd find out too, what a toad Samuel had turned out to be. She swung open the door.

The squire sat at his desk. He looked up, surprised. His face was like that of an innocent child. Round-eyed, round-cheeked, soft and questioning. He was so proud that Mrs. Farsyde was with child. Everyone knew that he couldn't wait to be a father.

"Afternoon, sir," she said. "I'm wanting to talk to you, if it's no trouble."

"Afternoon to you too, Jiddy. I need to talk to you too, it's about Jonas, I'm afraid."

Jiddy walked to the desk. "It's about Jonas I'm here."

"Now, I don't want you to be upset, but Magistrate Avery said there wasn't anything he could do. I'm afraid we can't bring Jonas back—"

"I've seen Jonas," Jiddy interrupted, fighting to keep hold of the angry words that tore up her throat.

"What?"

"He's going to France to fight, and I think Captain Ryethorpe's making him go. He's threatening him somehow, and I've to find the captain and ask him to stop it."

Squire Farsyde leaned his stubby hands on the desk and rose to his feet. "You've seen Jonas? How did he leave the ship?"

"He never went. They held him in Whitby and persuaded him to go to France. He won't listen to anything I say. He says he's got to go, so Captain Ryethorpe must be using something to make him. Where is the captain? I must see him."

"Well, I'm shocked. Surprised. It's good news, but I think I should talk to Jonas. I can't see why he'd agree to go to France, he's not the soldiering type, I would have thought, with his ideals."

She couldn't hold the tears in much longer. Her voice cracked. "You're right, he isn't the soldering type! But he's going! I tried to find out why and stop him, but he wouldn't change his mind. He was so adamant he wanted to go. That's why I've got to see Captain Ryethorpe. He must be holding something over Jonas, something instead of the prison ship."

"You say Jonas wanted to go?"

That was it. She had it. Of course. It made sense why he'd acted so strange.

"He's being made to go," she said. "I think Captain Ryethorpe has told him something about my father that's making him go."

"You've lost me."

"Jonas mentioned my father. My real father. Viscount Hartshorn?"

"Viscount Hartshorn? You mean the Hartshorns of Fulford?"

"I'm not sure, only that my father was called Hartshorn and Jonas has found something out about him."

"He's dead, isn't he?"

"That's what I were told," Jiddy said, "but I don't know what to believe anymore. I just know Captain Ryethorpe's said something about my father that Jonas won't tell me, and now he says he has to go to France. You saw Captain Ryethorpe in Whitby. He wanted Jonas on that prison ship. He must think fighting in France is many times worse than being trapped in bowels of a ship. He hates all of us. He just wants to punish all of us in whatever way his twisted mind thinks will hurt most."

"Now, I'm sure that's not true," said the squire. "And Viscount Hartshorn is dead. There was a funeral over in Fulford—it might even have been in York, I forget. There was no body of course, but the family—"

"Can I borrow a horse?" she interrupted. "I'll ride to Whitby. I'll bring Jonas back myself if I have to knock him out to do so and tie him up and hide him in caves so that man can't get him."

"No, I'm sorry, I can't do that. Ride over to Whitby and drag him back? Oh, no, that's not the way, Jiddy. It would be a fool's errand."

She was so angry, she'd explode. She wanted the squire's gun if she couldn't take a horse. Force Samuel to leave them be. She could do it. She knew how.

"Jiddy," the squire said, sitting again. "Jonas is an honest, young man, and he isn't the type to be bullied into anything. Please. Sit with me."

Jiddy strode to the door. "I've got to find Captain Ryethorpe. Will you help me or not?"

"He's gone to York, I'm afraid. I can have a word with him when he returns."

"It'll be too late, Jonas'll be on his way to France by then."

"I've come to know the captain well since he was posted here. He wouldn't force anyone to go to France unless they'd committed a crime. Has something happened to convict him again?"

She couldn't believe it. He thought he knew the captain? What if she told him that his wife were in love with him? He wouldn't be so forgiving then.

"Maybe Jonas wants to put on a uniform," he said. "He's not the only young man who's drawn to fight."

The awful truth seeped in. What if Samuel had nothing to do with it? That would mean Jonas did want to become a soldier. Anything rather than wed. The awful truth struck her. The kiss. They'd kissed different this time. Maybe he hadn't meant it. Maybe he'd hated that kiss as she'd hated Samuel's, and Jonas had done to her what she'd done to Samuel. Promised marriage then fled. No. She'd never believe that.

"We're wasting time," she said. "Jonas would rather go to prison than fight for this government."

The squire walked around the desk. "Jonas is in Whitby, you say?"

"That's where ships sail from, but I don't know if he'll be at dock now or where."

"If he's determined, there's nothing I or anyone can say, you know, Jiddy. I know what a young man can be like when his blood's fired up. If I were young again, I might very well make the same decision."

"But what about his da? I can't believe he'd deliberately leave his da to farm Meadow Bank on his own."

The squire thought for a few moments. "Mr. Chaplow will probably hire a lad while Jonas is away. I wouldn't worry, and at least France isn't Australia. Keep busy, that's my motto. Keep busy and don't dwell on things."

"I'm not worried. I'm…" What was she? Frightened for him. Afraid he'd never come back. Frightened for what she'd do?

"I really have to be getting on, Jiddy." The squire held the door open. "An estate doesn't take care of itself."

What was she to do if Jonas did want to go to fight? Scour streets and inns for him? Stand on the dock and wave him off? *Blast him, then. Damn him. Blast the squire and his puffed-up bravado.* She was back to her original idea. Keep busy. Do all the stuff Mrs. Farsyde wanted her to do. Spend time with Mary, and above all, avoid sodding Samuel Ryethorpe. And definitely avoid any thought of Jonas pin-a-medal-on-my-chest Chaplow.

***

Annie's face said it all. She gaped, wide-eyed when Jiddy opened the door to the sewing room.

"You're beautiful," she said, fingering the fabric. "Do you think Mrs. Farsyde will give me a dress to wear now I'm helping out too?"

Jiddy pushed back stray fronds of hair. "It's my dress, not Mrs. Farsyde's."

"Oh." Annie didn't hide her disappointment.

"She might," Jiddy said in reconciliation. "She gave me one when I first started, as she didn't like my skirt and shawl."

Annie smiled. "I hope she gives me a dress like yours."

"What are you doing in here?" asked Jiddy, walking to the large sewing table.

"I'm here to help. Squire Farsyde thought with two of us to see to Mrs. Farsyde and baby's clothes and linen and such, Mrs. Grainger can keep an eye on her health, or something like that."

"Violet will love that," Jiddy said, then, after a pause, "You know, I definitely think Mrs. Farsyde might give you a dress. She likes us to look presentable."

Annie's face lit up. "Do you think so?"

"If you've nothing to be doing right now, you can talk to me while I sew."

Annie couldn't stop smiling. "How come you're this dressed up? You're not usually."

Jiddy held out the red skirt and curtsied. Annie laughed.

"Jonas has gone off to France to fight," Jiddy said, standing straight again. "He's fighting for King George and to save us from the terrible Frenchies, so I'm going to swan around in my finery and not pretend I want to be a farmer's sweetheart any longer."

Annie's smile dropped. "What? What makes you say that? I thought he were headed for Australia."

Jiddy turned to the table again. She couldn't look at Annie or she'd not keep up the act. She rested her hands

212

on the cloth. *Chin up. Jiddy Vardy, you're a soldier too. You're in the Smugglers' Army.*

"I saw him. He came back to farm to pick up his stuff and say goodbye."

Annie slipped an arm around Jiddy's waist and peered over her shoulder. Jiddy dropped her head down, hair falling forward. Annie lifted back the strands and peered closer.

"Are you all right?" she asked.

That was it. Tears dripped onto the fabric, and Jiddy gulped to hold them in.

Annie pulled her into an embrace and held her, stroking her hair and not saying a word. Jiddy wiped her cheeks with her fingertips.

Annie's little face squinted. "Jonas don't believe in war, does he?"

"He does now. He said it were right thing to do. He'd rather fight for his country than stay fighting preventives."

"We don't fight preventives."

"He felt he were shirking his duty. Anyway, he's gone, and I don't care, so there's no point going on about it."

Annie took Jiddy's hands and played with her fingers. Jiddy watched Annie's hands. She couldn't bear it. She pulled away and wafted out the blue fabric that lay on the table, spreading it on the floor. Picking up the large, heavy pair of scissors, she turned them, making the blades gleam in the light from the window.

"Will this mean you'll go back to London when Mary... When..." Annie faltered.

Jiddy looked up. Annie coughed.

213

"I didn't mean…"

"It's all right," said Jiddy, even though she wanted to sob until she had no more tears left to fall. "I'll stay in Bay after Mary passes."

The door opened, and they both jumped.

Mrs. Grainger stared at the fabric over the floor before looking at Jiddy.

"I need you to fetch Mrs. Farsyde some hot tea and take it to her," she said. "Nobody thinks that I need to pee once in a while."

Jiddy didn't move.

"I will, said Annie, rushing forward and tripping over the scissors. She slid to the door, only narrowly avoiding crashing into the Fylingthorpe woman. "I'll fetch it, and I'll sit with Mrs. Farsyde while you do whatever you need to do."

Mrs. Grainger looked at Jiddy. "Too menial for you, is it?"

Jiddy looked at Annie's eager face.

"Annie's got lots of little sisters and brothers. She's looked after her mam when she were in this state. She'll know the right tea to make. Besides, I've a dress to cut out."

Annie followed the older woman out of the room, leaving Jiddy alone with the trampled fabric. After a few minutes, the door opened again. *What now?*

"Yes?"

"Come downstairs."

She looked up. Samuel stood at the door. She picked up the scissors.

"I can't," she said. "I have to make up this gown for Mrs. Farsyde."

She knew the way she stressed 'Mrs.' stung, but she didn't care. She remained kneeling, scissors raised. She'd snip him if he came any closer.

"I won't tell you again. Get up."

It galled her, but she had to do as he said in the squire's house. There were strict instructions to do as guests asked. Was a captain of dragoons a guest? Was someone who bedded your wife a guest? She didn't want that image in her head. She pointed to the sea of material.

"You can see I'm swamped," she said.

"Do you dare disobey me? I asked you to come downstairs."

That was enough for Jiddy. She dropped the scissors. The clatter as they landed reverberated across the wooden floor, hopefully along the landing, hopefully down the stairs and through the entire house. She didn't care who came running or if Mrs. Farsyde woke. He wasn't her employer. He wasn't a guest. He wasn't worth the mud on her boot. She looked at Samuel. *Come on, I dare you to order me again.*

"You cannot see Mrs. Farsyde, you know," she said. "Only her husband may visit her from now on. She has to rest."

Samuel trembled. She saw the anger in him. He might be able to hurt her, but he couldn't do anything to hurt the Farsydes. She'd see to that. If Violet were in the kitchen, she'd be up the stairs faster than a hare to see what was

215

going on. Samuel must have realised too. He cleared his throat.

"You think you're invincible, Jiddy Vardy, but no-one is. Least of all someone as lowly as you. No parents, no family at all, in fact. And a precarious occupation from what I see. As you refuse to come downstairs and talk in a civilised manner, I will have to say what I would have discussed rationally, in the plain language you understand. Now, are you listening?"

She nodded, taking in his words.

"Right then. Remember, I'm the one making the offer, there are no negotiations—"

"Just get on with it."

He clasped his hands as if praying.

"The only way you can save your farmer from being slaughtered on the battlefield is for you to give me the names of Robin Hood's Bay's smuggling ring. There. Is that plain enough for you?"

CHAPTER TWENTY-FIVE

As soon as Samuel marched down the stairs, Jiddy knocked on Mrs. Farsyde's bedchamber door. Annie had obviously not appeared, and the covers were pushed back on the bed, with one pillow slumped on the floor. The sight of Mrs. Farsyde peering into the empty cot made her cry out.

"You shouldn't be out of bed!" Jiddy hurried to her side. "Hasn't anyone been in?"

Mrs. Farsyde looked past her in eager anticipation, and Jiddy realised she must have heard Samuel's voice and had been listening for his tread. A moment or so passed before she looked Jiddy up and down.

"You look nice." She sounded distracted, staring at Jiddy's dress and touching the skirt. "I'm glad you've taken to dressing properly for me again."

"But of course," said Jiddy, watching Mrs. Farsyde's movements. "I know you like me to."

Mrs. Farsyde turned her gaze to the huge, ornate cot and stroked the side. "My baby's going to be in here soon."

"Let me help you back to bed." Jiddy took Mrs. Farsyde's arm to lead her, but she clung to the side of the crib.

"No, I need to be here." She stroked the lace hanging, pushing it back to pat the small mattress. "I nearly lost the baby, you know, so I had this brought in. I am going to keep it here until the baby is born. I told Squire Farsyde, and I told the doctor. It mustn't be moved."

"Of course."

"I mustn't let it out of my sight."

Crows cawed in the tall trees outside the window, and a lad in the yard shouted, but all those noises seemed separate to the strange atmosphere of the bedroom. Jiddy wondered if she should leave Mrs. Farsyde be, but she seemed so odd it didn't feel right. Maybe the loss of blood had affected her brain. Or the soft kiss with Samuel had made her lose her senses. It was worrying, whatever it was, and there was no chance of a reasoned conversation. What if Mrs. Farsyde said something she shouldn't to the squire, something about Samuel that came out without thinking? Samuel didn't deserve protection, but Mrs. Farsyde did, and if there was trouble, she'd definitely lose the baby, one way or another. *What I'm asking is small*, she told herself, *a legitimate reason to talk to Samuel. She'll thank me for that.*

"I need to speak to you," Jiddy said.

"Now?"

Jiddy nodded. Mrs. Farsyde glanced at the crib again then back at Jiddy. She shook her head. "It'll have to wait until later."

Jiddy leaned closer. Her lips brushed Mrs. Farsyde's hair.

"It's about Captain Ryethorpe," she said.

A pink flush seeped through Mrs. Farsyde's cheek and Jiddy took her hand.

"In the next room?"

Mrs. Farsyde shook her head and clutched the crib again.

"We don't want the nurse to hear if she comes back in."

Reluctantly and with head still turned toward the crib, Mrs. Farsyde let go, and Jiddy led the way into the adjoining sewing room.

"Keep the door open," Mrs. Farsyde said when Jiddy made to close it. "I want to see the cot."

The blue fabric Jiddy had been cutting still lay scrunched on the floor. The scissors poked out their pointed blades. Mrs. Farsyde looked around the room.

"Where is he?"

"Can we come away from the door a little?" Jiddy said. "You can still see the crib from here."

Apprehension flooded Mrs. Farsyde's face.

Jiddy tried to find the right words and she needed to be quick. Annie would be coming upstairs with the hot tea and knocking at the door at any moment. This was grown-up business. She needed Jonas. Jonas was good at persuasion and reason. *Say the facts. Just say the facts.*

"I need your help," she said.

Mrs. Farsyde frowned, clasping her hands together. "Why is the material for my new dress lying on the floor like that? You've not even cut out the skirt. I don't pay you to waste my time or my money—"

"I'm not. I wanted to ask you... You see, Captain Ryethorpe wants me to... Well, he's asked me..."

"Oh, I see! Of course! He wants to offer his best wishes for my health, and as I cannot go downstairs and he cannot enter...is he outside?" She moved towards the door leading to the hall.

"It's about Jonas Chaplow!" Jiddy blurted out.

Mrs. Farsyde turned around. "How dare you bother me with talk of that farmer's boy when Captain Ryethorpe is here to see me!"

Mrs. Farsyde looked at Jiddy with such distaste that Jiddy couldn't bear it. From Samuel, it was bad enough, but not from Mrs. Farsyde as well. This was the mistress of the house again, not the absent-minded apparition from earlier, swooning over the baby's cot. This was the lady of the house in all her authority. The emotion she'd been holding down bubbled to the surface.

"I know Captain Ryethorpe's been in your bedchamber," she said.

The shock on Mrs. Farsyde's face told her immediately that she'd said wrong thing. She rushed forward and took Mrs. Farsyde's hand.

"I mean, he isn't a nice man, and the squire won't like it. He won't like any of it."

Mrs. Farsyde pulled herself free. "I thought I could rely on you."

"You can, you can." Jiddy motioned to a chair, but Mrs. Farsyde ignored it.

"Has someone said something? Who? What are the servants saying?"

"No-one's said anything."

"It's lonely here." Tears welled in Mrs. Farsyde's eyes. "You have been my lifeline. Teaching you to dance..." She caught her breath, holding in the sobs. "Teaching

you to dance, dressing you so you seemed equal..."
She turned away, gasping in her tearfulness.

"Mrs. Farsyde?"

But Mrs Farsyde had changed again.

"How dare you threaten me! We have done nothing
wrong. I talk to him, that is all, and he listens. The squire
doesn't listen. He talks about shooting and managing the
estate and disputes over land and...and tedious, boring
things. We have nothing in common and..." She put
a hand to her throat.

"I didn't mean to make it sound as if I were threatening
you. You can talk to me," said Jiddy, "but you don't need
Captain Ryethorpe. I'll come up more often, especially to
spend time with you—"

"No," Mrs. Farsyde interrupted. "You don't
understand. I want to talk to him. He is on a par with me.
He understands me. He understands death, and that I've
lost so many..." She gulped in tears, staring defensively
at Jiddy.

The babies. Of course. All the babies that hadn't
been born.

"You mustn't tell anyone," Mrs. Farsyde said, squeezing
Jiddy's arms. "No-one must know. No-one." She raised her
voice, willing Jiddy to secrecy, fluctuating between sense
and fantasy. "It's the squire's fault. His babies wouldn't
hold and I had to try, and Samuel's young. He said it was
only fair for me to be a mother."

So it was true, and Mrs. Farsyde had admitted it.
Mrs. Farsyde and the captain had done what she and
Jonas yearned to do but had held off. Cold haddock,

sloppy-kissing Samuel had been in bed or some cupboard or stairwell with the lady of the house. Maybe in the ballroom. Maybe after a gavotte or a cabriole.

Mrs. Farsyde realised what she'd said, and her grip on Jiddy's arm grew tighter.

"We're in love," she said. "He loves me and I love him, and the squire could not give me a baby."

Jiddy remembered how tenderly the captain and Mrs. Farsyde had gazed at each other. Samuel had never acted like that before, certainly not with her. Babies must make you love each other, she decided. It had to be. Mrs. Farsyde gripped her hand so tight it hurt, her eyes locked with hatred.

"I will have Captain Ryethorpe arrest you and throw you on a prison ship. You will never see your farmer again, or Mrs. Waite. I'm going to call for Violet right this instant. You won't even be able to see Mary die. I'm going to have you arrested right now." She waddled to the door and grabbed the handle.

"You misunderstand me." Jiddy rushed to her side. "All I wanted was for you to ask him to stop Jonas joining the army. I thought you were the best person to ask him for me, as lady of the house."

Mrs. Farsyde, her hand still on the door handle, turned slowly. "I won't be put in this position," she said. "I am ill. I am frail."

"I wouldn't ask, but I don't know who else—"

"You think I have influence on the captain? Why would I? What are you saying?"

"You seem close. I saw you together, and you looked—"

222

"You have no right to ask me to do anything for you. You are here to work for me, not ask for favours. I can have my dresses made in York. London if I want. The squire is so happy, he will grant me anything. You are a grubby foundling, and I was merely being kind by offering you a place here when you had none in the village. Well, I've had enough of being kind to ungrateful girls like you." She scurried back into the room and pushed the material aside with one foot. "Do you think anyone would believe you over me?" She waved a hand at Jiddy. "You can't possibly think that that gown disguises who you really are, do you? The squire will have you thrown out if you utter one word against me."

The air rang with injustice, and Jiddy couldn't stop herself retaliating.

"I hope you enjoy Captain Ryethorpe's kisses more than I did. I found them disgusting, but then you have only the squire to compare—"

The slap Mrs. Farsyde gave her made Jiddy's cheek smart.

"Get out," Mrs. Farsyde shouted. "Get out of here before I set the dogs on you!"

CHAPTER TWENTY-SIX

Grabbing her cloak and rushing through the back door before anyone stopped her, Jiddy cut across the front lawns, scrambling over a wall and striding through an adjacent field of long grass that led downwards to the Bay. She snapped up her skirt as it bunched around her legs, wishing she'd never put the blasted thing on, cursing it for ever existing, cursing that she'd kept it. It was useless for making a quick get-away, and that's all she seemed to do these days, getting away from preventives, from Samuel and now from Mrs. Farsyde.

"Stupid, stupid," she muttered. "Why did you say that to her? That were worst thing you could have said. It were mean and nasty and stupid and it made everything even worse."

Slate clouds rolled away creating silver spaces. The wind caught her hair, and she dragged it off her face. Kicking at her skirt and cloak and the grass, she headed diagonally across the fields.

"Just because she were mean, doesn't signify you should be. You aren't her friend. How on earth did you ever think you could be? And why did you have to say you'd kissed Samuel when you needed her help?"

She stopped to listen for the sound of anyone following. What if Mrs. Farsyde really did send Samuel to arrest her and throw her on a ship? She listened for the bellow of dogs but only curlews cried out. Fields stretched empty in every direction, and she set off towards the woods.

"It's your fault, Jonas Chaplow. If you hadn't upped and gone, we wouldn't be in this situation. If we'd flaming well done it and had a baby of our own, maybe you'd have wanted to stay."

Clambering over a wall, she entered the woods.

"I don't want a baby and definitely not your baby now." She swiped fronds of bracken. "And I'd not want you to stay even if we had one. I still hate you, Jonas Chaplow! Don't think you've got away with me still hating you!"

She stopped, hands on her waist and caught her breath. She were so wound up, she'd explode. Trees cast a gloom of rustling shapes, and she looked over her shoulder. She couldn't go back to the hall ever again. What if Samuel did turn up to arrest her but if she gave him the names he asked for, would he let her go? Oh God, what if they took her away before Mary died? They couldn't do that. They wouldn't. But she couldn't give up Abe's and Silas's and Captain Pinkney's names for any reason. She couldn't do that.

"Agh!" she shouted and set off again. In the thick undergrowth, nothing stirred. Reaching a path, she wound through the jittering birches and wagging hazel catkins until she came out at the top of Fisherhead. Nothing would stop her from seeing Mary. No-one nor nothing.

She went home, Ran up the slope to Sunny Place and through the door as she had done many times after fights with Nellie or fallouts with Jonas or merely because it was home. She ignored Helen Drake and her sister, as she had come to do, and bounded up the stairs and into Mary's bedroom where, after throwing off her cloak, she paced up and down in the small space at the end of the bed. When it came to it, she didn't know what to say. She was too ashamed to tell Mary what she'd said to Mrs. Farsyde and too scared to worry her that preventives could burst in any minute and drag her away. But she did have a decision to make.

"What do I do?" she said. "There's no way I can give up Big Isaac's or Abe Storm's or Silas's names, but I don't want Jonas to be killed, Mary. I don't want him to die in a field somewhere in France or in Paris with his head chopped off!"

It was a tester, that's what it was. She'd be a traitor if she gave Samuel the names of Baytown's smuggling ring. And they'd be dead men if she delivered up their names. But if she didn't, Jonas would certainly die. Damn it. She didn't want to care, but she couldn't help it. She couldn't let Jonas die, no matter how much she tried to hate him. Sodding Samuel Ryethorpe and Viscount bloody Hartshorn. They'd made Jonas go. The fact that they had ever existed and all of them together had made it come to this.

"Captain Ryethorpe wants names. What do I do?"

"What do you want to do?"

"That's not point. That's why I'm asking you."

"On your death bed," said Mary, "what will you say is most important?"

Jiddy stopped pacing. "I'm sorry, I'm sorry. I didn't mean to be thoughtless. Of course you're more important. I'm sorry to bother you with this."

Mary attempted a smile. "I'm ready to go, Jiddy love. Others may look at me and say, 'What's she done with her life? She's done nothing big. She's not built ships or explored the world.' But that's not always the most important. Small things, daily things, are what affect those around you. Small things, to some, big to me."

"I don't understand."

"I've had a good husband. We took in a baby who turned into a challenging, headstrong little lass, and she gave our life purpose. And here you are, still pacing and ranting and not seeing how good you are."

Jiddy shuffled along the side of the bed and took Mary's hand. She couldn't speak. She couldn't trust herself not to cry.

"You ask me what you should do," continued Mary. "You tell me your worries, you always have. And you spend time with me, taking care of me. My life has been a good life because of you. When you have all these memories, you too can look back and say that. For me, it don't matter about doing anything grand, but for you, you're different, Jiddy. Some people have to build ships and make life better that way. That's why you're given these big decisions to make."

227

Jiddy waited for her to say something else, but Mary didn't speak again.

"I don't want to be different. I want to do small things. I want to be the same as everyone else. I just want Jonas not to die because of me, and I don't know how to do that."

Mary contemplated the cup by the bed. Jiddy held Mary's head and tipped it to her mouth so that she could drink.

"Thomas and me wanted a baby," she said when Jiddy placed it back down. "But there were nothing we could do for me to have one. Then Captain Pinkney brought you to us."

"I'm glad," Jiddy said. "He did right thing after killing so many people."

"I always knew there were a reason for it."

"But what about Jonas? I can't give up names. What would you do?"

"That's what I'm saying. Whatever is meant to be, you must accept it."

These were riddles. Mary sounded like the minister.

"I can't be like you, Mary. I can't accept it. If I give up names, Jonas will be back but I'll be a traitor, and if I don't give up names, Jonas will most likely die fighting."

"And what would Jonas want?"

"I could kill Captain Ryethorpe. I could get Squire Farsyde's pistol and do it." She sat back. "But how would Jonas know it would be safe to come back? Only the captain knows where in France he'll be stationed.

D'you think the squire would know? He didn't seem to when I asked…"

She had to do something, whatever Mary said. She couldn't let her best friend be killed. She loved him too much not to try.

"Maybe I don't need to give up names," she said. "Big Isaac knows sailors and ship captains."

"Shhh. Shush, not so loud," said Mary, closing her eyes. "Think about what Jonas would do."

"I'm sorry." Jiddy watched Mary's face. The skin sank where round cheeks had once been, her eyes like upturned shells in dips of sand, shadowed dark.

"D'you want anything?" Jiddy asked.

"No." Mary silently mouthed the word.

"Do you think I should talk to the squire again? Or Isaac? Who would be best? Squire? If only Captain Pinkney were here."

Mary remained quiet and tucked in on herself.

"I'll head off back to hall, hope I don't see Mrs. Farsyde, but so what if I do? What d'you think, Mary? D'you think squire will sort it? I can't think who else."

Mary didn't make a sound. She lay very still and small, and Jiddy slumped on the bed, cradling the cloak in her arms.

"You do think Jonas wants to come back?" she said, more to herself than expecting an answer.

Mary touched Jiddy's hand with the lightness of thistledown.

"This is his home," she said. "France isn't home."

Home. What did that mean anymore? Jiddy could be at home in Naples or in London with Signora Maria Vardarelli or on board a ship heading who knew where. She'd throttle Jonas if he didn't stay alive and come back to his farm and Robin Hood's Bay. She'd give him home.

"Please help me. Don't fall asleep. I need you to help me decide what to do because I don't know. I can't see what to do."

Purple-red patches speckled Mary's dry skin that sagged over her bones. This wasn't Mary, not the Mary Jiddy knew, full of opinions and advice and an inability to sit still. The wax-coated skin toned pale yellow and mauve, faint colours like the contraband silk that had caused all the trouble.

"Mary?"

"I'm tired, Jiddy. Let me be."

"I can't do nothing," Jiddy said.

Mary turned her eyes to Jiddy.

"Fetch Captain Pinkney," she said. "He's back from his travels. Tell him I want to see him. Tell him Mary Waite has one last request."

CHAPTER TWENTY-SEVEN

Pulling her shawl close, Jiddy bounded up Jim Bell's Stile, muttering Captain Pinkney's name under her breath. Mary wouldn't explain how she knew the captain was back in the Bay or why he'd returned. It seemed impossible a man like him could do anything for a good woman like Mary. She was as honest as it was possible to be, while the captain stole ships and threw people off them. Jiddy stopped to catch her breath. Captain Pinkney was the main name Samuel wanted.

But, Captain Pinkney had seen something in her when she was a bairn. He'd given her that first bag of salt and made her a smuggler. If Mary had any influence, he'd help her in what she had to do in return for everything. He had to.

Fisherhead loomed across the field. She studied the sloping row of houses, roof tiles uneven and front doors weathered by salt winds. The door had been mended, the cupboard one too, but he wouldn't take kindly to intruders having been in his house. Mary must be mistaken. He couldn't in a thousand years be there. He'd been away for months, and it was common knowledge that he'd sworn he'd never return. He'd be arrested if he ever came back, and that was exactly what Samuel wanted.

She contemplated the rough path. It must have rained at some point. The earth was darker than that morning, and the air dripped neglect. Doors closed. Windows dark. No-one about. Her belly rumbled, and she put her hand over the gathers of her skirt. A lone gull swooped. It promised to be another difficult day.

A noise behind made her look up the hill. Silas Biddick shambled out of Captain Pinkney's cottage. Flabbergasted, she watched him walk down the slope towards her.

"Silas!"

She hurried towards him. He'd know if the captain was angry somebody had broken in.

"Keep your bloody voice down," he said, ambling down the path and spitting mushed tobacco out of the side of his mouth.

"What are you doing in Captain Pinkney's? Is he here? I need to speak to him."

"You'll do no such thing." Silas pulled her with him back the way she had come.

"So he is back?" She couldn't believe how easily some folk let out secrets. She yanked her arm free and strode towards Fisherhead.

Cursing and puffing, Silas followed, but she hurried ahead and, reaching the patched oak door, pressed the latch. Nothing happened, so she snapped it down and shoved. It was locked, even though Silas had just left.

Silas was fast approaching, face set and fist raised, ready to land her one. She battered the door with both hands, kicking with the toes of her boots. Someone had mended it as strong as ever.

"Captain Pinkney!" she shouted. "Open door!"

Silas grabbed her mid-beat. Face shoved pungently into her own, fingers taut around her arm, he dragged her away.

"Shut your gob," he menaced. "Shut your fucking gob."

She wriggled, shoulders, arms, fist, struggling against him. He may be old, but he was strong.

The door opened. She shoved as hard as she could, kicking out for good measure. Silas couldn't keep hold, and he stumbled against the wall. It sounded as if the wind was knocked out of him. Unbalanced herself, she lurched for the open doorway.

Sandy Kellock blocked her path, arms folded across his chest, legs splayed against a barrage. She hit him, full pelt.

"Let me in," she shouted, barging into him again.

He didn't move. He was a stone-solid wall.

"I want to see him. I need to. Let me pass."

Silas had got himself together and with arms similarly folded, leaned against the door frame. If he could have struck her, his face told her he would, but he was holding back for some reason. She shoved Sandy in the chest, but still he didn't move. Behind him, big Isaac McCaw appeared. There was no way she'd get past him.

"What's going on?"

"Mary sent me. She's ill as if you didn't know. You can't deny her last dying wish."

The silence grew as big a wall as their thick bodies. She was worn out, but she was determined not to lose face by walking away.

"Captain Pinkney!" she shouted as loud as her lungs would allow.

Her voice carried right across the ravine. Mary in her bed must have heard her.

"Christ, let her in." A voice she knew well rasped out to meet her.

Unsure, Sandy shifted. Big Isaac looked over his shoulder into the gloom, and Silas straightened himself. Slowly, Sandy moved aside, and Big Isaac stepped back. Jiddy pushed past them. It was a bright morning now the mist had lifted, but the contrast with the dark, unlit interior made her stop.

"You tried to shoot me last time we met," came a familiar voice. "You bring preventives into my home. Give me one good reason I should let you within ten miles of me."

This wasn't going to be easy. Captain Pinkney didn't trust her, and she couldn't blame him. She didn't trust him either, and saying Mary wanted to see him wasn't enough. He'd no heart in that big chest of his, but she'd have to crack it open, nonetheless, and wring out some nugget of compassion.

Big Isaac, Sandy and Silas crowded in, closing the door behind them. Abe Storm lit a lamp and placed it in the middle of the table. Captain Pinkney sat at its head, big black hat in front of him, face a bag of shells. He slid the lamp to one side.

"Thanks to you, whole of Bay will know I'm here. Wouldn't surprise me if preventives come bashing on door to arrest me any second. Is that why you've come, so keen to see me dragged to gibbet?"

With a firm hand, Abe guided her to sit in a chair facing the captain.

The men, ruthless, vicious men if need be, towered over her. No-one knew where she was, and Mary had probably fallen asleep so couldn't tell anyone. They could do what they liked and nobody to stop them. She held tight onto the edge of the table, feet pressed to the floor, ready to jump up and head upstairs if necessary. Head straight for the dodgy back window and out and away.

"Mary wants to see you," she said, keeping her eyes on Captain Pinkney's. If he checked with any of the others, she'd be ready. They'd not snap her neck or stifle breath out of her so easy. He didn't break her gaze.

"You don't know how ill she is," she said. "She wants to see you right away."

Saying the words out loud hit her, but she'd not let them see how it hurt. She'd not let them know the details; that Mary whimpered with pain sometimes but never cried out. That sometimes she withered as if she'd already left this world.

Captain Pinkney lay his long fingers on the table. The lamp tinged them warm, but she knew, underneath, they'd be brutal.

"Why else do you think I'd risk my neck?" he said, deep and growling.

"You're…" She couldn't believe it. "You're scared," she said.

The noise of him shoving back his chair made her jump. It made Abe, Silas, Sandy and Big Isaac jump too. They were all nervous; she noticed that now. Nervous as rabbits sensing the whiff of a fox.

She stood. Slowly. Holding her nerve in her grasp of the table.

"I'm sorry I shouted so loud," she said. "I wouldn't have had to if you'd let me in straight off."

Captain Pinkney's heavy boots clomped around the table, bearing down on her.

"Now listen to me, Jiddy Vardy," he said, brandy rich on his tongue. "I'm here for one purpose, and I'll not be caught by any over-zealous preventive. If I catch even a glimpse of blue jacket or a red snatch in the tail of my eye, you'll be the one wishing you'd never survived beyond cradle."

"Not my fault you nearly made me a complete orphan. Women in my family are not so easy got rid of. I'm not frightened of you. You can't do owt to me. Mary won't let you."

"Thought Mary were on death's door," said Silas. Even in shadow, she sensed the grin on his face.

"You're an insensitive toad, Silas Biddick," the captain said. He waved his arm, and Silas retreated. The captain turned back to Jiddy. "Only reason you're alive is because I handed you as a bairn to Mary Waite. You mind your manners, little girl. I've come to pay that good woman my respects. Then I'll be off."

"No!"

"No?"

"I need your help," she blurted.

His laugh made them all tenser than taut catapults.

"Last time I helped you, you aimed an effing pistol at my head. I go away for a couple of months and you and yon lad break down my door. Give me one good reason why I should ever raise a finger to help you again."

Jiddy clutched the table harder. If he was here for Mary, he obviously cared about her. He couldn't do anything that would hurt Mary. She took a deep breath.

"Captain Ryethorpe of dragoons wants me to give him name of each man in this room."

"I'll break your neck first!"

The men loomed around her, and she knew they were capable of it.

"You didn't give me to Mary for that," she said.

"I can give and I can take away. Life's funny like that, isn't it, lads?"

The men grumbled laughter, but their faces gurned insults.

"You wouldn't deny a dying woman's last wish, would you?" Jiddy kept her eyes on Abe, who came closest.

Abe glanced at the captain, but Pinkney didn't take his eye off Jiddy.

"Right," he said eventually. "We need a bloody good plan if we're going to pull this off."

CHAPTER TWENTY-EIGHT

An hour or two later, Jiddy headed along the clifftop path. Far below, the tide drew out, and the beach exposed its stone and sand banks. She scurried down the bank to Boggle Hole and along the beach, keeping Musgrave Inn, towering on the tops at Ravenscar, in her sight.

The size of the place made it forbidding, today more than any, with the task she had to accomplish. She puffed her away up the steep bank to the clifftop, stood a moment before approaching, then pushed open the front door.

Inside, soldiers sat with their ales slopped on tables, muskets between knees, cleaning and rubbing and smoking tobacco. The air was thick with it. They were clearly celebrating and not worried about drinking so much and it only being mid-afternoon. As she weaved through, Jiddy wondered if they were smoking smuggled tobacco and liquor. And if they knew.

Sidling around their leering faces and groping hands, she reached the bar. Jane Bell eyed her while pouring ale into two mugs and taking the coins for them. Jane took her time, wiping the counter with a cloth and checking the dribble on the jug spout.

Jiddy waited. No point in rushing Jane Bell. She'd learned the hard way not to. She watched Jane carry a cold slice of pie to a table where Deputy Staincliffe sat. Jane said something, and he laughed. This place were like a wolf's den. That's what made Musgrave's so successful. Jiddy was good at making soldiers laugh too. She and Jane had that in common, but right now, she wished Jane would stop flirting. Jiddy had never been good with patience. Soldiers were getting noisier too, and she didn't want to hang about longer than she had to.

The door opened then banged shut. The two new preventives Jiddy had tricked into going up to the hall and demanding a welcome drink had come in. Those nearest whooped. Someone shouted.

"Please may I have my glass of sherry, Squire Farsyde?" More whoops and stamping of boots on the floor.

"Please may I wipe your arse, Squire Farsyde?"

The newly arrived preventives, heads down, walked towards the bar as the noise and taunts grew louder.

Typical. It would have to be those two coming in. Trust word to get round what fools squire had made of them. Soldiers took ages to quit joshing any newcomers, and these two had given them plenty to josh about. Or rather, she had.

Turning her back, she leaned her cheek on her hand, praying they'd yell out from their table what they wanted and Jane Bell would take them their drinks and they'd not come near the bar.

But they didn't shout out. Jane Bell didn't stop them either, and Jiddy listened as their boots approached. If she moved, they'd definitely spot her. Who was she fooling?

A female in a sea of men, of course they'd spotted her. There was nothing for it.

She turned around and prepared to brazen it out. The bigger one met her eyes first. The surprise on his face almost made her turn away. He pushed out his chest and nudged the other one, whose face glowed scarlet. That one didn't react straight away, but when he did, a second after being nudged, she could tell he recognised her all right.

"You wee bitch," he said.

Jiddy's smile faded. The taller one put a hand on the other's arm.

"Let me have a word," he said. He side-stepped his friend, barring her view of the room.

She couldn't see anything but a great, hulking chest, but she could tell that the men at the nearest table had stopped talking.

"You're blocking—" she began, but he grabbed her jaw in a firm grip and she couldn't speak.

The force of his fingers cut through to her teeth. She grasped the edge of the bar. His mouth belched dog breath. She pulled away, but the pain shooting up her jaw prevented her escaping. She stamped her feet, fumbling to find his feet without being able to see where they were.

"Think you're smart now, do you?" he snarled.

Spittle spraying her face, she closed her eyes. He squeezed her jaw tighter, and sharp pain shot through her cheekbones. He was going to break her jaw. She felt the bones cracking. Shattering.

Moving her hand over the bar top, she searched for a beaker or the jug that Jane had been meticulously cleaning, anything she could reach. Opening her eyes, she tried to glimpse sideways, but she couldn't move her head, he held it so tight, forcing her to look at his battered face.

Her jaw ached. She feared he'd snap her neck, but she couldn't open her mouth to yell. Straining her throat, a noise came out. No-one could see or hear her behind his enormous frame and the goading, red-faced bullfrog blocked any other view.

She felt over the wood again and touched something made of pot. Wriggling her fingers to slide it nearer, she gained a hold. He was squeezing, though, and leering in her face, and the other one's breath had come closer. She felt her way up the smooth pot. She had the handle and gripped hard.

"Make her sorry," said the shorter one.

With all her strength, she swung her arm. The one gripping her face didn't see it coming. It broke as it hit his head, and ale splashed out, soaking his hair and beard. At the same time, he released her jaw, and she fell backwards. Catching herself on the bar, she readied to ward him off, but he was shaking his head and spraying droplets of amber liquid, and for the first time in all the ordeal, she could see the room.

Jane Bell charged towards them. Soldiers pushed back chairs, silenced and gawping. The man in front clenched his fists. Jiddy readied to duck.

242

"What's going on?" Jane Bell shouted, shoving the red-faced preventive aside and pushing to stand between Jiddy and her assailant. Voices broke out. Some were laughing. They all merged in the heat and smoke.

"I said, what's going on?" Jane demanded.

The bully grabbed a cloth from the bar and wiped his face. He was fuming. The other one peered around his arm. More were closing in. Jane raised her hand, stepping to avoid pieces of broken pottery.

"Show's over," she said. "Back to your seats, gentlemen."

Some moved back, but others hovered. Jane inspected the dripping preventive.

"What can I get you, Horace?" she said. "Brandy? Anything. It's on the house." She glanced at Jiddy while he made up his mind. "What d'you mean coming in here causing bother?"

Jiddy didn't need asking twice.

"Is Captain Ryethorpe here?"

Eying her suspiciously, Jane pointed a tobacco-stained finger towards a door leading to the back.

"Let me pour you a large one," Jane manoeuvred Horace to the bar. "And you, Callum. What'll you have?"

Jiddy could take a hint. She didn't wait a moment longer.

In the room at the back, Captain Ryethorpe sat at a table with a plate of stew and a glass of wine in front of him. He looked up. Closing the door behind her, the noise of the bar receded. She pressed her hands to her face. She could still feel the impression of fingers and the tension in her jaw bone. She took a step forward.

"Good day, Captain Ryethorpe," she said.

Her voice sounded funny.

He stared at her without any emotion. At least luck was on her side on that score. He'd obviously left Thorpe Hall without seeing Mrs. Farsyde. Otherwise, he'd have been gripping her throat too by now. She took off her shawl and draped it over one arm, placing her other hand on the thick embossed skirt of her dress.

"I'll give you names," she said, "if you promise to bring Jonas Chaplow back from France."

He put down his knife and fork.

"All of the names I asked for?"

She concentrated on the heavy feel of the material, reminding herself that it was a costume and she was playing a part. A frond of hair draped over her forehead and curled into her lips. She'd learnt her lines. She only had to speak them.

"Hercules Storm, Lancelot Biddick, Percivell Kellock, Big Cuthbert McCaw and Captain David Pinkney."

There. She'd given him the names. But would he keep up his end of the bargain?

CHAPTER TWENTY-NINE

O nce she started running, she couldn't stop. She had to keep out of the way now. She'd given names, nonsense names, but Samuel didn't know a Biddick from a Drake. If she'd stayed any longer, she'd not have kept up the pretence. Who could say ridiculous names like Percivell and Hercules without choking over them? She needed to be outside, on the tops and far away from Samuel, from Jane Bell and that roomful of preventive soldiers. Hopefully, Jane Bell had filled those bullies so full of contraband rum they'd be unconscious for days. Hopefully, Samuel had remained as clueless about the names of Bay men as he'd always been. Samuel didn't listen to anyone who'd contradict him, she had to hold on to that. But then what? *Don't think about it.* If her lungs didn't feel like they'd burst, she'd keep on running until she reached Saltburn.

She'd not come away unscathed even if she liked to pretend she had. No-one had clenched her jaw in a grip like that before, and she'd never have believed how much it hurt. It didn't seem credible that someone holding her chin could stop her entire head from moving. The pain had reached every nook of her skull. Running made her feel different pains. Running put distance between her and them.

She leaned on the farm gate. If her face didn't hurt so much, she'd be bawling for all Yorkshire to hear. As it was, she could barely catch her breath.

Helen Drake's words snuck into her head with their lasting refrain. If she hadn't thought she was so clever, none of this would have happened.

She untied the gate and pushed it open. The hayloft seemed the most tempting place to be, and no-one would know she was there. She could make a bed in the straw. She could imagine being cuddled up with Jonas and no worries to trouble them. She could imagine soldiers had never found the silk and she'd not been arrested, nor Jonas, and he'd never spoken to Samuel.

As soon as she'd clicked the gate shut, Rex barked.

"Thank heavens!" Mr. Chaplow hurried across the yard, the dog scuttling around his legs and almost tripping him up. "You'll know what to do about this."

Mr. Chaplow never said this many words all at once, and definitely not to her. She'd never seen him move so fast either. If he hadn't looked so serious and she didn't feel so battered, it would be comical.

"Come wi' me."

She had no choice. Bed would have to wait. She followed his brittle, wide-legged gait across the yard. He hoisted open the barn door, scraping it as it caught the uneven ground. The dog pushed round his legs, and Jiddy followed them both into the shaded interior where she could barely make out his face.

"We've got to get rid of them," he said.

Jiddy studied the barn. She couldn't see anything amiss. "Who?" she said.

He jabbed a mound of sacks on the back of the cart.

"This lot. I can't have them here. Preventives are searching every nook and cranny of moors trying to root out poor saps to man their ships."

"What is it?" Jiddy lifted the flap of heavy cotton.

"Bloody salt," he said, glancing towards the open barn door. "I don't know what to do with it, and every lad around is busy sorting their own business. I thought Jonas had got rid of it before he went, but he must have forgot."

"He didn't take the cart to collect goods that night," Jiddy said. "I think one of Storm lads borrowed it. They should have got rid of stuff, not left it to Jonas."

"Well, hop on over and tell 'em to tek it away, won't you?"

He was already making for the door.

"Mr. Chaplow?" she said. "I'll take cart to Saltergate Inn. Storms have enough to be doing for themselves."

He shuffled around. She couldn't see his expression, only the silhouette of his cap.

***

It couldn't be that hard, she reasoned as she jigged the reins to keep Boy moving over the ruts of the road. This would get her further from Musgrave's and the Bay than she'd have dreamed. Stop her thinking too.

"Come on, Boy," she said. "It's all right. It's only you and me."

Nearing the Buttercross on the top road, Jiddy slowed Boy down. The gibbet that split the sky with its hard lines glowered empty, but Jiddy could still picture Nellie hanging there. It wasn't right, Nellie dying on gibbet. She was only a few years older than Jiddy. All she'd wanted was to escape Robin Hood's Bay, and that had been Jiddy's dream once. Always someone else's rules making them suffer.

She kept Boy moving, trying not to think of Nellie's cracked feet and ashen face with its grey tongue and bruised eyes, but the sound of creaking wood made her jump, and she gathered the reins tighter. Dry wood, a swinging rope. It was enough for anyone to believe ghosts walked along the crossroads on top of the moor. She pictured Nellie floating in the sea, caressed by waves and held in a hammock of seaweed. Jiddy made a clicking sound. "Walk on."

People left things behind when they departed in a hurry, she saw that. Storms had left contraband in the Chaplow barn. By leaving the farm, Jonas had left danger behind. She'd left a suspicious nugget in Jonas's heart when she'd escaped to London. She'd seen it as a necessary escape, only now she realised, Jonas had a different word for escape. Desertion, more like. Shame was, there was no going back once you'd done something. Or started something. Then Helen Drake's words made a persistent pursuit.

"You think you're so clever, Jiddy Vardy."

If she hadn't thought she was clever finding that skein of silk in the cave and wrapping it around herself as she'd seen others do, Jonas would still be here. That was the bottom line. Didn't matter if she was eight or seventeen. Her cleverness had caused bother for them all.

She flicked the reins again. At least she could sort this problem out for Mr. Chaplow. Then she'd think about the rest.

As they mounted the hills, she gazed at the vast moors rolling to the horizon, and she began to fear her rash decision. Clouds billowed low and grey. It must be late afternoon at least, and if she was caught in the dark on this track, she'd be in trouble.

Nor did the journey stop her thinking as she'd hoped. Boy knew the route well and needed no guidance, so her mind was free to roam.

The rise and fall of moorland stretched on and on with purple heather months from flowering. It gave her plenty of time to start blaming Jonas again. It was all Jonas's fault for wanting to give up smuggling. That was the real crux to it all.

If he'd have reminded her about her silk that he was keeping in his hayloft, she'd have taken it and made it up into a dress years ago, then Samuel wouldn't have had an excuse to pack Jonas off.

Mary was right. None of it was fair. Unfair taxes that made them smugglers. Unfair arresting men and shoving women on ships for stealing a bit of bread to feed their bairns. Sod King George and his sodding government.

And sod Jonas. Sod James Lanskill too for turning Betsie into a bitter, frustrated whinger.

I've every right to run away for a while after all that's happened. Mary will understand when I tell her about it. Later.

Sod preventives as well. Sod that officer for breaking his promise to Nellie and probably being the reason she turned on folk in Bay.

Jiddy eased Boy on. It was women who always had to pick up pieces, whether men disappeared in the sea off whaling ships or left to fight in some stupid war. They went anyway. They went as if that was all there was to it, but women had to sort out the mess they left behind.

She twitched the reins again. It was a long way to the Saltergate Inn, and yes, it was one straight road, but she didn't know if she'd meet anyone on it or not. She clicked her tongue. "Keep on, Boy."

It was past dusk when she saw the inn loom ahead. Unsure, she took the cart into the yard, looking around for someone who'd know what to do. They were obviously experts—whole of Yorkshire knew this was the place to come if you had contraband to pass on. She'd barely pulled Boy to a standstill when two lads appeared. One grabbed Boy's halter and began leading the horse and cart towards a large barn, all the while talking to Boy in a hushed voice. The other gestured for her to follow him.

"Get yourself some stew while we unload," he said.

"How do you know what's...?"

"We know this horse."

Jiddy didn't need telling twice. She'd heard Jonas tell many a time of the generous platter of stew and hunks of bread at The Saltergate. She hurried inside, into a large room with a great fire burning in a huge inglenook. A figure, seated at a table, turned to watch. He was on his feet and walking towards her before she'd got her proper bearings.

"What are you doing here alone, Jiddy? Please, come and join us."

She looked around. People stared. Those further away hunched over mugs of ale or slurped up a meaty-smelling dish. A dog curled by its owner's chair, one eye open.

"Jiddy?" He touched her elbow, acting as if he was a long-lost friend.

Lord Ryethorpe. The last person she expected in a place like this, but there was nothing to do other than follow someone you knew in a strange place. Halfway across the room, she noticed the other figure sitting in shadow in the dim corner of the high-backed bench. Lord Ryethorpe wasn't on his own. The man looked up from his plate and smiled, his dark-grey eyes twinkling with mischief.

Everything she'd promised she'd say to him flew from her head.

"Jonas!" she cried out, stumbling over herself to reach him. "Thank God. Are you all right? Thank God you've changed your mind and not gone to France!"

CHAPTER THIRTY

The smile on Jonas's face disappeared and his features aged. His figure withdrew into the cocoon of the alcove, and Jiddy realised her mistake at once. This man wasn't Jonas. He wasn't her Jonas, yet the resemblance was uncanny. She looked at Lord Ryethorpe for an explanation.

"May I introduce Lord Hartshorn?" he said. Remaining in shadow, the man nodded. "Hartshorn? May I introduce Jianna?" He paused, "Jiddy. Jiddy Vardy."

It wasn't Jonas. That's all she could take in. She saw that clearly now. This man was much older, flabbier. Alike, but not Jonas. She stepped back from the table. The excitement that it could have been him waned, leaving a weight in her chest.

"Sit down, Jiddy." Lord Ryethorpe, obviously unsettled too, pulled out a chair and waved a hand towards the bar. "The boy will bring you some food."

"It's a pleasure to meet you," the man said, remaining swathed in his dim corner.

Words dried in Jiddy's mouth. It didn't matter who he was. He wasn't Jonas, and she'd assumed and then hoped. The man resumed eating, and Lord Ryethorpe pretended to eat as well, but he didn't put any in his mouth. It was a relief when a boy brought a plate of steaming stew and placed it on the table.

Jiddy picked up the spoon he'd brought. Food mattered, and she was hungry. She blew to cool it and slid the spoon into her mouth. It tasted good. Perhaps she could take a pie and bread back with her and tempt Mary with a morsel. She took another spoonful, Ryethorpe had too, and with them all eating, she relaxed until she caught sight of the stable lad looking around the room. They must have unloaded, and it was time to go, but she was halfway through the stew, and it was too tasty to leave. Dark gravy, rich. It took over her senses, heating her mouth and stomach, cheeks flushed from the steam.

She glanced sideways at the stable lad then looked away. He got the hint and disappeared outside again. The cart would be safe for a while. She hated to admit it, but she didn't fancy the long drive back in the dark. Who knew what folks she might meet or what sort of ghost? With only a lantern to light the way, she could easily lose the path however sure-footed Boy seemed. Maybe she could sleep in the barn until it got light; they'd surely let her do that. She might even get something to eat in the morning, and by the time of her return, the bedlam that must have occurred in the Bay would be over.

She dunked a chunk of bread and sucked the tasty juice.

"Jiddy?"

Lord Ryethorpe's face radiated kindness. She'd forgotten that. Samuel had seemed kind when they were in London, but his father truly tried to be. She checked her mouth for gravy trails with her finger and thumb and gave him her attention, wondering if she could clean the bowl with the remains of bread without them noticing.

"How are you?" he asked.

She looked at the man in the corner. "Are you my da?"

The man choked, coughing and spluttering while he dabbed his mouth with a cloth.

"What are you doing here so far from Robin Hood's Bay?" Lord Ryethorpe acted as if she'd never asked the question.

"Is Lord Hartshorn my father? Is that why you're here?"

They both seemed to draw themselves in.

"No, I am sorry, Jiddy, your father is dead, but this is—"

"I am not your father or anybody's as far as I am aware," the man interrupted.

"But your father was Lord Hartshorn's brother, Jiddy. This young lady is your niece, Harvey."

The man choked in a cough. "My deceased brother had a bastard?"

Jiddy broke a chunk of bread and swept the rim of her bowl. She chewed the gravy-soaked portion before turning to Hartshorn.

"I know what a bastard is," she said, but before he could respond, she turned back to Samuel's father. "So you didn't lie to me? My father is dead?"

"I'm afraid he is. He did die in the sea off the coast of Robin Hood's Bay."

"Is my mother still in London?"

"Yes."

She turned to the other man again. "What is your business in Yorkshire, sir?"

He seemed at a loss. Lord Ryethorpe touched her arm.

"Let's talk about your mother," he said. "We didn't get a real chance when you visited."

"I know her well enough to know all I need."

"But I never told you about the place your mother was born, did I? You know it's called Naples?"

She didn't care. She didn't want to know about Signora Vardarelli and where she'd come from. She knew all about tactics, and there was no way she was going to be distracted. She looked at the man sitting deep in the shadows and pressed her hands down on the table.

"I've got to be going home."

In her haste, the chair toppled, but she grabbed it and held it still. She no longer wanted to linger and scrape the bowl of all its juices. She mumbled words of thanks, goodbye. Turned.

"Don't go, Jiddy. You've had a shock," Lord Ryethorpe said, rising to his feet. "Have something else to eat, and you need something to drink."

Lord Hartshorn leaned forward. "People tell me my brother and I look alike," he said, "Perhaps I remind you of him."

Out of the shadows, she saw he had thick, wavy, copper-brown curls and dark-grey eyes and that skin, that indefinable skin that ranged from rosy to freckled brown. He looked so much like Jonas not to make it feel odd.

"My father were killed minutes after I were born, so I wouldn't know," she said.

Lord Ryethorpe took her elbow and guided her to sit. "Have some wine. Please. Stay."

Night clung to the windows. It would be cold out there. She sipped the wine he poured while the man began talking. His words coated her mind like honey, and the warmth of the fire and of the wine lulled her away from the Bay and the farm and her own thoughts. She'd stay for a bit, and the wine and flames would help keep her warm for the journey home.

"Listen to what Lord Hartshorn has to say. Go on, Harvey, speak to the girl about her father."

They were all succumbing. Lord Hartshorn shook his head, but eventually, after another glug or two of wine, he began to speak.

"I know Lord Ryethorpe through my brother, Gregory," he said. "He's told me how they travelled together and he was with my brother when they met your mother, Maria?" He let the words, the familiar names linger for her to register, but she noticed the slur in his voice.

"Would you like to know more?" Lord Ryethorpe asked.

She shook her head. No. They'd abandoned her. Both her mam and da. That were enough. She did not want to know more.

"Let me tell you about Naples instead," he continued as the other gentleman leaned back into the shadows again, his slurring all done. "I've found out that the Vardarelli family is large and prosperous. That is good news, isn't it?"

"That has nothing to do with me," Jiddy said. "They're not my family."

Neither of the men said anything. She must remember that she was good at shutting people up.

"I believe Mrs. Waite is not well," Lord Ryethorpe said. "I'm surprised to see you so far from home and unaccompanied."

That was enough to haul her back to reality. They knew how to shut a person up too. She pushed back her chair again.

"Yes, and I have to get straight back."

"Jiddy? I believe your name is Jiddy? May I call you that?"

Her father's so-called brother reached his hand across the table. He rested it by her own. It was a strong hand. A square hand. Square nails. Made for swatting.

"My brother would want to make amends."

She'd not listen to excuses. "Then why didn't you do that? Why didn't any of you come and find me and claim me as kin?"

Calm as calm, he answered, seemingly not affronted by her bluntness. "My brother would have liked to make amends to your mother too. Gregory took her away from her native Naples with a promise of a new life here in England, but as you say, he was killed. I am sure he would wish you to return to Naples in Maria's place. Make up in some small way by them having their daughter return in the form of a granddaughter. What do you say? Exciting prospect, returning to the bosom of your family. A girl like you won't get an offer like this every day."

Jiddy looked at Lord Ryethorpe. "Is my mother dead?"

He coughed. "No, no, of course not."

"Then she can go back to Naples to the bosom of her family."

"Maybe she will, Jiddy. Now wouldn't you going together be a kind gesture to make?"

The other man leaned forward again. "Aren't you curious about the land you came from? Lord Ryethorpe has told me you have been searching for where you truly belong, and I take it you've not found it here."

Heat flared in her cheeks. He shouldn't have told anyone she'd been searching. She shouldn't have told anyone that. How dare they use it against her? Of course she was curious about where other people had skin like hers and looked like her. Who wouldn't be? She'd never stopped imagining the land across the sea where people who resembled her walked and laughed and lived. But she'd met her mother, and that hadn't turned out well, so why on earth would she repeat such a disaster? No, there would be no circumstances she'd go anywhere with her mother.

Lord Ryethorpe took a long drink before placing his glass down.

"I fell in love with Naples," he said, "as did your father. The orange Naples sun shining on soft Mediterranean stone is unforgettable. People bathe using almond and orange oils, and the scent lingering on your skin is like resting in a lemon grove."

Orange sun and warm stone and scented oil. Naples sounded like a different world entirely. She would love to feel hot sun on her face and smell such oils. Robin Hood's Bay stood exposed to a freezing northeast wind, persistent rain and sea frets chilling your bones. She'd lived there all her life when instead she could have bathed in warm sunshine all year round. She didn't know what almond and orange and lemons were, but they sounded delicious.

"You have cousins there," Lord Ryethorpe said. "Young people like you to talk with and enjoy."

"Like me?" She was different to everyone here in Yorkshire, but there, there he suggested, she would fit in. Young people like her.

"Naples is made up of people like you, Jiddy. People who love eating outdoors in the warm sunshine and where there is no shortage of food. Think of how you devoured that bowl of soup. You'd never be allowed to go hungry in Naples with your family to feed you."

She looked down at the dish caked with an unappetising brown ring.

"You ate it as if it was the best food you had tasted in a long time. You could do that every day."

They were embarrassing her. What if that was true? So what? She was hungry. They'd eaten too. Why pick on her eating habits?

"They eat a great deal of fruit there. It grows on trees, and it's natural to harvest it. Not only would it taste delicious but it would keep you healthy as well. Fruit the colour of bright red and vibrant green. Yellow sunflowers that turn their large heads to follow the sun under deep-blue skies. You would fit in there, Jiddy, with your colouring and vibrancy. You're too big a flower for this dismal place. Too exotic. Naples is the place where you belong. Trust me, I know."

"I belong here," she said.

"But think about being with people who understand your personality. A place where you will look around at people who have the same skin as yours."

"I don't care."

"As your father's brother, I have to agree with Lord Ryethorpe," the other man said. "You may think you belong here, as you put it, but in a pitiful place like Yorkshire and by uneducated, ignorant people, you can never be deeply understood. Anyone who says that they'd rather live in this godforsaken hole rather than in a beautiful place like Naples must be demented." He looked at Lord Ryethorpe before picking up his wine glass.

Clutching her hands tight together. Jiddy watched him. She counted in her head. *One, two. One, two.* She took a long breath.

"They're not demented, as *you* put it," she said. "They feed me and show me things you don't know anything about." She thought of Mary rubbing whale fat on her arms and legs and feet to stop them cracking with cold. She thought about Jonas hiding the roll of silk in his barn so Mary wouldn't get in trouble if it were found in her cottage. And Rebecca who'd mothered her as Mary had.

"They're kind and generous. You don't know nothing about people in Robin Hood's Bay and what they know. They know tons. They're not demented or ignorant. No-one I know is ignorant because they all know how to do something. Bet you don't know how to catch crabs or skin fish or mend nets or how to get salt from the sea."

She shoved back her chair, standing defiant, daring them both to insult her people again. Lord Ryethorpe looked surprised. The other man looked shocked. Well, good. She was full of surprises.

"You are right," said Lord Ryethorpe. "We know none of those things."

Jiddy flashed her eyes at the other man, waiting for his apology. He bowed his head.

"Mary may not have set up an emporium selling fancy cloth and expensive jewels, but she gave me a home and she cared for me. It might not sound much to a gentleman like you, but it's made me who I am, so it's big, it's huge. Don't call people I know ignorant," she said quietly, letting her hands drop by her sides. "And don't say Robin Hood's Bay is godforsaken. We all go to chapel. John Wesley's been to speak at Chapel Street, and you can't get more godly than him.

"And I do belong. I love Bay. I love the sea. It's the most special place in the world, and I thank God every day I live there. I've seen London. Now that's a godforsaken place.

And water there is rank, not sharp and fresh like here. Those people you say I look like in Naples don't know me. They don't know me as Mary knows me. I have nothing in common with family I've never met, nothing but how we look, so you say.

"Well, how you look's nothing. It's what you have in here." She hit her breast bone. "I may not look like anyone here, but I have everything in common with them. Everything. They are not ignorant, and I'm not ignorant. It's you who know nothing."

She was halfway across the room when Lord Ryethorpe's voice stopped her.

"Jiddy, this is for your benefit and that of your true family. Naples may well be the best place for you when you hear what I have to say. When you hear this, you may well want to be far from Robin Hood's Bay. Please, please listen to me."

She couldn't deny him when he pleaded like that, an old man who tried to be kind. She could show that she would listen and show that folk here weren't ignorant. She strolled back to the table.

"Please, let's sit again."

She pulled out her chair and sat at a small distance. Ryethorpe sat and waited for a few moments before he looked up.

"You see, Jiddy," he said, "you need to know that you do have family of sorts in Robin Hood's Bay. You are related to the farmer at Meadow Bank Farm, near Fylingthorpe. Jonas Chaplow? I was in Whitby, visiting my son, and

I heard that he has left the area. I'm sorry for your loss, but it is a good thing, Jiddy. I know about him, and you, and for your sake and to dispel your memories, this is why we mention Naples. It would be best for you if you left Robin Hood's Bay as well."

"He's not family," she said. "We aren't married. It's not a loss, I'm not heartbroken and in need of distracting. He were free to go."

Ryethorpe took his time. "I mean, good. That is good because, well, as I said…you are…" He said it slowly this time. "You and he are related."

She watched the look of horror on Lord Hartshorn's face and the frown returned by Lord Ryethorpe, and deep in her belly she felt a stab.

"It is good you are not married, otherwise…you have heard of incest?"

"No," she said. "I don't know that word."

"It means if you and this Chaplow had married, it would be a sin. As brother and sister…"

In that moment, she knew Jonas had been told about incest and about them. He knew. He knew everything that they said. That's why he'd blanched and run away when she told him Gregory Hartshorn was her father. That's why Jonas looked like the man in the corner. They were related. Jonas knew they were linked by blood, and he'd never come back. It didn't matter that pact with Samuel. It didn't matter if she gave every name of every living man in Robin Hood's Bay. Jonas would never return. She'd risked Abe Storm and Isaac's and Silas's names for nothing.

There was no reason to stay and every reason to leave the Bay and find a new life, far, far away.

They were right. She should get away, and Naples could be her haven. The place she was destined to be.

CHAPTER THIRTY-ONE

The seeds Jiddy had sown sprouted anger amongst the preventives more quickly than she'd expected.

"Hercules Storm? Lancelot Biddick? Percivell Kellock and Big Cuthbert McCaw?" said Deputy Staincliffe. "Are you serious? The only name I recognise there is David Pinkney."

"The entire place is teeming with Storms," Samuel argued. "And I've heard of Biddicks and Kellocks and that other one. They're all interbred. Go and dig them out."

"With due respect, sir, you don't go down to the village. You don't mingle the way the other men are forced to do. I've asked. No-one has heard of any local man named Hercules, Lancelot or Percivell, never mind Cuthbert. These are not the names of Baytowners."

Samuel glared at his deputy. "These names belong to somebody. Are you telling me it is too much trouble to sort one man from another when I give you a direct order?"

Staincliffe had never heard the captain raise his voice before. Drinking at the inn, they referred to him as 'Lady Ryethorpe'. Robin Hood's Bay got to them all at some point, driving them to their wit's end with their inability to fathom the Bay's hiding places and the locals' belligerent violence, but it surprised Staincliffe how quickly the captain had been affected.

"But sir, these names…"

A shadow of doubt passed over Captain Ryethorpe's face. "These are the names Jiddy Vardy gave me under the proviso I gave her. She will not have lied."

"With all respect, sir, she's a local. They're known to lie."

"Not under the terms we agreed."

"I can't see any terms she'd—"

"She wants to trade one person for these, and I agreed."

Staincliffe looked at his feet then back at the captain. "Must be an important person."

"Not to us. You needn't concern yourself with that. He's a farmer, he's nothing." Ryethorpe hesitated.

"Even so, sir, you do know what this Jiddy Vardy is like, don't you?"

A sheen of pink blotched Captain Ryethorpe's cheeks. "She would not lie to me," he insisted. "Why are you quibbling? Get the men together and make the arrests."

"But those men don't exist."

"I gave you an order, Staincliffe. Gather your men and make these arrests. The more we delay, the faster these blighters will disappear into the peat bogs whence they crawled."

***

At Sunny Place, the stubs of three candles filled the room with shadows and little light. Captain David Pinkney breathed in the scent of sickness. He'd never understood why Thomas and Mary Waite had agreed to take in the day-old baby all those years ago. The rum, salt, tea and contraband diamonds he'd given to compensate for an extra mouth to feed wouldn't have lasted a year, never mind seventeen. No wonder this honest couple had had nothing to do with him or his smuggling gang before or since. And now Mary had sent for him, heard somehow that he had returned. Of course, he was unable to refuse the wishes of a dying woman, but he'd have decided to come anyway, to explain, comfort, do whatever he could to tell her he was grateful. Well, something like that. Nothing too embarrassing. He must be growing soft in his increasing years. Thing was, she'd sent for him. He was standing in her bedroom of all places, and now he was there, she couldn't see him clearly, let alone say anything.

He closed the door. He wouldn't stay long. It was dangerous enough that he'd come at all, plus, he didn't want any of the women downstairs seeing him so awkward. The once bright-eyed Mary Waite stared without seeing. He checked himself. He didn't usually spook easily. He had expected to find her if not asleep, with closed lids, resting away the hours, but she gazed at him with sunken eyes so different from those that had stared at him when he'd turned up on their doorstep with a basket and asked them to take the baby. He recovered his shock when her once-warm voice scratched bare. He perched on the edge of the bed. No-one must see this. A big man like him, sitting on an old woman's quilt. He didn't want to touch the purple-stained hand, but he forced himself and was surprised by the fragility of the bones and parchment-thin skin. It was cold. She wouldn't be alive for long, with her eyes, lost of pigment, staring into the beyond.

"You asked to see me."

She barely moved her head, but he caught the shadow of her breath.

It had been a large ship. A strong, solid ship with its sails full-rounded by the wind and gulls noisy in its wake as they picked off supper waste in the waves. The setting sun had been bright on the North Sea, and one particular passenger had given birth while he and his gang murdered the crew. He'd been a different man then.

"You promised," she breathed out.

He leaned closer.

"What did I promise?"

He couldn't remember. Heaven help him for what he might have said in desperation to get rid of a sallow-skinned bairn nobody else would touch. Was she making it up? A woman on her death bed could make up anything. She could ask for the world.

She opened her mouth. No sound came out, only a droplet of breath.

He'd have said anything to appease her back then. What had he gone and promised?

He could have shut the ship's cupboard door in the hot disarray of the cabin and convinced himself he'd never seen the tiny bundle. Nobody else had been there at that point. Nobody else would have known. He could have thrown it overboard after its mother and the other poncy gentlemen. He'd initially thought they'd thrown the dead corpse of the rejected bairn with the woman's soiled clothing. If only there hadn't been that basket to hand. Blasted basket. Blasted baby. If Mary Waite had said no like all the rest, what would he have done? *Don't think about it.* And every time he'd come back to the Bay from a voyage, he'd been astonished how they'd taken to her. She was more like family than the skivvy he'd thought she'd be, coming to belong in a way he'd never expected.

He took Mary's silence for accusation, but what more than diamonds could he have offered to help the couple feed the child?

Flames in the grate caught in a gust of wind and a shiver of sound down the chimney. He wished he hadn't closed the door. If only Grace or Helen would think to check in on them, he could go. He'd done his duty. Said goodbye. Now he could escape before preventives closed in.

The chimney gusted a down-draught again. He picked up his hat. She couldn't be aware of him any longer. He could up and off. He gathered his cloak. She didn't move. He looked down at her hands, unsure about going with the reason for her calling him still not sorted.

***

Mary wanted to shout but she couldn't get out a sound. She could barely move her mouth. His breath and fidgetings came to her through fog. She tried to move her hand, but she couldn't feel her arm. If only she had written a note in the hope that Jiddy would know what she felt. But she didn't know how to make marks on paper, and she didn't know who to ask. She'd left it too late, anyroad. Too late for a letter. Too late for words. Anyway, what would she say?

I love you, Jiddy lass.

How could she have said that? They were words people like her didn't say. Yet each day, the words whispered in her head on wakening and returning to sleep. And each day, they were more insistent, but she still hadn't said them aloud. Jiddy had accepted Robin Hood's Bay as her home. She'd chosen her to be a mam in all but name. And she still hadn't told Jiddy that she loved her. She wondered if proper mothers said those words, passed down through generations like a family heirloom. Those words that she couldn't say. She yearned to hold again that little baby the smuggling man had brought to their door.

"Mary?"

Whose voice was that? It sounded familiar. Someone repeated it. Her name. In her mind, she put the baby back in the crib. Something rose up her throat. It must be a tear, but she could not cry. Her throat blocked full. She could hardly breathe. *Jiddy*. She wanted Jiddy. She wanted to cuddle her little girl. She couldn't breathe. It was rising, that sludge of coffee grounds. That smothering, festering mud that filled her lungs.

The figure leaned closer until his head filled her view. He loomed so big. She recognised the shape. A big hat. A triangular hat.

"Home," she breathed in his ear, words drowning with the suffocating silt. "Give her a home."

She grasped at the air. She hadn't expected this fear. She believed in God. She believed in heaven and Thomas waiting to greet her, but now the time approached, she was scared. She wasn't ready. She couldn't breathe. She wasn't ready to leave Sunny Place and Jiddy, and that made her afraid.

CHAPTER THIRTY-TWO

Jiddy stood in the inn yard. A lamp illuminated the stable. Apart from that, the night enveloped all light. A voice made her jump.

"We've stabled your horse," it said. "You can kip in hayloft."

The inn's hayloft was bigger than Meadow Bank farm's, and it had a lot more straw. She was exhausted and too hazy to attempt the track to the Bay; it was the perfect choice. Trouble was, she couldn't sleep with her head churning about what the two men had said.

How could the man who supposedly loved her mother so much have had a child with someone else, and someone here in Bay at that? How come Mr. Chaplow didn't know? How come nobody knew? Yet Jonas obviously believed it. She shuddered. They couldn't be brother and sister. How could they feel the way they felt for each other if they were brother and sister? They'd sense something was wrong, wouldn't they? Surely, instinct would have told them that? This was Jonas they were talking about. Her Jonas. She'd kissed him. She loved kissing him, and she'd wanted to do much, much more than that. It hadn't felt wrong. Surely, it would have felt wrong if they were really related? They'd told Jonas as well. That's what hurt most. They'd told him, and he'd walked away without telling her.

"It will be incest if you marry." That hateful man had said. *"I'm your uncle. I have to protect you. Protect both my niece and my nephew."*

"That is why I suggested Naples," Lord Ryethorpe said. *"A new start. A new life."*

When she finally fell asleep, straw softening under her weight, she slept in snatches, waking to a blustery dawn. She didn't have the luxury of thinking about it anymore. She had to get back to Mary, and she'd wasted so much time. She should have eaten her stew and gone. Straight away, not drunk wine, not stayed by the fire, not left it too late to make the journey back.

As soon as the sky turned from black to grey, she harnessed Boy to the cart and clambered up. Boy's hooves clattered over the cobbles then became muffled on the earth track leading back along the salt road towards the coast. Jiddy urged Boy on, putting as many miles as she could between her and that hateful word. Every time they'd said it, it sounded spiteful. She'd never heard it before, but now it was ingrained in her head. Incest. Pinched and nasty.

She cracked the reins. "Come on, Boy."

Jonas knew. That's why he'd asked if she had heard the name Gregory Hartshorn. He must have realised when she said that was her father's name. She hated it. Hated all of them. Gentry most of all. Roaming the countryside, ruining people's lives. Jonas would never come back. Half of her didn't care if they did commit incest. What if they'd never known, either of them. Would it be incest then? Could you commit a crime if you didn't know what it was? She tried to remember the expression on Jonas's face when he'd said he was leaving.

Don't die. That's all she hoped for him. *Don't die.* They'd told Jonas, and they knew he'd have to go away when he realised what they meant. It was Samuel. He must have done it. He couldn't stomach that she preferred a farmer to him. Gentry thought they were above farmers and fisher folk. They thought women should drop at their feet because gentry wore expensive clothes and could read and write and talked as if they'd a gob full of pebbles. And she couldn't tell anyone. They knew that too. All this clever talk about how beautiful Naples was and how she belonged there and they were her people. They didn't even speak the same language! She'd bet all the dresses in Mrs. Farsyde's trunks that they'd not know you could carry brandy and salt and who knew what under your skirt. Her folk weren't ignorant. They were clever. She was working herself up again. She could feel it. Her chest was thumping and her thoughts were all over place.

Boy was reliable, keeping a steady pace and not giving any trouble even after standing all harnessed up. Lads at the inn must be wondering who'd been daft enough to trust her with delivery. Damn it. She was good at what she did, and she'd not have people thinking otherwise.

She kept her eyes on the road ahead and her mind on getting back to the farm, trying not to spook herself by listening for horses in pursuit or accents not from hereabouts. *Don't look for distrust or malevolence in the faces*

273

of passers-by. Avert your eyes from the gibbet where Nellie hung.
Look for the first glimpse of the sea and that first smell of salt air.

Mr. Chaplow didn't appear when she drove into the farmyard, and she wondered if, worried, he'd gone searching for her. She unharnessed Boy and held a bucket of water up for him to drink. Giving him a rub down, she left him chomping through a trough of bran.

Strangers stood in the kitchen.

"My nephew and his wife, John and Kate," Mr. Chaplow said. "They've come over from Pickering."

"How do," Jiddy said, shaking their hands.

They appeared different to Jonas; Jiddy was noticing these things now. She even noticed that Mr. Chaplow seemed awkward in his own home. Rex lay in a corner, snout in paws as if he too didn't know quite what to do.

"I've brought cart back, and Boy's stabled down," she said.

Luckily, Mr. Chaplow barely acknowledged the fact. She didn't know how much Jonas's cousins from Pickering knew about local goings on.

"My nephew's stopping for time being," Mr. Chaplow said.

"We're here to help Uncle," the man said, "since Jonas has gone off."

Jiddy looked at him more closely. He was thin like Mr. Chaplow, but he didn't look as if he could plough a puddle.

"Jonas hasn't gone off," she said. "He's coming back."

Mr. Chaplow patted Rex to his side, and the dog obediently shifted to its feet and padded across the floor.

"We don't know that," the woman said, filling the silence. "And a farm doesn't run itself."

"I need help," Mr. Chaplow said, ignoring Rex now that he sat at his side, "and John has kindly offered to take over running of place."

"But Mr. Chaplow," said Jiddy, "I can help."

"You're not family," John said.

"Thanks, lass, but you've got Mary to take care of," Mr. Chaplow said more kindly.

"There's more to farming than helping out," Kate said. "What's needed is someone who knows what they're doing and is young enough to do it. Like my John."

Jiddy didn't see how someone from Pickering was any more qualified, but she had no answer that wouldn't come out rude, and she wasn't ready to be rude in front of Jonas's da. She told herself it wasn't her business. Mary must be her main concern.

"You're going to take it easy now, Uncle," John said. "If I'd known situation earlier, we would have been here before now, but not to worry. We're on track now."

She couldn't believe it. They were taking over. Mr. Chaplow trembled like he'd been mowed down by a stampede of bulls.

"But Jonas will be back, Mr. Chaplow—"

"Jonas is not coming back," said John. "We've got to face it."

275

All the anger she'd suppressed over the moors and dusky hours passing fresh crops and brightening woodland bubbled to the surface.

"You don't know that," she said. "You haven't spoken to him. He is coming back. Meadow Bank Farm is his, and he'll be working here with his da, not you."

"Forgive me, Mrs. Know-it-all," said Kate, "but you do not know that Jonas is coming back or if he can, for that matter."

They were right. Of course they were. They knew it. She knew it. He would never come back and reclaim the farm, but she was the only one who knew exactly why he couldn't and wouldn't return, and for the first time in her life, she sagged, defeated.

CHAPTER THIRTY-THREE

Meadow Bank Farm would never be the same again. Everything was changing, and Jiddy couldn't do anything about it. What she could do, though, was show it didn't bother her. She closed the farm gate carefully as if she agreed this was the right course of action. She walked along the path holding her skirt in clenched fists so she didn't grab a stone and chuck it or a stick and crack it to show she thought otherwise. She held it all in and walked until she knew she was out of sight of the farm, and then she stopped and she screamed as loud as she could.

When, finally, she ran out of breath and the scream stopped, she gazed, exhausted, at the view. Hills sloped down to the coast where the sea shone flat. Lapwings darted over the scrubland. Gulls, mere specks, wheeled nearer the water. She had thought she'd not be able to stop herself running once she was away from their sight, but instead, she wanted to make the walk over the grass last as long as possible. She wanted to creep like spring into Robin Hood's Bay, not spin like a winter storm. She held on to her skirt the entire way until her knuckles hurt.

Rather than take the steep incline of Main Street, she walked around the back ginnels until she dropped down into Sunny Place, mounted the front steps and pushed open the door.

"Where the heck have you been?" Helen Drake demanded.

"Now then, lass," said Gracie. "Go on up."

Something in their tone made her afraid. She clattered up the narrow stairs, wishing she had run instead of taking her time to adopt a calm and peaceful manner, which were the last things she felt at that moment.

"Not so much noise," shouted Helen Drake.

Jiddy didn't take any notice, the words a background to her clomping feet. All that quiet and control and now she was shaking. She needed noise, as much noise as possible. She opened the door, heart pounding. She should have run. Run every step of way.

"Mary, I'm sorry. I'm so, so sorry."

The fire spat, making her jump. This room was all that mattered. Mary lay in the bed completely still, eyes staring at the ceiling. She was smaller than yesterday. Jiddy's breath filled the room. It sounded so loud, but Mary didn't seem to notice. She was dead. Dear Lord, Mary was dead and she was too late. She grabbed the door latch. A noise made her turn around. Mary's chin were raised, her mouth wide. Jiddy rushed to the bed, sitting on the stool directly next to Mary's pillow. Taking hold of her hand, she cupped it in her own.

"It's all right, I'm here now," she said. "It's me, Jiddy."

She forced herself to remain still. This was Mary, Mary who had brought her up, and this was what Jiddy could give in return. Give her hand and give this time. Make the most of it. Be with her. It's all she'd got. She remembered

Lord Ryethorpe saying something about that when he talked to her in London.

"Birth and death are what holds us together." Something like that.

"And love," she'd added.

But Mary was dying and Jonas had gone and she'd nobody else to love or love her.

"Thank you, Mary, thank you, thank you, you know that, don't you?"

Mary couldn't have heard. She didn't say anything or even look at her. *Don't cry, don't cry. Don't go, please don't leave.* Jiddy had never been entirely alone before. Even if Jonas wasn't with her, she'd always known where he was but not anymore. Mary was always somewhere about. Waiting for her to come back, stropping about something or tired from a night's run. In the Bay, you were never fully alone. You could always hear someone, know someone was on the other side of a wall, someone who'd watched you grow and been some part of your life. But nobody but Jonas and Mary cared properly for her. And she didn't properly love anyone but them.

She looked at the tiny shape outlined under the cover. It was a child's shape with a wizened face and arms. Her sunken cheeks, eyes, chin, neck and shoulders didn't seem like Mary's. Two twig-like arms lay still, hands unmoving. Gently, Jiddy stroked the cold hand. An autumn leaf of a hand. A winter hand.

"It's all right," Jiddy leaned closer. "I'm here."

Downstairs seemed very far away. The farm, another country. Saltergate Inn, someone else's life.

"It's me," she said. "Jiddy. Can you hear me?"

She could recount stories. Tell the tale about Mary sitting with a barrel under her skirts while preventives prodded and banged around the room looking for it. She could talk about the afternoons sewing around the table with Annie, Betsie and Nellie. How she had moaned and whined about Nellie Ashner. The smell of rabbit stew and roasted fish and the day a gull fell down the chimney and blacked everything it touched as it tried to find a way out of the room, and how Mary had screamed the roof down until Jiddy opened the door and ushered it to freedom. Vibrant Mary, the woman full of life.

She leaned even closer. "D'you want anything?"

She didn't know what to do when no answer came. Gobbit had been a slick of clothing when he died. Rebecca had been a whale of a corpse. Bodies lost at sea, prayers and stern faces on shore.

"You needn't worry," she said. "I'll be all right. Everyone will be. You don't need to worry about me or anyone."

Mary was hardly breathing.

What else can matter if you can't breathe? You need air in your lungs. Mary should be on the beach or on tops; she'd breathe proper there, not in this stifling hot room where anyone would struggle to breathe. This was drowning. Drowning in a room without air.

Mary's eyes searched for something, staring at Jiddy but not seeing her.

"I'm here," Jiddy said.

Mary's open mouth didn't say a word, but Jiddy felt it was trying hard to speak.

"Can you see me?" Jiddy squeezed Mary's hand.

Mary's eyes pulled and pulled for her to understand. Mary could see something and wanted to tell her something, but she hadn't a voice anymore, and Jiddy could only guess.

"It's all right," she said. "Gracie's moved in with her family, and Annie's earning up at hall, and I'll be all right. You don't need to worry. We will be fine."

Mary's eyes unsettled her, her face so gaunt with its dark, yellow skin, sucked-in cheeks and mouth. That moment, Jiddy realised how frightened Mary must be. She fought for breath. She was drowning. Whatever that tea-leaf mixture had been that Mary had spewed, it was clogging up Mary's throat and stopping her from breathing.

Jiddy sat rooted to the stool. She couldn't move. She couldn't speak. Reality disappeared with the dwindling candles. Tomorrow would be the same and the next and the next and she'd sit, holding this hand, its cold and its shrinking size always in her own, watching Mary's face fold up. The fire burned too hot. Gracie or Helen had stacked it to last, and it made her cheeks burn. Her bum, far too close, scorched. She rested her head on the soft pillow next to Mary and closed her eyes.

She must have dozed off. She woke with a jump, not sure what had made her wake. She'd let go of Mary's hand while she slept, and she stroked it back into her palm. Mary reached for breath. Anxiety filled her eyes. She reached and reached for air. Jiddy watched her face, willing her to breathe, but Mary stared, mouth open, eyes afraid. Jiddy leaned back, she couldn't watch, this wasn't something she should see. It couldn't be.

For a moment, Mary looked fearful, and then the sound of her breath filled the room in one massive exhale. And then it grew quiet. Jiddy couldn't even hear her own breath. She shifted her feet. Leaned in again. The eyes didn't see her. Cheeks hollowed, the open mouth held in a small oval. Jiddy didn't know what to do, so she remained still. So still, she couldn't even cry.

CHAPTER THIRTY-FOUR

At some point, she'd gone downstairs and told Gracie and Helen Drake that Mary had died. Neighbours around the Bay heard as if by magic and crowded into the house. She couldn't bear it. What right had they? How could they find things to say, and what did they want? Being outside seemed the only alternative. She walked slowly up the hill. Dull. Numb inside, but she kept walking. Kept moving. She walked on through Fylingthorpe and took the familiar track to the farm. She found Mr. Chaplow on the bottom field where he puzzled over a section of dry-stone wall, Rex lying amid the heap of stones strewn across the grass. Jonas would never have fixed a wall like that. Jonas would pick up a stone, gauge its weight, give it a look over and wedge it in place. Mr. Chaplow was doing none of those things.

Rex raised his head as she approached, then lowered it again and rested it between his paws. His master studied a stone as if he'd never seen one his life.

"How do, Mr. Chaplow," she said.

He barely acknowledged her.

"You've got a lot of stones," she said.

He looked at her as if she was an idiot. It did seem a daft thing to say when there were so many stones on the ground and in the wall. Everywhere it seemed.

"Mary's dead," she said.

He looked at the rock fortification. "Sorry to hear that."

"How's your nephew settling in?"

"He's about."

"We've got a full house today."

She bent to rub Rex's head.

"When's funeral?"

"Day or so."

Mr. Chaplow studied the stone before dropping it to the ground.

"Bet it's grand having your nephew's wife...Mrs. Chaplow here. Bet she's making the farmhouse homely."

"Farmhouse is right."

"D'you wish you could tell them to beggar off?!" Laughing, she stood up. It sounded pathetic.

Mary's dead! She wanted to shout it over and over. She wanted to throw those stones and break the wall down. Instead, she pressed her hands together.

"I'm going to be chucked out," she said. "House were only rented." Rex's paws covered his head. "Can I help?

"Have you fixed a wall before?"

She shook her head, glad of the shawl shading her face. She'd never live at Meadow Bank Farm. Not now. She had to find out truth, though. Know for sure and not waste time when she'd a new home to find and an empty heart to fill.

"D'you think Jonas'll come back?" she asked.

"How do I know when I don't know where he's gone?"

"He's gone to France."

Mr. Chaplow shrugged. His jacket draped too big. He'd lost weight. She'd have words with that cousin and his wife if they weren't feeding him proper.

"Didn't Jonas tell you he were going to fight?"

Mr. Chaplow nestled a stone onto the structure. It wobbled. He needed Jonas to help him for more than mending walls, she could see that. Whatever had happened between her and him, Mr. Chaplow needed Jonas back at the farm.

"Mr. Chaplow?"

"What d'you want, lass?"

Her eyes welled up. *Don't be kind. Not you.* She looked over the fields to the sea. It was one of them fretful days.

"I were wondering, as I've met my real mam now and I found out who my real da were, even though he's dead, at least, I mean, I can choose where I want to live. You see, knowing who my real mam and da are, I know who I look like and who I don't..."

Mr. Chaplow gazed at her as if she had twigs shooting out of her head. She could tell he hadn't a clue what she really wanted to ask. This was hard, but she had to know for sure, and he'd know, wouldn't he? You'd surely know if a child was yours or not.

"Everyone says I'm spit of my mother," she said. "Black hair, black eyes, my skin. My bony fingers." She wriggled them for him to see.

"Jonas never met his mother," he said.

"Well, I don't suppose he counts that he has, when she died giving birth to him."

Mr. Chaplow wiped his nose with his crumpled square of frayed cotton.

"Did you tell him much about her?" she asked.

Again, he looked at her as if she was half a basket full.

"It makes sense if you and he don't talk about her. Must be difficult."

He stuffed the handkerchief back in his jacket pocket.

"We talk about land and livestock," he said. Contemplating the stones, he picked one up and dropped it onto the wall.

She didn't know how he stood it. This was such boring work. At least Jonas got through it quick. Seemed like Mr. Chaplow would be at it all week.

"Does Jonas look like his mam?" she asked. "Did she have russet hair and dark-grey eyes and…?"

The distant crinkle of sea filled the silence.

"Why d'you ask that?"

"Have you heard of Gregory Hartshorn?" she pushed on in a hurry.

It was like waiting for a run to start but without any of the excitement. She knew it was true, and even though she'd asked, she dreaded hearing his reply aloud.

"Jonas's mam were a young lass from a farm over Pickering way," he said. "I knew her da from markets. She were in family way, but beggar that did it disappeared off."

That was the most personal words Jiddy had ever heard him speak. She waited.

"I needed a son to pass farm on to. She needed a home."

"Why didn't you marry someone else?"

286

"Her da paid me."

Jiddy thought about it. From what she knew, and if his brother was anything to go by, Jonas's father was handsome. Like Jonas. Mr. Chaplow weren't handsome or charming or funny or any of the things a young girl would like.

"Did she want to marry you?" she asked.

"She agreed, and she came here for a few months before she died."

It was Jiddy's turn to be silent. There was nothing more to say. Jonas was born, his mam died, and Mr. Chaplow got his heir to the farm.

"You must be disappointed Jonas has gone," she said.

"Aye. We got close with it being just him and me."

He pressed his hands on the stones. The rocks on the ground held his attention again.

"I'll leave you to it," she said.

He raised a dry, lined hand.

"Hartshorn's right name for the beggar," he said, "but it weren't Gregory. It were more like Harold."

"No, it's Gregory."

Heart pounding, she made her way up the field, her boots sinking into the moist ground.

"Harvey!" Mr. Chaplow shouted, and she turned around to look. He strode towards her, Rex bounding in front. "It weren't Gregory, it were Harvey. I remember, two H's. Harvey bloody Hartshorn."

"Are you sure?"

"Think I'd forget his name?"

287

Harvey, not Gregory. Lord Harvey Hartshorn. Double H. She headed back up to the track. It wasn't Gregory. It wasn't the same man as her father. Harvey was the beggar who'd put the local Pickering lass with child then run off, not Gregory. No wonder he'd hidden from her in that alcove, the lying coward. Maybe Lord Ryethorpe had known, maybe he hadn't. Didn't matter, now she knew the truth. She and Jonas weren't brother and sister, they were cousins, and cousins were allowed. Cousins married all the time, on every farm from here to York. It were all right. Jonas could come back when he learned the truth.

She reached the road and turned to look back down the field at Mr. Chaplow. Rex stood halfway, but Mr. Chaplow returned to the wall and stood gazing down at his hands.

CHAPTER THIRTY-FIVE

Jiddy looked around the room. It seemed smaller without Mary. The empty bed had been stripped of its covers, and embers crumbled in the grate. Already, the room smelt damp. She put a hand on her chest and breathed out to hear the sound.

She needed to keep calm. Keep herself busy. If she kept her mind on finding where Jonas had gone and telling him the good news, she wouldn't fall down into a slump of grief.

Jonas's face breaking into that great smile of his when he found out they were cousins and not brother and sister was what she should concentrate on.

She picked up the bunch of daffodils lying on the table. At last, she was ready. She would make it a ritual, closing the door, treading on each step. No jumping. Walk down the slope. Up the steps to the graveyard. It came as a surprise, how the quiet and peace took over. Mary and Thomas together again, in one place. A chill wind blew, and she was glad for the thick shawl. Mary's shawl containing Mary's smell.

Long grass straggled between the graves. It would be good when the sheep were let in again to keep it down. She paused. Someone bent over Mary and Thomas's grave. It wasn't Gracie or any of the women who were still checking on Jiddy. Hands moved quickly. Jiddy tiptoed forwards. They were shifting stones from around the edge of the grave.

Violet Ashner hadn't noticed her approaching because she was intent on lifting one stone after another and putting them back in place. Unnoticed, Jiddy crept closer. Finally, Violet touched the white stone.

"Searching for something?" Jiddy said.

Fumbling, Violet replaced the stone. So, Violet had seen the diamonds hidden underneath. Before she could stand, Jiddy knelt beside her and laid the bright flowers on the rough earth of the newly dug grave. Violet froze.

"I'm not going to do anything to you, you ninny," Jiddy said.

Violet rested her hands in her lap and kept her eyes down. "I couldn't come to service, I were needed at hall. Sorry."

She was a stringy girl, and she was growing quickly. Her dress, too short in the sleeve and hem, showed she was now the older sister with no hand-me-downs to be had.

"Thanks for coming to grave then," Jiddy said.

"I'll be going now."

They spoke at the same time, shutting each other up. Violet stood frightened and defiant all in one. Jiddy felt sorry for her. She wouldn't have, months ago, dismissing her as another shifty Ashner. Not anymore.

Something had changed. Maybe it was the day they'd pegged out the washing and Violet had volunteered to keep the squire out of the way so he wouldn't discover Mrs. Farsyde and Samuel. No Ashner was that unselfish. She'd never told either. Nellie certainly would have used that information to her advantage.

"How's Mrs. Farsyde?" Jiddy asked.

"Fine."

"Have you got afternoon off?"

Violet fidgeted. "I'd best be off."

Jiddy looked up, past the thin wool skirt, tightly bound shawl and purple-tinged hands, to Violet's clenched face. She was only a lass. She wasn't strong and sharp like Nellie. She wasn't funny like Nellie could be. She was thin and too young to be keeping squire out of the way and holding secrets.

"Violet?" Jiddy reached to take the younger girl's hand, but Violet drew back.

Jiddy's skirt, trapped under her knees, held her down, and she tugged but ended by falling sideways. Violet didn't offer a helping hand or say a word.

"As you can see, I'm a tad clumsy today," Jiddy said.

Dampness pressed cold through her skirt, and she scrambled to a crouching position. Studying Violet again, the situation made her want to laugh, in spite of where they were. It was ludicrous. Violet all self-contained and Jiddy scrubbing around at her feet.

It took another second for her to realise that if she stood up, Violet would bolt. She had to remain crouching even if it did numb her legs. She felt for the bag tied to her waist and pulled out the small wooden box she kept hidden. She held it out.

"Here," she said. "This is what you're looking for."

Violet put her hands behind her back.

"I want you to have it," Jiddy said.

"No, ta."

"It isn't charity." She held it out further. "Take it or I'll lose my balance and fall over again."

Violet still kept her hands behind her back.

"I know you saw what's in here," Jiddy said.

"So?"

"So open the box and have a proper gander."

Violet pressed her lips tight. She was on the brink of running.

"It's for you. It's yours."

Nobody could look more suspicious.

"I don't need it," Jiddy said, "and I know what it's like. It's right tempting to think you could fall in love with a soldier or even a captain, or even a squire. Gotta set your sights higher than any of them." She smiled. "Diamonds are better."

Violet's body remained rigid with distrust.

"This means you don't need to," Jiddy said, pressing the box forwards. "Go on, open it. You want to, you know you do."

Violet's fingers moved over the box, but she didn't take her eyes off Jiddy.

"If Nellie had had this, she wouldn't be dead now," Jiddy said. "Go on, take a look."

Violet took the box and opened it. The diamonds sparkled.

"All that makes us different from gentry is a brooch like this or a necklace or a big house and fine clothes," Jiddy said. "The brooch won't buy you a grand house, but with it, you won't need the squire or anyone else to be kind to you."

Shuffling on her knees, Jiddy wrapped her arms around Violet's waist and held her head against the girl's belly.

Tears spattered her head, and Violet's body shook.

"You should make up with missus," Violet said.

"What?"

"She misses you. She don't talk to any of us, she always talked to you. Can't you go and say you're sorry for whatever's upset her?"

Jiddy leaned back.

Violet wiped her face. "You can make her a present for the baby," she said. "She'd forgive anyone if they did something for her baby."

CHAPTER THIRTY-SIX

Jiddy and Violet walked back to Thorpe Hall together, cutting through the fresh-leafed trees with their budding blossom and over the field rather than up Main Street then along the lane, just as Jiddy had done the last time she'd visited the hall. Neither of them, in all their years, would ever live in a place like Thorpe Hall with its many rooms and elegant furniture and heavy window drapes.

Jiddy would rather live in a cave for what it cost your soul, but you could only think like that when you had other options, and she had none. Maybe she could make a present for the baby. A shawl or a nightgown. Let Jonas make his own way back to Bay. Do as Mary said. Be kind. Don't hold grudges, say you're sorry. Small things. Gestures that affected people around you. She'd almost decided when they heard shouting as they cut across the front lawn. Violet glanced at Jiddy, worry erupting all over again.

From the backyard, they heard the kitchen bouncing with voices. Mrs. King spotted them first.

"Where the hell have you been?" She grabbed Violet's arm and pulled her into the room.

Annie jumped up from her chair and ran to Jiddy, who hung back in the corridor.

"It's bedlam," she said. "Mrs. Farsyde is upstairs in tears. The squire can't stop shouting. Captain Ryethorpe, my god, Jiddy, I've never seen anyone so angry. He's so different from his usual self, and he's demanding to see you. But I wouldn't go in. Go home, go anywhere. He's saying the names you gave him are wrong, and he's going to punish you something rotten."

"They arrested all of them," said Mrs. King. "Every Storm, every Biddick, all Kellocks, even Big Isaac's mob, and not one of them named same as ones they were looking for."

Others were crowding around, speaking all at once so that Jiddy couldn't make sense of them.

"Come in here." Mrs. King looked down the corridor from where loud voices came. Annie and Jiddy followed back into the warmth of the kitchen, jostled by the other maids and stable hands. They were all there, every one of them.

"They picked up Isaac McCaw, Abe Storm—they even arrested old Silas, can you believe it?" said Mrs. King. "Had them all manacled up, and then Squire showed and said what they were doing were illegal. They'd got wrong men!"

"You knew, didn't you?" said Annie, "Were it you gave 'em such stupid names?"

"You gave him names of Storms and Biddicks?"

Jiddy contemplated the faces watching her. "I gave up wrong names. Captain Pinkney knew. His were only true name, and he ordered me to give it."

"Just like him to act hero," muttered Mrs. King.

"They couldn't find him, though, he made sure of that," added Annie. "He didn't want to be a martyr."

"Thank heavens. They'd never let him go," said Mrs. King.

Jiddy sensed that some were none too happy, and it made her nervous. It had been a risk, she knew that. There were no end of Storms and Biddicks in Bay, but that didn't mean they were protected or that they wouldn't come looking for her.

"So, what's all fuss about with Squire and Mrs. Farsyde?" she asked, hoping to change the mood.

"They thought they had 'em," laughed Mrs. King, clasping her hands together and ignoring Jiddy's question, "and then they found out they had the names of imaginary men!"

"They had to let them go," said Annie. "That's why Captain Ryethorpe is so furious."

"Squire insisted. The law were on the men's side."

"And not on Government's."

"That captain's got smoke coming out of his arse!"

"God knows why Mrs. Farsyde's so upset. She's nowt to do with it, must be noise," said Mrs. King.

"She's emotional," said Violet, and they all turned to look at her. "Mams are always crying and then laughing and then crying again when they're in this state. Everyone knows that."

"Well, hark at you," said Mrs. King. "Now who's the expert?"

Violet slumped into a chair at the table and picked at the crust of a loaf that stood on a tray. "Mam's had lots of babies," she said under her breath.

"So," Mrs. King turned back to Jiddy. "Now we know why captain wants to see you?"

They all fell silent.

Jiddy regarded the faces, even Violet's watching her.

"It were Captain Pinkney's idea," she said. "I wanted to find a way of making Captain Ryethorpe bring Jonas back, and Captain Pinkney said to give him names that don't exist."

"Jonas Chaplow?"

"Where's he gone, then?"

"It sounds an odd business to me."

"Sounds right clever!" burst out Mrs. King.

It was like a wave breaking. Laughter. Exclamations. Pats on her shoulder.

She glanced at Annie.

"I'd best go and face gunfire," she said.

"They can't do owt to you," said Annie.

"That's made my day," chuckled Mrs. King.

"Where's Isaac, Abe and Silas?" Jiddy asked. "Are they all right?"

Mrs. King waved the cloth in her hand. "Oh, they're all right. Supping beer and making their part in it bigger than it is. Bloody heroes they think they are."

So it had worked, and Captain Pinkney had managed to avoid capture. All that needed to happen now was that

Jonas returned. She'd done her part. Wasn't her fault Samuel didn't know the names of Baytowners.

Violet stopped her in the doorway. "Thank you," she said.

***

Samuel's voice greeted Jiddy before she reached the study door.

"She gave us these names!"

And then the squire's voice, so excited he'd lost all airs and graces.

"They're the right family names, I'll grant she gave you those, but you didn't think to ask anyone, did you? It were you who assumed. Just because Abe Storm's grandpa were a smuggler doesn't mean anyone round here would name a bairn Lancelot."

"I've been made to look a fool."

"Not at all," said the squire. "It were merely your mistake."

"Where is she?"

This was it. Samuel was spitting fire, but the squire was right, Samuel had assumed, and there was no way he could go back on his promise when she had given Baytown names. That's what he'd asked for, and Baytown's family names were what she'd given. She pushed open the door.

The squire, Captain Ryethorpe and Deputy Staincliffe turned to look who had come in. She kept her chin high, determined not to be cowed by the three men.

"When will Jonas Chaplow be coming back to Bay?" she said.

298

Deputy Staincliffe put a hand on his captain's arm.

"You can't blame Jiddy," the squire said. "You asked for names of smugglers, and she gave you them. Not anyone's fault that she gave you names of folk who are dead. Maybe these men were smugglers once upon a time. You wanted names, and she probably saw names on headstones when visiting Mrs. Waite and gave you what she thought you wanted to hear. No harm done. What do you say? You put her in an unwinnable position. The poor lass had to give it a try."

The captain shrugged himself free. He pointed a finger at Jiddy. "You gave me false names and made me look a fool."

"Are you going to make good on your oath and bring Jonas Chaplow back?"

She looked at him straight, daring him, in front of everyone, to deny he'd struck a bargain and made a promise to call a man back from exile.

CHAPTER THIRTY-SEVEN

The squire's words rang in her ears as Jiddy walked down Main Street, Annie at her side, smiling when someone stepped out of ginnel clapping their hands, while others watched from their windows with typical underplayed approval as the girls passed by. Everyone knew about the ruse, and it had worked. All the way to Sunny Place, there came more nods and mutters of commendation.

Inside, though, were only kind, sad faces. A basket with Mary's belongings stood on the floor by the door. Helen Drake put a broom back in the cupboard. Gracie rolled down her sleeves.

"All done," she said.

"I've swept entire house," said Helen. "We've got to give key back now."

It was so soon. Jiddy hadn't expected it to be so soon.

"I don't know where to go," she said.

Helen busied herself closing the cupboard door. Gracie took Jiddy by the shoulders, glancing at Annie to step back.

"I'll ask our Jack," she said. "You can sleep wi' me in my cot. We'll pull it out and make it up together."

300

Annie piped up quickly. "You can sleep in bedroom with me, twins and Maggie. Mam won't mind. You can stop with us, until…"

Jiddy stared at Gracie. She knew Jack wouldn't have room for anyone else in their tiny cottage, and she could tell from Gracie's eyes she knew that too.

"Thanks, Gracie, and you, Annie, but I'm best renting a bed at boarding house."

"But how will you afford that, Jiddy? I thought Mrs. Farsyde—"

"I'm sure Mrs. Farsdye'll give you a grand room of your own, you being such pals," interrupted Helen before Annie could finish.

Jiddy nodded. "Yes, I'm sure she will. A right big one, with drapes on bed and everything."

They weren't pals, though. Mrs. Farsyde never wanted to see her again. Gracie's son, Jack, lived in a tiny triangular end cottage with not enough room for Gracie to have anything but a pull-out cot, and Annie's house overflowed with brothers and sisters. She ran her fingers over Mary's belongings in the basket rather than have to look at any of them.

Gracie put on her outdoor shawl, and Helen walked to the door. Jiddy kept her eyes on Mary's cup and bundle of cutlery.

Mary was in her new home in the graveyard. Sunny Place was ready to be handed over to Kitty Trueman's son and his dynasty of fishermen. How could she have thought she belonged? Of course she was being kicked out now that Mary was gone. She wouldn't be able to afford the boarding house. By the end of the week, people of Baytown would be wishing her gone and be relieved when she had to head to Whitby, though likelihood of finding enough work would be remote. Baytowners wouldn't give her much thought after that. They'd be relieved not to be made uncomfortable any more by a foreigner. Their sweethearts would be safe from the flirtatious incomer, and they'd be all locals together.

Even Gracie would find it easier not to have to act as peacemaker between Jiddy and Helen Drake. Annie and Betsie's friendship could grow closer with just two of them. Three was an awkward number, especially when there was an odd one in the mix from the beginning. The expression on Helen's face spoke volumes on what she thought.

Well, Jiddy would manage. She'd cross the sea and find a new place to live, a place nobody else from here knew about. Not Naples. She'd stop in France if she found Jonas or no. She'd disappear and become a myth, that's what she'd do.

"Will you take Mary's things and keep them safe for me, Gracie?" she said. "I've a few errands to run before I head up to hall."

Annie didn't say anything. Jiddy kissed her cheek. "It'll be all right," she said.

***

Jiddy didn't head up to Thorpe Hall. She went down to her beloved beach to clear her head and form a proper plan.

She left her boots, shawl, woollen dress and jacket on the sand and walked into the sea. Cold clutched her ankles. When her cotton underskirt clung to her thighs, she flung herself forwards, closing her eyes as water engulfed her body. A second later, she was under, the depth of swell blocking out the world. Ignoring the cold, she swam until forced to resurface, and stood, thigh-deep, wiping her face with wet hands. The shock of chill water invigorated her heart. She'd been right to follow her instinct and took a few steps, moving further from the beach. This was the best place to be. Water lapped her shoulders. She could go out further still, see how far she could swim, then for how long she could float. She wanted to wash it all away. Use salt to scrub herself raw.

Jonas couldn't be with her here. He couldn't swim, even after all the times she'd tried to teach him. Saved him. It didn't matter. He might never hear they were free to love each other and he might have stopped loving her. He might never come home, now she knew gentry, captains—men like Samuel, who it turned out, weren't to be trusted to keep their word.

Feet adrift, she gazed at the sky. It was so big. The world so huge, and she felt free. She looked back to the beach and her small pile of clothes, then to the cliff, meandering green and brown. The causeway lolled empty. She dipped her head under again. Her forehead numbed. Spearing her hands through the water, she kicked inland. Mouth clenched so tight her teeth hurt, she ploughed forwards.

She'd not leave Robin Hood's Bay. She'd not give anyone that satisfaction. She couldn't leave Mary's belongings with Gracie. She'd find work. She'd take care of herself. She'd become a myth by becoming the most famous smuggler in England. Jonas would want to come back when he heard tales of her bravery while he shivered round a meagre campfire with his fellow soldiers. He'd hear about her and come back. She'd make him come back by being the bravest and strongest and hardest smuggler on the whole Yorkshire coast. No-one would drive her out, and Mary and Thomas would be proud of her. Robin Hood's Bay would end up treasuring her enough to write songs about her.

The beach was no longer empty. Two figures stood next to her pile of clothes. Wading slowly towards them, she squinted to make out who they were. The one with a livid face held her jacket up on a stick. The other leaned against a boulder.

Twisting her hair to wring it dry, she walked slowly, keeping her eye on them. She stopped. That wasn't a stick holding up her jacket. That was a rifle. A preventive rifle, and she did recognise them. They were the two new preventives she'd sent up to Thorpe Hall to demand a glass of port as a welcome from Squire Farsyde. The one leaning against the rock stood up. It was the big bully from Musgrave Inn. Horace. The one who'd gripped her jaw so tight it still ached. He took a step towards her.

"Think we've caught ourselves a mermaid," he said.

CHAPTER THIRTY-EIGHT

Jiddy didn't need to think twice. They weren't getting charming Jiddy Vardy after what they'd done. They were getting tidal wave, shove words down your throat Jiddy Vardy.

Swivelling on one foot, she spun and kicked Horace's rifle out of his grasp. It hit the beach with a thud, and he stumbled, trying to regain his balance. Caught off guard, the other one, ruddy Callum, fumbled to get his rifle out from under her jacket, which slid down the shaft over his hands.

Reaching for her boots and skirt, Jiddy flicked her head back, whipping his face with her wet hair.

"Didn't know you were interested in lasses' clothes," she said. "If I'd known, I'd have arranged a fitting for you."

Her jacket dropped onto the sand; red-faced Callum hoisted his rifle up and pointed it at her. Horace shifted his feet and waited.

She could outrun them, she knew she could, but they held all her clothes and she needed them. She'd shamed them too, and that meant they would not let her go without some punishment.

She swiped for her jacket. Next moment, massive Horace had clasped her arms from behind, encasing her so tight, she dropped her boots and skirt and released her tentative hold on her precious jacket.

"Get off me!"

She twisted and kicked her legs, knocking the rifle from Callum's hands. As he bent to retrieve it, she threw her head back, butting her captor's chin. His grip loosened and he cursed, but he didn't let go, so she beat her heels into his thighs, shins, knees, anything she could reach, squirming and bashing her head backwards into the hardness of his face. He swung her from side to side, but she didn't stop. She wouldn't stop. She pounded and yelled and screamed and kicked.

Callum became a blur. He didn't seem to know what to do. She kicked and twisted. She still couldn't move her arms, and she was tiring. This was hard to keep up. Horace was tiring too, and his curses faded to grunts. She caught his thigh with the round of her heel, and he lost his hold enough that she could turn and look into his sweating, stubbly face. She could do it. She had to. She bit the side of his jaw. Hard. Yuck. She had his dirty skin in her mouth. She let go. He fell backwards, pulling her with him. Off-balance, she couldn't stop herself and landed on top of the lump of his body. Rolling quickly, she grappled to escape his flailing arms. The other preventive lunged, and she scrambled, knees, hands, anything to be on her feet and get away. She'd never retrieve her clothes from these two. Not now.

Callum stood, legs splayed, arms out, determined not to let her pass.

She looked at the cliff. Pebbles would hurt her bare feet, but she had only one choice.

Clutching her still-wet underskirt, she kicked against the prostrate preventive's reach for her legs and dodged the other's lunge. The pebbles did hurt, and the sharp edges of shell cut, but she ran.

"Get up!"

"Stop her!"

Heart pounding, she slipped and slid on the stones. What were they doing? What the heck were they doing? She couldn't look to check. Preventives weren't their friends but they'd never behaved like this before. *Don't panic. Keep moving. Dodging.*

The cave entrance gaped a couple of yards away. The men's boots churned up stones behind. She had to be quick. Really quick. Her heart thumped so hard she thought it'd crack her ribcage. Briefly touching the rocky edge of the entrance, she staggered into the dark, tracing one hand over the wall to keep her bearings. She had a moment to find it before they appeared. Their shouts filtered in. A change in the atmosphere told her they'd come to a standstill in the cave entrance.

"We've got you, mermaid," the huge bully said.

"Give yourself up now."

With both hands, she felt her way over the rough surface, fingers fluttering across the stone. She trod carefully, trying to be quiet. The sound of their boots kicking pebbles made her hurry, but at least it covered any noise she made. *Please, please.* She had to find it.

307

"We know your name, Jiddy Vardy."

She almost missed it in her panic. One hand caught the edge, and turning sideways, she slipped through the crack. Straight away, it widened; with a hand on either wall to steady herself, she stepped as quickly as the uneven ground and carved rocks would allow. *Keep calm.* She stopped and caught her breath. She was breathing so loud. Too loud. Unlit and alone in the dark, she could easily lose herself. Where did she want to go? Where would be best? It would be a chance in a hundred thousand that they'd find the crack in the wall, and even then, they'd struggle to fit through or think to squeeze their bodies into the space beyond. They'd come for her if she went to Sunny Place or chase her round the ginnels and flights of steps until they wore her down. She couldn't turn up at Thorpe Hall. Samuel wouldn't believe anything against his men. The only person she'd feel safe with was Captain Pinkney, but she couldn't bring herself to rely on him even if he was still around, which was doubtful. She'd have to think hard where to go.

At a junction, she turned left. The tunnel grew steeper, and soon she had to crawl. She'd not been this way before, but she'd heard of it. Annie's Andrew said there was a way out onto the tops, and she had to believe it was true. If not, she'd have to scramble backwards, back to the cave.

Breathing became harder and harder with panic setting in. It was so dark. She could get lost. She could get stuck. She could die here and her bones would be all that were left of her. *Don't panic.*

Maybe she'd have been better taking her chances on the beach in the open air, but she couldn't think about that now.

Head low, she crawled forward, keeping thoughts at bay that the tunnel narrowed, that she had to bend her elbows more, hunch her shoulders, drop her head and lower her back. One hand in front of the other, right knee, left knee, wincing as hard rock sent arrows of pain through her kneecaps, feeling the heat steam her damp clothes and not being able to see in the pitch-black.

Don't panic, don't panic. Her underskirt kept pulling and jolting, and she wriggled it free time and again from under her knees. It could go on forever. Andrew wouldn't lie, would he? She stopped. Maybe she should start inching backwards. The dark heaved with her breath. Her head filled with dense air. She couldn't think. She couldn't see or breathe. She couldn't move. *Help.* She couldn't even shout for help when no-one would hear.

She reached one hand forwards. Leaned with it. Her shoulder scraped the wall. This was it. This was where the tunnel ended. She dropped her head in despair, resting her forehead on the stone floor a moment, readying for the long retreat.

CHAPTER THIRTY-NINE

The cold surface felt solid—a relief until she realised her forehead rested on grains of sandy soil rather than rock. She ducked lower to move forward. The tunnel curved, and she rounded the corner, grazing her other shoulder. Light shone ahead. *Thank God. Light.*

Pushing through tufts of grass, she dragged her battered and aching limbs through the narrow hole. Storm clouds had never looked so welcoming, and she filled her lungs with the freshest air she had ever breathed. Sprawling on her back, she looked up. The sky mixed white, slate, dove grey, mauve—every shade, in fact, but the black of the tunnel. Clouds moved swiftly, drifting high and skittish. Fresh, luscious grass tickled her cheeks. Tears trickled over her temples, and she closed her eyes.

The grass and soil pressed cool, and her underclothes stuck damp to her skin. She had no boots or jacket or skirt or chemise. Sitting up, she looked at the water lapping over the beach far below. So that was where the tunnel ended, high on the clifftop, as Andrew had said. She sniffed. Traces from the alum mine filled her nostrils. The wind blew in the right direction though, taking the smell of urine and something equally pungent inland.

Wrapping her arms around her knees, she gazed at the horizon. Somewhere out there lay Holland. Somewhere out there spread France. The sea wavered so big between here and there that she couldn't imagine a ship sturdy enough to cross it. But ships did make it to the other side

"What's happened to you?"

A pair of boots, her skirt, jacket and a shawl tumbled at her side. They were the clothes she'd left on the beach. She looked up. A black cloak billowed out. Captain Pinkney stood, his great boots heavy on the ground, his large triangular hat silhouetted against the sky. She looked at her clothes, dry and intact. She didn't ask him how he'd got them back or what he'd done to the two preventives. He took a few paces and gazed out to sea while she dressed. Sitting to pull on her boots, a heavy, dark waft of material fell around her shoulders, and she sagged under the weight.

"I thought you'd have gone," she said, pulling it close around her neck.

They sat in silence for a few minutes listening to the wind in the grass and the waves hitting the beach. Jiddy could have sat like that for hours, the cloak so comfortingly heavy and warm.

"I'll be leaving from the cove here tonight," he said, breaking the easy peace. "I wanted to check out the tide."

"Can I come with you?"

"You don't know where I'm going."

"I don't care."

"I can't look after you."

"I'll look after myself."

311

She couldn't face him, but she knew he was looking at her.

"You weren't waiting up here to shoot me again, were you?"

"I couldn't hide a pistol in what I was wearing."

He laughed so loud, she smiled.

"You still had a good life, didn't you?" he said when he'd stopped.

"You know what my life's been like."

"Nobody knows what your life has been like but you."

"Then why did you say I've had a good life?"

She plucked repeatedly at the grass. The skin on her shoulders and elbows had begun to smart, and underneath the thick cloak and dry clothes, her damp undergarments made her shiver.

"Why d'you want to leave now then?" he asked.

"Because Jonas were arrested and Mary's died."

"That's not a good reason."

"I'm going off to find him," she said, plucking at the fluff on the cloak.

"No, you're not."

"Yes, I am. You can leave me in France, and I'll find out where armies are and I'll find him. I'm good at finding my way places, and I'm not frightened of doing it alone."

He didn't answer for a while, and she wondered if he was deciding to help her.

"Captain—"

"It won't work," he interrupted. "It's not about finding him. You can't force the lad. He'll come back when he wants."

"But—"

"If he wants. You've got to let him be and make up his own mind."

She stood, dragging off the cloak and stepping out of its dark waves.

"But he don't know facts. He'll come back when he knows truth, and I'm only one to tell him."

"Stop being a daft beggar." He tried to pull the cloak back around her.

"If you're not going to help me, I'll say good night."

"Give over. Get off your high horse."

She sank to the ground and pulled the cloak back over her shoulders and head.

"Remember when I told you to meet me on this beach when you were still but a bairn?" he said, breaking the tension. "Said I'd show you how to get salt from the sea?"

She cast her eyes down to the stretch of sand and shingle. She didn't want to think about the eight-year-old Jiddy who had been excited that the head of the smuggling gang had singled her out.

"I need to be cleverer, don't I?"

"You're a canny lass," he said. "You're doing all right."

"No, I mean clever in everything. I can fool preventives and see how we can avoid them, but I always make a mess of other stuff. I've not been clever up at hall,

I upset Mrs. Farsyde because I blurted out something that were right mean."

"You can't change your nature. You are who you are."

"Don't say that. There's loads I do that's wrong!"

"Saved me from a few close encounters, so you must be doing something right. Trick is to accept who you are and use it. Yes, you're hot headed but you're canny. I can be generous when time's right, and I can be selfish. Trick is knowing when to be which."

Jiddy puzzled over it. The trick was knowing when to be which. Could she do that? Could she think before she reacted? That would be a challenge.

"I'll see you here at dusk tonight if you want to come with me," he said. "If you don't come, then get yourself up to Fisherhead. I'll leave something on mantel shelf for you in case. Now, give me back my cape, I've got places to be, and you've got to get yourself warmed up proper before you catch your death, or you won't be much use then, will you?"

CHAPTER FORTY

Jiddy remained on the clifftop, waiting for the sun to sink below the horizon. She could have been eight years old all over again, meeting him at dusk to discover what the sea brought in and thinking about what the captain had said and about Jonas and letting him have his own choice whether to return or not. Thinking about it made her notice the time passing until dusk and his return less than she would have done otherwise.

When the sun drew an amber glow across the waves, she'd made up her mind. She'd make her way to Naples and her family, watch sunsets like this and feel a hot sun on her skin. Turn brown and not have to worry that anyone would comment, make jests or even make her conscious about her colour. That would be a plan. A good plan. Captain Pinkney would see her safely over the sea, and she'd find her way in whatever way she could to her new home. Or was it old home? Home. That's all that mattered, and Lord Ryethorpe would be pleased she'd gone. Maybe even Samuel would be pleased.

She tightened her grip around her knees. It'd be strange sharing her thoughts with the captain, but she couldn't tell Anna and there was no-one else, and if she didn't share her thoughts, they would melt away and be lost forever. And what thoughts. Thomas and Mary gone.

Robin Hood's Bay, the only place she knew, left behind. If she never saw it again, she might forget its corners and crevices. She could wander around Bay with her eyes shut, she knew where to find wild garlic and dock leaves and where the densest blackberries grew. She'd learned when the tide would strike rocks and when it revealed sand banks. Where cliff crumbled and which caves held secret passageways. She'd do the same in Naples and learn every house, street and corner. But Annie...

She hoped Annie would forgive her leaving without saying goodbye; she hoped she'd understand.

The sun sank rapidly, beaming its last over Ravenscar, and dappling the water with blinding brush strokes. Sun did the same world over. It would set over Naples, kiss a similar hill that she'd heard loomed over Naples' harbour. She'd been pleased to hear Naples was by the sea. A home from home. It pulled at her more and more.

Would it smell the same? Would the sea hit the beach as it hit here? At least there'd be no stinking alum mine there. There'd not be stench of piss to remind you of the work done in its tunnels.

Captain Pinkney arrived as promised, standing tall on the beach. He looked up, and she began the steep descent down the cliff.

"Are you sure about this?" he asked when they stood in the dark shallows next to his waiting rowing boat.

A large schooner rocked further out. This was it. He stood up to his knees, holding the boat steady, and he'd not wait forever. She grabbed the side and, lifting her sea-drenched hem, climbed on board.

"We'd best be off," she said. "If preventives hear you're still in Bay, they'll be down here before we take another breath."

He placed one oar in its cradle, then the other, dipping the paddles into the water. Jiddy looked at the towering outline of cliff against the sky and pulled her shawl around her head.

"I take it you've made your farewells to Thomas and Mary?" Pinkney said. "Because you'll most likely not be back this way."

She nodded, not trusting herself to speak for fear of shedding tears. Thinking about their headstone turning green and weathered from lack of care wasn't an image she wanted in her head.

Water lapped the boat as it rocked, and she shivered. A fresh start beckoned, she reminded herself. She'd get all she needed when they reached the schooner.

He rowed slowly, easing the oars back and forward again. She looked at the waves furrowed dark and smelling cold, then at the schooner, waiting to take her to a new beginning. Glancing over her shoulder for a last glimpse of the cliff, she gripped the side.

"I can't do it."

The boat dipped in the rising waves, oars sending up spray, as if he hadn't heard.

"Stop!" she shouted. "I want to go back!"

"Flaming hell. Has water filled your head? You've wanted to go to sea ever since I gave you that first bag of contraband salt. Now shut up whining and let's get off before morning sun's beaming down on us."

"I can't. I have to stay. I'm being a coward if I leave, and I'm not going to let Captain Ryethorpe or fear of being on my own drive me out. I'm not alone, I have a purpose, don't I? And folk will be kind. I'll show them I'm thoughtful and think of others and I'm not selfish. Please, Captain Pinkney. I'm sorry to mess you about, but please row back. It's right thing, you know it as much as me."

He threw his hat at his feet. "You test the patience of a saint, Jiddy Vardy. Are you saying you now want to stay?"

"Yes."

"Fuck's sake."

"Thank you, but if you could row back faster..."

"That's it then, I'll not be back. I've paid my debt to you. There's nowt else between us. We're done. You've house of your own. Take it and be bloody grateful."

"What?"

"Fisherhead. I'm giving you Fisherhead. Now bloody take it and let's have done with this to-ing and fro-ing."

The boat turned, and he heaved the oars with the current.

"You'll kill me, you know," he grumbled. "Boat could smash—"

"I can get to the beach from here!" she said, pointing at the strip of land. "I can wade back. You don't need to come closer..."

He rested the oars in their cradles. "All I know is, I'll be a dead man if I ever return to Baytown. Fisherhead is yours. Use it to make your place here, understand? It's what Mary wished, remember that. She wanted you to feel you properly belonged in Bay. 'Give her a home,' she said. No better way to belong than with a home, so, I'm giving you mine. Take it. You've made your choice, now accept it and get out of my boat."

Accept it. His house. A place to put her things, to wake up in and return home every night. A place to call home. Not someone else's home, but hers. Not flee to a place her mother had escaped from.

She clambered over the side of the boat and paused, holding on to the gunwale.

"You've given me a chance three times now," she said. "I didn't waste first two, and I won't waste this."

Holding her skirt high around her thighs, she splashed through the water towards the cliff.

The sound of oars made her turn for one last look as Captain Pinkney rowed out to the schooner. There could be no changing her mind now. She'd decided to stay in Robin Hood's Bay, and that was that.

The sea was rising fast and changing rapidly, dusk brought great whaling clouds with it, and a wind stirred from the waves, making swells and troughs. *There. The path.* She grabbed tufts of grass and hauled herself up. The sea had turned dark, and she couldn't see the captain or the schooner any longer. Wind slipped through the grass, and gusts stirred the trees. The spring tide crashed hard on the rocks.

North wind chilled, though she sweated as she pulled and half-crawled up the path, her skirt dragging heavy with wet.

Panting, her nails filled with soil, ingraining her palms. Sodding, sodden skirt slapped hard. *Strong Jiddy Vardy. Warrior Jiddy Vardy. They'll write songs about me.* Going to Naples, she'd be forgotten; staying in Robin Hood's Bay, she'd be a legend. Her mother had left for a reason. They'd be a reason her mother had not gone back either. She'd made the right decision. She had to give her life here, her adult life, a proper go.

She'd almost reached the top. Pulling, heaving, she placed one palm on the flat clifftop, and drove her toe caps into the earth. She'd made it, and she rolled over, breathing hard. Clouds scuttled away, revealing stars that splattered in hundreds, maybe thousands of tiny dots so far away, no ladder or chimney would ever reach them. There'd be stars like that all over the world, but there wouldn't be a clifftop like this anywhere else.

One minute then she'd get up, but for a moment, she'd enjoy the bliss of lying still. The night breeze tussled the long grass, and waves foamed below. She pressed her palms into the ground. Cool and solid. Wind gusted stronger. She loved that wind, blowing frets in from the sea, bringing the taste of salt and promise of ships.

The air smelt more briny than it usually did at night. The sudden swell in the tide brought in seaweed, that was all, and it would linger until morning—popping brown bladderwrack and bright-green slime to slip on.

You wouldn't find any of this in Naples. She'd popped seaweed ever since her first day on the beach, holding Thomas's hand and smelling the strange scent from his pipe mingled with the smell of the ocean. Thomas and Mary were ingrained in the Bay. Every accent she heard echoed back familiar at her. She could fall asleep, listening to the swell.

Struggling to her feet, she looked out over the water. She could just make out the schooner. Captain Pinkney would be on board by now. With Mary and Thomas and him now gone, she was finally a grown-up. She pushed back the hair that had escaped her shawl and watched light glint on the waves as wind ballooned her skirts.

CHAPTER FORTY-ONE

News travelled fast in the Bay. Some weren't happy that Jiddy Vardy had become Captain Pinkney's heir. Many didn't believe it to be true until they saw for themselves the piece of paper with his signature and that of Squire Farsyde's and a legal man from Whitby. Some of the women brushed past Jiddy with a sideways look of distrust. Several of the Storms shouted and railed against the announcement, but the squire made it known that the property belonged to the name on the document and there were to be no acts of violence against the young woman or her home.

And then there were the constant visitors, friends and neighbours and those so nosy they couldn't keep away.

"I can't believe Captain Pinkney left you his house, Jiddy. Can you believe it? D'you keep having to pinch yourself?" Annie's voice brought Jiddy out of her reverie.

"Thank heavens for Squire Farsyde and the law!" She laughed. "I never thought I would ever, ever say that!"

She had much to thank him for, not only curbing any protests about her legacy but suppressing her fears that Samuel Ryethorpe might still retaliate.

"Don't you worry about him," the squire had said. "He's new fish to catch now Pinkney's gone and you're a respectable homeowner."

She picked up a stack of plates. All the things that had been Mary's and Thomas's at Sunny Place were now at Fisherhead, jostling with Captain Pinkney's pots and dishes. He'd said he didn't need them, not on board ship or wherever he was going to end up. She couldn't stop thinking about that, about not needing anything and about how Fisherhead belonged to her because he'd never come back to Yorkshire.

She put the four plates on top of some larger ones, closed the cupboard door and let her palms rest on the wood. Its warm roughness always steadied her, and this was her cupboard door. Those were her plates inside. No-one could tell her to leave. Samuel Ryethorpe couldn't touch her now. This had been her choice—her choice to stay—and no-one could take it away from her.

"Jiddy, are you happy?" Annie stared at her, all flushed smiles.

"I'm not sure what I feel." She moved the jug of daffodils for the tenth time.

"You're a woman of property."

Jiddy looked around the room. It was much larger than Sunny Place. Everything was bigger. Windows, door, furniture. It didn't seem possible that she owned them.

"The table's huge," she said.

Annie slipped an arm around Jiddy's waist, and together, they stared at the long surface of oak.

"I can see Jonas sitting at that end and you at this and a gaggle of little Jonases and Jiddys in between." She looked sideways. "Some'll have black eyes and copper curls, and some'll have grey eyes and black hair."

Jiddy covered her face. She didn't want to see any images like that.

"Oh, Jiddy, I'm sorry." Annie pulled her close and hugged her. "I didn't mean to upset you."

Jiddy wiped her face with the back of her hand before repositioning the jug of flowers. "It's stupid. I don't know why I'm blubbing. I should be happy. I've got all this."

Annie put her hands on the back of a chair. "Now Captain Ryethorpe's gone, and you don't have to worry about him no more, Jonas could come back. If someone knew where he were, they could tell him."

"He's in France."

"You should have asked Captain Pinkney to find him."

Jiddy sniffed. Jonas could be dead, but she couldn't say that aloud. Saying thoughts aloud made them real.

"Captain Pinkney's got his own life to sort out," she said instead.

"Well, Jonas'll have to come home sometime," said Annie. "Wars don't go on forever."

The fire crackled. Jiddy pressed her fingertips along her closed eyes. Taking a deep breath, she turned to Annie and spread out her arms in a gesture of bravado.

"I'm going to give up smuggling."

Annie laughed. "'Course you are!"

"I'm serious."

"Being a woman of property has done something to your brain."

Jiddy walked around the table, touching each chair with her hand.

"My plan is to open a sewing school. Like when Mary taught us...but without Nellie and her vicious needle."

Annie followed Jiddy around the table, but Jiddy kept walking.

"I can't carry on doing it, Annie. Jonas wanted to give up smuggling, and I made him do another run and he got caught. He were right. You can't do it forever. I can't do this year after year until I'm forty or fifty and doddering around with a walking stick. I want to look people in the eye and tell them what I do, like Jonas said. I don't want to hide anything."

She stopped. She couldn't look at Annie, even with her standing right by her side.

"But..." Annie said. "But we all know smuggling ring wouldn't do as well without you. You find out things, like whenever a set of preventives are coming or when dragoons are making a round. I remember what you've done. Isaac and Abe and everyone need you. I couldn't do that, nor Betsie."

"I suppose."

"Bay can't do without your tricks, Jiddy."

"I just think there are other ways." She turned to her friend. "Besides, as you said, this can't go on forever. Wars'll stop, and then taxes will be lowered again, and prices will fall. No, I'm going to fill these chairs with your sisters and their friends. I can help Bay folk in other ways, better ways, I think."

Annie followed Jiddy's gaze as if imagining the room filled with little girls.

"I want them to get jobs in the big houses and maybe shops in York."

Annie walked around the table, tapping each chair as Jiddy had done. "Can I help?"

"I'm going to ask Violet to join us as well."

"Violet Ashner?"

Jiddy nodded. "I think she'd like to come. Be a way of having Nellie with us. Though we might have to give her a blunt darning needle rather than a sharp one."

Annie's face flushed pink. "Will you ask her or shall I?"

"Do you want to?"

Annie's face flushed deeper. "I will if you want me to."

Jiddy smiled and placed her hands on the table's smooth surface. "Think of it, Annie. I'll teach proper pattern cutting and hemming and embroidery. We'll fill the fine houses and shops with Baytown lasses. They'll make their own wages and not be relying on any man. What d'you think of that?"

Annie pulled out a chair and sat. "I think you're going to be right busy."

"*We're* going to be right busy."

Jiddy went over to the fireplace and straightened a ladle hanging from one of the hooks that opened the hidden cupboard.

"Wish I had my own home," said Annie. "You're so lucky."

"You could wed a certain stableman and be in your own place next year. That is, if you change your mind about you-know-what."

Annie shook her head vigorously. "I'll never change my mind. Memory of that thing Billy Hardcastle got out of his breeches makes me wonder how any lass can do it."

"There'd be no more people in world if all lasses felt like you." Jiddy laughed.

"I can safely say, there'll be no more little Annies." She folded her arms. "I know it'll not be easy being a spinster. I'll have to wash and scrub and sew until I drop, but I can put up with that much more than I could put up with... you-know-what."

"We can grow old together," Jiddy said. "We can rattle around here getting on each other's nerves and laughing about Billy Hardcastle's jigger as it shrinks smaller and smaller."

They held each other's gaze before bursting out laughing.

"But you'll wed, Jiddy, you know you will, and you'll have strong bairns just like you to fill up this cottage."

"No, I won't," Jiddy said certainly. "There's more to life than that."

"Jonas'll come back. He'll be back as soon as he's able. You'll see. He could turn up anytime, and then you'll change your tune."

Jiddy gave a brief smile. "Maybe." If he believed they had the same father, he'd never come back even if he did survive fighting battles, but she'd never tell Annie that. Never tell anyone.

Voices trickled up from Jim Bell's Stile; Jiddy crossed to the open door and looked out.

"Now then, Jiddy."

Helen Drake and her sister Dottie approached, blocking out the light.

"How do?" Jiddy said, stepping aside.

Helen moved first, whisking the cloth off the plate she carried.

"These are best apples," she said, putting the plate on the table. "I only use best for my fruit pies."

Dottie put a small bread loaf next to the pie. "I baked you this."

"Anybody brought you 'owt else?" asked Helen, eyeing Annie, then the rest of the room.

Jiddy and Annie exchanged a quick glance.

"Jane Bell sent a meat pie," said Jiddy.

"Jane Bell? You are favoured to have her attentions."

Annie pointed to the jug filled with yellow flowers. "I brought daffs."

Helen folded her arms. "So, he's not coming back, then?"

Jiddy felt the flood of emotion rising and kept her mouth closed. Annie touched her arm.

"Captain Pinkney told Jiddy he'd never come back and the cottage belongs to her. It's all legal. Squire Farsyde sorted it, and no-one can take it away from her. It's Jiddy's for life."

"Can't Jiddy speak for herself?"

"He signed the papers for the house over to Jiddy. Squire Farsyde and magistrate have signed them too," said Annie, unable to restrain herself and nodding at Jiddy for reassurance.

Jiddy smiled. She loved that Annie wasn't going to let Helen Drake spoil it.

"Well." Helen clasped her hands as tight as her jaw. "Who'd have thought it?"

"Someone's looking after our Jiddy, and his name is Saint David Pinkney," said Gracie shadowing the doorway with her great figure. "Jiddy, Helen." She nodded to Dottie and Annie, stepping inside as she did so. "I've brought you a pease pudding. I hope it's the only one you've got." She eyed the table with its recent offerings.

"Thank you," Jiddy said, taking the dish and kissing Gracie's cheek.

"You didn't thank me," said Helen, coming closer to study the dish Jiddy carried to the table.

"You didn't give me chance," Jiddy said, kissing Helen's cheek. "Thank you for the apple pie, Mrs. Drake."

Helen narrowed her eyes but didn't say anything.

Gracie waddled around the room, taking in the comfortable chairs and big table. "Seems like you and Annie have been busy," she said, approval rounding her voice. "Mary would be right proud."

***

Jiddy was glad when she could stand outside the front door and watch them all make their way down the run of cottages until they dropped out of sight. Clouds still billowed high. The setting sun bounced off the sandstone.

Standing completely still, she listened. Waves tripped over themselves. Wind stirred in the trees around the back. The storm hadn't completely blown itself out. Nearby, someone tapped pots together, and elsewhere, someone hummed a favourite hymn. But there was something else. It wasn't the wind. It sounded at her shoulder. She looked behind, but there wasn't anyone coming down the path or over the field. Gracie would be heaving her frame towards Chapel Street over the other side of the little valley, but this sound, this sense, was different. She glanced through the open door. It remained all quiet inside. Peat, burning in the grate glowed without calling for attention.

She halted in the doorway. She'd no cat nor dog that kicked in its sleep or snuffled in its dreams. No bird had flown in by mistake. It felt like someone had strolled in, lingered for a bit, then out again, leaving their presence behind. It couldn't be Captain Pinkney. She'd seen him sail away.

"Mary?" she called tentatively, watching for an apparition as she stepped inside.

She waited, hoping Mary would appear, either in the chair by the fire or sitting at the table, but the room remained empty. Wishing she'd asked Annie to stay after all, she crossed to the hearth and turned, the heat warming the backs of her legs. The room gleamed neat and tidy as the women had left it. The pies stood on the table, cloths wrapped taut around them. Captain Pinkney's trinkets lay on the window ledge. Papers that said the house belonged to her were tucked safely away.

She was imagining it. She wasn't used to being alone in a house. That was it. Stupid imagination playing tricks. This was her home. She didn't need to create phantoms and worries. It was legally her property. She owned it, and nobody could take it away.

"Thank you, thank you, thank you," she said, bringing her hands to her cheeks.

She would have sewing circles and lots of visitors. She would bake pastries and tarts for Christmas and Twelfth Night. She crossed to the door and pressed it closed. The cottage belonged to her. The noise she'd heard was probably a mouse behind the wall or a gull scratching on the roof. Normal sounds. Homely sounds. She could rest easy.

The room was so quiet, though. She touched a piece of wood, forked like a catapult, lying on the mantel shelf. She glanced around again. It must be her imagination or an invisible spirit, but she was positive she sensed something.

"Stop it," she said, touching the ladle, then caressing the hooks that protruded from the cupboard door. This was where it had started. If it wasn't for this cupboard, Jonas would be settling Boy for the night or she and he'd be off canoodling somewhere.

"Don't think on it." She pressed her palm to the panelling. She couldn't bear the thought of never kissing again. It was her favourite thing, but there was nobody else she wanted to kiss.

"Stop it, stop it, stop it." She tapped the wall with her fingertips.

331

She leaned against the door, minding the hooks above her head, and sighed. She'd have to go out. If she stayed in, she'd wind herself in knots. Pushing herself away from the wall, she swept up her shawl.

A faint noise made her look behind as she reached the front door. The air flickered like sea spray. And there was a sound, like a tiny beating moth. The fire burned steady. Light through the window dimmed. She wasn't mistaken. A noise seeped from somewhere in the room. A rubbing together of cotton. Boots shifting weight. There it was again, coming from the cupboard. Grasping the ladle from its hook and holding it ready to strike, she pulled the middle peg and abruptly opened the door.

"All right," she ordered. "You've had your fun."

Someone stooped inside. She trembled, fear and excitement jumbled together.

"Come on out. I'll not hurt you even though you deserve it."

A pause. She opened the door wider. Her body fizzled with anticipation. She clutched the ladle tight. A boot and a leg appeared.

"Jonas?"

CHAPTER FORTY-TWO

S he dropped the ladle, and it clattered to the floor. Captain Ryethorpe stepped into view, crinkling his eyes as he left the dark of the cupboard. He straightened his hat and then faced her, hand on his sword.

"You didn't think I'd let you get on with your life just like that, did you?"

She looked past him at the open cupboard door, then at him again.

"You told me about this hidden cupboard, don't you remember?" he said. "And how it leads into next door? Mr. Biddick was very obliging."

"Get out," she ordered. "This is my home, and I say who can enter here."

She crossed back to the door and stood, gesturing for him to leave.

Samuel touched his hat. "Very well. I am going, but once you step over this threshold, I will have you."

She swallowed hard and relaxed her shoulders, moving from the door so that he could pass. His silhouette framed in the orange glow of sunset. Night would soon be setting down its chill, and he'd have a lonely ride back to Mulgraves. It struck her how lonely he must be, surrounded by men such as Horace and Callum. Samuel was too refined for this posting.

He didn't move. The deep-orange glow dipped deeper, and the tendrils of dark gathered across the field.

"Good night," she said.

He turned slowly. She stepped back, and he took one pace into the room. "Is that it? Is that all you have to say?"

He loomed over her, his hat making him taller and his sword hanging from his waist making him appear wider.

"What do you want me to say?"

His eyes met hers.

"I'll not be bothered by you," she said. "I gave surnames of men you either hung or exiled or packed off to war. King George calls them smugglers. Thought you wanted smugglers' names."

He stepped so close his sword brushed her skirt. The buckles and buttons of his jacket pressed against her, and his breath gusted her face. He could cut her and who would know if he closed the door and let her bleed on the slabs until she died? Her heart raced. She hated it. Being so close to someone she'd once cared about caught her off guard.

"What do you want?" she asked.

He took a step back and appraised her again. Usually, she'd play up to any member of the preventives, any dragoon and even a captain, but the fact she'd known this captain—had her arms around him and kissed him—made anything she said that was not a matter of fact completely insignificant.

"Fisherhead is mine," she said. "I have documents to prove it."

"When you wed, this property will become your husband's." He spoke quietly, calmly.

"I'll not wed," she said.

For a moment, he looked unsure, and then he smiled.

"Of course. Mr. Chaplow is not a resident here anymore."

"He'll come back."

"But you'll not marry him? Maybe you should have stuck to your promise to me?"

She pressed her hands into her skirt and felt the taut muscle of her thighs. At the point when she thought she could stand it no longer, he turned away and walked to the window. Taking off his hat, he ran a hand over it. She waited. Wood on the fire powdered into ash.

"It's late, Samuel. It's not right you're here."

"I never understood," he said. "We returned to Robin Hood's Bay, I to capture Captain Pinkney, the leader of the local smuggling gang, but I was never sure exactly why you returned."

He caught her eye again. She hadn't expected him to talk about their return from London. He cleared his throat. The fire shrank.

"I never understood at the time why you kissed me in the inn yard at York while we were waiting for our horses, either."

"*You* kissed me," she said.

He raised his hands. "You changed after that. You were no longer on my side."

335

"What do you mean? We rode back together to Thorpe Hall. You went off to arrest Captain Pinkney, and I..."

"Yes? You retired to bed? You stayed up and talked to Squire and Mrs. Farsyde? You snuck back to your home in the Bay? Or did you go somewhere else?"

"It was late—"

"We never found Captain Pinkney, you know. Or any smugglers, for that matter. Instead, I lost men and two horses in the marshes, and you kept away."

"I'm sorry," she said. "For your men and horses." She stroked her palms down her skirt.

He bowed his head.

"I realised," she said. "I mean, you know it weren't right I were seen with you."

"We were to be married, Jiddy."

"I apologise. I were happy to be in Bay again. I were that thrilled to see Mary and be by sea, I got swept away with seeing folk again. And you know I were unhappy in London." She stepped towards him. "But you've behaved worse than I could ever do."

"We are not discussing my behaviour."

"You deceived me."

"You led me on."

"You were playing with the hearts of two of us, Samuel."

"I don't know what you mean."

"I were at hall, remember? I know what's gone on between you and lady of the house."

"Mrs. Farsyde is the only lady of standing I have met here. Naturally, I would speak with her. She was my hostess. Politeness dictates."

"Does politeness dictate what you did? No! Don't say anything. I don't want to hear your excuses."

"Jiddy—"

"You are not the caring person you pretended to be."

"Jiddy, you were a temptation. I mean, an unexpected treasure. That is meant as a compliment. How could I refuse? How could I not—"

"Would you really have wed me?"

It was his turn to hold back his words. He ran a hand over his hat again. He walked to the fire and, resting his hat on the shelf, studied the embers. His rigid back to her, loose curls crept over his collar, and she found anger dissipated. He stood out more in Bay than she did in London, and who'd be alone in a place like this?

"Let's forgive each other," she said.

He turned and locked eyes with hers for a moment, and she saw again the shining blue that had originally fascinated her.

Picking up his hat, he tipped a salute. "Yes, we can do that. You have a home of your own." He waved his hat before repositioning it on his head. "And I am leaving."

"Leaving? But why, and what about your..." She stopped, unwilling to say it out loud.

"The child is Squire Farsyde's," he said. "Everyone's lives will continue as if I'd never been here."

He strode to the door but stood aside and waited. She crossed the floor quickly and took hold of the latch. It was her turn to hesitate.

"I'm glad we can forgive each other," she said.

"This is a harsh place, Jiddy. If you want, I'll take you to York or London. It could be better for you there."

"No, thank you. Funny how so many folk want me to leave, but I'll not. I were brought up here, and I won't feel right anywhere else. I'll take my chances."

He nodded. "Goodbye then."

"I wish you well, honest I do," she said, pulling the door open.

Cold night air wafted inside, and two faces peered out of the dark.

"Silas told us he were here," mumbled Sandy Killock.

Before either of them could react, Abe Storm reached out, pushing Jiddy aside and grabbing Samuel by his epaulettes. Jiddy stumbled backwards as Sandy punched Samuel in the stomach, making him slump between them.

"Stop it!" Jiddy reached to grasp him, but Abe held her back, turning a scowling face in her direction.

"We'll deal with him now. Get yourself to bed and sleep tight."

"But he's leaving Bay," she said, clutching his sleeves. "Let him go, then there'll be no reprisal, no nothing, and we'll be able to carry on—"

"We'll escort him out," said Abe. "Make sure he doesn't change his mind."

"Or be able to," added Sandy.

"You can't kill him! Be sensible if nothing else."

Abe shoved his face up close. Sensing the anger in him, Jiddy backed off.

"You were lucky Mary stepped in when you helped this beggar escape last time," he said. "Now, you don't want to be accused of being a traitor again, do you?"

The memory of Nellie standing on the top step of Sunny Place and whipping up the crowd with fists holding stones made her flinch.

"It were me that were escaping, not him," she said. "I would have been stoned cos of a false accusation, and you well know it."

"One act of loyalty don't mean—"

"I am always loyal!"

"Every action." He glanced at the sagging figure hanging between him and Sandy. "Every action, Jiddy. It's not only Sundays. Every day has to be for Bay. There's no picking and choosing, lass."

Lost for words, she watched them drag Samuel down the path, but she couldn't give in.

"Where are you taking him?"

"It's high tide," said Abe. "Dangerous down in dock at high tide."

CHAPTER FORTY-THREE

Closing the door quietly behind her, Jiddy glanced up at Silas's dark windows to see if he watched what he'd set in place, but she couldn't see him. She turned and hurried in their wake, careful not to be heard or seen. Reaching Main Street, she saw Sandy holding Samuel up while Abe extracted the pistol from Samuel's belt, and then they continued, dragging him between them. All the houses remained closed in and dark, even though the two men scraped Samuel's boots along the ground and panted and groaned. Sounds of the swell striking rocks reached her ears. They hadn't been lying; they were heading exactly where they'd said, down Main Street towards the dock.

Abe and Sandy appeared nervous, dropping the body and rolling it with their feet. They glanced up King Street and then the steps to the right. A surge of water lapped towards them, but Samuel's body remained untouched.

"Move," Jiddy whispered.

The men looked at the sea then, in silent agreement, headed up to the left, up King Street, leaving Samuel splayed on the ground to meet 'a natural death', as they'd have it said the following day.

Tiptoeing forwards, Jiddy watched Abe and Sandy disappear. A surge of water sloshed around her feet, taking her unawares, and she jumped, hitching up her skirt. Samuel's body drifted a moment before being left as the tide sucked back. Dropping to her knees, she shook him, but he didn't stir. She glanced up. The swell readied again, deep and dangerous, but she couldn't leave him. She couldn't leave anyone in an unfair fight against the sea, and Samuel, lying there helpless, had no clue that in a few moments, he could be struggling for his life.

She bent over his ear, pushing away his damp hair.

"Samuel! Get up, Samuel!" She shook him hard, keeping her eyes on the slipway. They had minutes only. "Get up, get up!"

He weighed heavy, but she slipped her arms under his and pulled as hard as she could. Sensing the muscle of sea building, she shook him again. The sea readied.

"Help me!" She shook him and shook him, and he came round at last. Hatless and dishevelled, he was upright again, yet he'd never looked more vulnerable.

A wave rolled its froth around their feet. Letting go of her arm, mesmerised, Samuel viewed the bulk of water swaying where the causeway should be.

"Sea's at full tide," she said. "It'll flood here in a minute."

"It won't come this far."

"We'd best move up street."

The sea breathed height and weight into the surge, flexing muscles to hold on to anyone who stood too close.

She splashed a few strides before turning to tell him again, but he remained where he was, hypnotised.

"Samuel! Move before it comes in."

341

He'd no idea. Sea stopped you thinking straight. It put you in a trance, and then it pounced. They all knew that. *Don't stare too long. Don't listen to its lullaby.*

Waves were building.

"We have to shift," she said, grabbing his arm.

Lifting her skirt as water pooled around her ankles, she let Samuel wade in front, where she could keep an eye on him. Heart racing, skirt heavy around her legs, she followed. He strode easily, white breeches and bright jacket. This time, she didn't have to persuade him. He'd listened.

"Jiddy!"

Water thumped the back of her knees, bashing her calves, and she splayed her legs and arms, staggering to stay on her feet.

Samuel stumbled with the force.

"Keep on," she shouted. "Run, you have to run."

He twisted around to see what he should run from. Unbalanced, he side-stepped, twisting like wrung washing as the sea breathed in, and then gallons bellowed onto the dock, slapping walls, submerging steps, and they both fell, splashing and blind. Her fingers fluttered in the water for his hand. *There.* She had it, but then it was gone. His arm brushed hers. Shoulders, legs, fingers again. She snatched at him. The ebbing tide sucked them along, the pull so strong, she didn't even feel the hard ground, only the roll of it as his hand slipped from her grasp.

In that moment, she knew. She wasn't meant to escape. She'd been in the dock before, with the tide dragging her skirts, and she'd escaped then. But this time, she would go with the tide. Swallow mouthfuls of it. If the sea took her, she'd belong in Robin Hood's Bay forever, her name whispered in the shallows with the shingle. Blown with the cotton grass on the tops. Rustled in dried seaweed. She'd already thought about it, heard her name sung in ditties around the streets. It was fate. It was what she should've done before. Mary and Thomas would wrap her up in their arms. She'd smell his baccy and feel the warm, noisy embrace of Mary's morning sleep.

Caught in the undertow, she scraped over the causeway stone. One minute above, the next below the surface, she couldn't scream. The thought of water flooding into her mouth, down her throat, pooling in her chest, sloshing in her belly, made her clamp her lips tightly together.

The sea gripped her in its ebb, holding her in its belly. Next moment, surfacing, she spat, eyes smeared with brine, and saw how far she'd come. Buildings bobbed beyond reach, the outline of rooftops black against a granite sky. Her legs dangled with no ground beneath, and she held herself in the swell, searching for Samuel.

A wave swamped over her head, and she sank, heart pounding, frightened as she turned with the current. Arms outstretched, she readied for the wall of rock to pulverise her. She didn't want this, now that it was real. This wasn't the way to die. Up again, spluttering, directionless, the weight of her saturated skirt pulled one way, the waves pulled her the other, battling for her to mould with them. Buildings loomed closer but blurred. Water lapped her chin, and then her head submerged again. She couldn't hear anything but the sea thundering into her ears. She couldn't escape. Her chest stung sharp as a slap, and the blanket of water crushed her breath.

Air. Snatches, then holding breath and dank cold pressing her body. Cloud and stars then dark. The gap of the dock then nothing but sea. She gulped. Spat. Spread her arms.

She'd saved Jonas when they'd fallen from the clifftop. What was that for if she couldn't save herself? This was punishment because she'd contemplated the sea taking her. She'd let the idea in. She'd let the sea in. *Don't panic. Don't let the high tide better you.* She tried to swim, but the rise and fall locked her in its arms. She kicked her legs, but her skirt clung taut. Her arms ached. They were tired. Too tired. The black dot of death were approaching, so close she could almost see it. Rise and fall, rise and fall and fall and fall.

Was she dead yet? Were Mary and Thomas calling her? She couldn't see them, couldn't see anyone, only a dark shape. A wave of death come to smother her.

CHAPTER FORTY-FOUR

Something hard touched her shoulder. Nudging her. Bruising her. She looked up. A boat loomed out of the water, and she recognised it. Had Captain Pinkney been careless, or had he left it on purpose as the type of gesture he'd make to see what would happen?

Grasping the side, she held on as it tipped, then settled. She rested her forehead against the wood and caught her breath. Waves sprayed up, slapping the hull. Fingers wet and cold, she clung on, spitting out brine. The boat rose and fell. She couldn't hold on forever.

Throwing an arm to catch the boat's edge as it dipped, she held her body higher. Every effort to haul herself up concentrated her fear. Kicking, scraping her boots, she tried to climb. The edge of the boat cut hard into her belly and scraped her hip bones. She pulled. The boat plunged, then righted. She lifted one leg. The sodden folds of her skirt restrained her, preventing her getting her foot over the side. She lay half in and half out. It dug into her crotch. She dragged one leg up out of the water. Her heel caught. The boat ducked. She screamed, heaved herself over and tumbled inside, spewing brine into the hull, her skirt pooling around her legs and her hair laying in sodden strips across her face and streaking onto the wood. Sick in her belly. In her chest. In her throat.

Waves splashed over the side, drenching her again. Droplets beaded the air. Dark, rolling shapes lifted and dropped the boat. She tried to rise but to no avail. She tried to sit, but the boat knocked her back. Her head bumped the wood. Feeling around, she found an oar. It didn't matter why Pinkney had left it. She'd found it—or it had found her—and she had to use it. She grasped the other oar and, sitting, began to row. Samuel was gone. The sea had taken care of that. If the boat cracked open on the rocks, she would be gone too. She pulled with all the strength she had left. Moonlight showed up the cliff and waves battering the base like angry white ghosts.

The coast loomed nearer. Dark, jagged silhouettes broke through the water, splurging so that surf exploded high. Each swell took her closer to the rocks scattered randomly to catch boats like this. One bash and it would splinter open. She gasped. The pit and swell twisted. The cliff threatened, closer and closer. *Pull, pull.* Her arms ached and her shoulders hurt, but she dug in the oars, turning the boat little by little.

Shapes projected out of the waves, rising dangerously close. Another dip, another rise, and the tide spewed forward. Striking a boulder, the boat's hull cracked open, and Jiddy slid out, plunging feet first under the water.

Resurfacing, she gulped in air, splashing to push away the debris before it struck her. All around, rocks loomed out of the surf, and splintered wood bobbed in the swell. She pushed her hands against a stone as a wave swept her with it. Gasping, she spun with the pulling tide.

Underwater again, she reached out with her hands, readying for another pulverising strike. Her leg hit something, then her shoulder. She couldn't breathe. Pain shot through her knee as it struck something hard. She surfaced into a mass of foam and spray and then dipped under again, churning over, unable to stop. Her boots struck rock and her head scraped ground as she tumbled in the surf, round and around.

Finally flung from its grip, she slapped into shallows, palms flat on firm ground. The backwash tugged at her skirt, but her body cramped down and the tide dragged back. Sinking her fingers deep, she clung to pebbles and sand. The water sludged under her. Scrambling forwards, she clawed at the shingle until she couldn't crawl any further. Cradling her head onto the sand, she collapsed. She'd made it. She'd reached land. She was alive.

ABOUT THE AUTHOR

Ruth Estevez lives in Manchester where she works as project coordinator for The Portico Sadie Massey Awards for Young Readers and Writers, based at The Portico Library.

Ruth is also a writer of fiction, with place, identity and voice being at the forefront of her work. Born in Yorkshire, her novels are frequently set there, and landscape as well as character are what stand out. A believer that we should be heard as well as seen, she feels voice, in her case the Northern voice, is important to be found in books.

Ruth has previously worked as a scriptwriter on the children's TV series *Bob the Builder* and worked in theatre and TV from Opera North, Harrogate Theatre-in-Education Company, Pitlochry Festival Theatre to *Emmerdale*. She has also taught scriptwriting on the Contemporary BA Film and Television Course at Manchester Metropolitan University.

When not writing or project coordinating, Ruth is either dancing or indulging in her latest passion, long-distance walking.

You can contact Ruth on...

Instagram @ruthestevezwriter
Twitter @RuthEstevez2
Facebook @RuthEstevezM
Website: www.artgoesglobal.wordpress.com